SERGEANT
SALINGER

Praise for *Sergeant Salinger*

'Supremely engaging… A smoothly told, unexpectedly affecting foray into a lesser-known chapter of the literary giant's life'
– *Kirkus* **(Starred Review)**

'In this literary tour de force… Charyn vividly portrays Sonny's journey from slick short story writer to suffering artist. The winning result humanizes a legend' – *Publishers Weekly*

'Nuanced and acutely perceptive… Charyn offers an astute psychological portrait of an elusive yet vastly compelling subject'
– *Booklist*

'Charyn peers into the traumas that formed the lifelong recluse and his enigmatic stories… An engaging and informative rendering of an important American author'
– *Historical Novel Society*

'Charyn, who at 83 has had a remarkably prolific career, has an affinity for literary sphinxes… *Sergeant Salinger* is true to history… but in this novel, as with much of Salinger's life, we have to accept a certain amount of mystery' – *Washington Post*

'A tour de force… Charyn is a master of the written word'
– *Jewish Journal*

'Charyn deftly leaves the reader wondering whether Holden Caulfield's teenage angst was really Salinger's personification of post-traumatic stress disorder… Engrossing' – *Library Journal*

'Masterful… Grounded in biological fact and topped with a generous helping of imagination, Charyn's novel wonderfully recreates the war years of J. D. Salinger' – *Michigan Daily*

'An in-depth look at one of our most celebrated of writers… Complex and full of intrigue' – *Comics Grinder*

'Intense and absorbing' – *The Reporter*

Praise for Jerome Charyn

'Charyn is a one off: no other living American writer crafts novels with his vibrancy of historical imagination' – **William Giraldi**

'One of our most rewarding novelists' – **Larry McMurtry**

'Charyn is one of the most important writers in American literature' – **Michael Chabon**

'Among Charyn's writerly gifts is a dazzling energy – a highly inflected rapid-fire prose that pulls us along like a pony cart over rough terrain' – **Joyce Carol Oates**

'Charyn's sentences are pure vernacular music, his voice unmistakable' – **Jonathan Lethem**

'Charyn, like Nabokov, is that most fiendish sort of writer – so seductive as to beg imitation, so singular as to make imitation impossible' – **Tom Bissell**

'Absolutely unique among American writers' – *Los Angeles Times*

'Both a serious writer and an immensely approachable one, always witty and readable' – *Washington Post*

'Charyn skillfully breathes life into historical icons' – *New Yorker*

'One of our most intriguing fiction writers' – *O, The Oprah Magazine*

SERGEANT SALINGER

JEROME CHARYN

NO EXIT PRESS

First published in the UK in 2021 by No Exit Press,
an imprint of Oldcastle Books Ltd,
Harpenden, UK

noexit.co.uk
@noexitpress

ISBN
978-0-85730-471-1 (Paperback)
978-0-85730-472-8 (Ebook)

2 4 6 8 10 9 7 5 3 1

Typeset in 11 on 14pt Garamond MT
by Avocet Typeset, Bideford, Devon, EX39 2BP
Printed and bound by CPI Group (UK) Ltd, Croydon, CR0 4YY

Contents

PRELUDE

Oona

April 1942

1

VOLUPTU-U-U-U-U-OUS.

She was sixteen and entitled to sit at the king's lair, Table 50, where Winchell presided. Tonight, on a whim, he wore his lieutenant commander's uniform with his initials embroidered in gold near his heart. He was dying to serve on a battleship. But FDR said he was much more valuable writing his column and protecting the home front. He had vitriol for everyone – J. Edgar Hoover, Errol Flynn, Charlie Chaplin, Mayor La Guardia, Ethel Barrymore, and Eugene O'Neill, the father of this voluptuous child.

She'd been coming to the Stork since she was fifteen and a half. Winchell called her 'New York's New Yorkiest debutante' in his column. She had dark lashes, dark eyes, and dark hair. She'd arrive at the Stork in her school uniform – she went to Brearley, the swankiest prep school on the Upper East Side. The headmistress had complained about her dual role, as a Brearley girl and nightclub debutante. But Winchell was her protector now, and he could ruin Brearley's reputation with the bat of an eye. No one, not even the devil, wanted one of his barbs in 'On Broadway,' with all its syndication rights. Winchell could drown Brearley in a sea of print.

He pretended to cover his eyes with his tiny, childish paws. 'Oona, I can't bear to look. You break my heart every damn day of the week.'

She pouted at him with her bloodred lips. 'You wouldn't be happy, Uncle Walt, unless I did.'

She had her own closet at the Stork, where she could park her

Mary Janes and put on peep-toe pumps. She wore a strapless affair tonight that she had found while rummaging through Klein's bargain basement. She couldn't afford to shop at Saks, even if her daddy had won the Nobel Prize and was the most pampered playwright in the Free World. She'd only seen him once or twice since she was two. He'd abandoned her and had another wife – a real witch – while Oona and her mother had to live on crumbs at a crappy hotel.

Table 50 could seat Winchell and nine other souls, but since he was feuding with everybody except Frank Costello, the club's master table looked like a gallery of ghosts. Costello sat in his usual spot, with his immaculate fingernails and silver hair. Next to him was Mr B, the owner of the Stork. Mr B had been a bootlegger and had spent time in Leavenworth, but that didn't keep high society away from the Stork. He was the one who had the idea of luring debutantes into the club. He called them 'jelly beans,' with a touch of ridicule. But it was good business. They pulled in all the traffic. Besides, he liked the constant allure of young, pretty girls. And Oona was the prettiest and most voluptuous of them all – a timid tigress, ready to burst out of the seams of whatever dress she wore. She seemed distracted tonight, guarding the chair next to hers when she should have been concentrating on Winchell and his wants. He had made her a celebrity, a girl whose only career was to sit and pose at Table 50 while the Stork's female photographers snapped her picture. Her daddy had seen shots of his debutante daughter in *Redbook* and *Mademoiselle* and the *New York Post* with her bosoms on display and her lips as swollen as a vampire about to suck some blood. He had telephoned Winchell at the Stork a month ago. The captains didn't have to bother carrying a big black clunky phone into the Cub Room. Winchell always had a black telephone near him at Table 50. He took Eugene O'Neill's call. The playwright said that Walter Winchell was turning his daughter into a whore, and that she would be much better off studying to be a nurse or getting a job in an airplane factory after she graduated from high school, or perhaps she could be the first lady announcer at Ebbets Field and dance with Leo Durocher when the Dodgers went to bed.

'Gene,' Winchell said, growing familiar with the playwright, 'do ya know how many soldiers and sailors populate the Stork every night? It's a regular serviceman's paradise. And your luscious daughter, sir, gives them a few moments of delight just by sitting at the debutantes' table... and dancing the rhumba with a general or two. I wouldn't let your little girl dance with Durocher. Good night, good night, Mr O'Neill,' he shouted within earshot of the entire Cub Room. And he didn't attack O'Neill in his column when he could have. *The Iceman Never Cometh. He wouldn't dare.*

FDR also telephoned him at the club. The Boss might want some political favor, and Winchell was prepared to deliver at any cost. But he didn't like *his* debutante coveting an empty chair at Table 50. It unnerved him. He'd made the Stork, and could unmake it if he moved to another club, just as he could strip Oona of whatever polish she thought she had as the club's Debutante of the Year.

And then this lanky boy sat down next to Oona, with big ears and olive skin and a Gypsy's dark eyes. *A tall Yid*, Winchell muttered. He himself was a Yid who never got beyond the sixth grade.

'Oona darling, where did you find this squirt?' He didn't wait for an answer, never did. He stared at Mr B. 'Sherm, how did Big Ears get through the gold chain? Did he fly into the Cub Room, like Dumbo?'

'He's on Oona's guest list,' Mr B said, having to pay court to Winchell at his own club.

'He's still a squirt.'

'He is not,' Oona said, her shoulders bristling. 'He's one of my beaux, Sonny Salinger, the short-story writer. And you can call him Jerry or J. D. if you like.'

'I'll call him "squirt".'

Costello had to intervene. 'Winchell, be nice to the kid. This isn't a barroom brawl. Apologize to Oona and her boyfriend.'

Frank Costello didn't own the Stork Club, even if some people thought he did. But he owned Manhattan. Every mobster south of Boston paid fealty to him.

'Apologize,' Costello sang, with a slight scratch of menace in his musical voice.

'I can't,' Winchell said. 'It's not in my nature, Mr Frank.'

'Sir,' Sonny said, standing up and towering over the table at six feet two and a half. 'I can defend myself.'

'Call me Frank,' Costello said. 'You're a writer, and you should be afraid of Winchell. He could wreck your career. That's what he is, a wrecker.'

'Damn right,' Winchell said.

Oona panicked over her latest cavalier. 'Jerry's had a story accepted by *The New Yorker*. They had to postpone the story on account of Pearl Harbor. They couldn't publish a Christmas story after Pearl. He's been in *Esquire* and –'

'We don't need a list of Sonny's accomplishments, sweetheart,' Costello said. 'He's welcome at the table. He'll be our guest of honor.'

Winchell brooded for a moment.

'Hey, Sonny,' he said from under his elbow, 'who would ya like to meet?'

Sonny wasn't shy about his own worth as a writer. He'd told Oona how much he despised the Stork Club and all its glitter. The famous were like lapdogs waiting to lick and be licked. But he still grabbed at a chance to enter the lion's den. It was a writer's privilege, his education, his descent into the dirt.

He recognized Hemingway a few tables behind him, with that rugged handsomeness – this wasn't the Hem he admired. He worshipped the apprentice in Hemingway, writing like a trapped panther in Paris cafés, not the sanctified and fêted 'Papa' of Key West and Cuba. The panther had broken out of his cage. He must have come to Manhattan to meet with his publisher and rub elbows at the Stork. Early fame had ruined him.

'Isn't that Mr Hemingway sitting there?' he asked.

Winchell didn't even bother to look behind him. '*Hemmy*,' he shouted, 'come over here! A kid wants to meet ya, a member of your fan club – Sonny Salinger.'

Sonny heard a weak, high-pitched midwestern twang. 'Winchell, I thought we were having a feud.'

'We are, Ernie boy. But I'm calling a truce.'

Hemingway rose up from his banquette with a boxer's litheness and danced over to Table 50 on the balls of his feet. He kissed Oona's hand with that resolute charm of his, that irrepressible smile. 'How are you, Miss Oona? Has Sherm been looking after you?'

'Mr Billingsley is very kind. He pays for all my meals.'

'As he should,' said Hemingway, 'as he should. You're his ideal ornament… Hello, Mr Frank.'

Sonny could feel Hemingway's admiration for this prime minister of the mob who behaved like a country squire. 'How are they treating you in Cuba, kiddo?'

'Swell,' Hemingway said. 'I've been chasing Nazi submarines.'

'How many subs have you lassoed so far?' Winchell asked. 'Five – six? Two dozen?'

Hemingway ignored him. He looked at Sonny Salinger with the same irrepressible smile. It was hard to resist. He had a shyness, despite the iron grip of his hand. 'Pleased to meet you, kid.'

Sonny froze. He'd never been tongue-tied before, even in the tightest situation.

'Cardinal-Lemoine,' he finally blurted out. 'Street where you lived, with Bumby and your first wife. I – I went on a pilgrimage to Paris, sat at your café on the place de la Contrescarpe. I gave a few centimes to the clochards. I only had a week, only one. That's all my budget would allow, but I drank in as much as I could.'

Hem lost his enchanted smile. His eyes wandered. He wasn't that young writer freezing his ass off in a café on the Contrescarpe, uncelebrated, with a wife and child, scribbling muscular, modernistic tales in a blue notebook.

'Contrescarpe,' Hem muttered. 'It was a long time ago. I can't work in cafés. I have a bad back. Have to stand when I write… I don't have Walter's clout. FDR will send him anywhere. I'd have to join up as a war correspondent. What about you, Salinger?'

'Tried to enlist,' Sonny said. 'They wouldn't have me.'

He had a slight heart murmur, the docs had told him at his physical, and he was a ball-less wonder, born with an undescended testicle.

Winchell was seething. It was his table, and he was abandoned, left out of the little tête-à-tête. 'What does your father do, Big Ears?'

Sonny would have liked to slap Winchell's own big ears, but he was Oona's guest. And he didn't want her to be banished from Table 50 by this petty tyrant in his toy uniform.

'My father imports Polish ham,' Sonny said.

'Then he must be rich,' cackled the king of the Cub Room. 'Where do ya live?'

'On Park Avenue,' Sonny said.

Winchell couldn't stop cackling. 'Mr Frank, now I get it. Oona has brought her own playboy to the Stork.'

'Walter,' Costello said, 'stop riding the kid. You can't hold Park Avenue against him.'

Sonny could see that flair of madness in Winchell's eyes, like a white-hot maze. 'Who's riding him? I'm the innocent party.'

'You're always innocent,' Hemingway said. 'Can I leave now, Walter?'

'No,' Winchell said with that same sinister flair. 'Sit. Keep us company.'

Hem could have gone back to his own table – that's how Sonny saw it. Hem was the most celebrated novelist we had, while poor Scott Fitzgerald, who had died over a year ago of a broken heart, was half-forgotten. Hem wasn't a ghost, like Scott. He could have laughed in Winchell's face, but he sat down at Table 50, a good little boy. He was angling to become a colonel with his own battalion.

But the War Department was deaf to his pleas. And he knew how close Walter was to FDR. So he hunkered down and ate a chicken hamburger à la Walter Winchell, like everybody else at Winchell's table. The chef prepared it with relish and onions and sweet potato pie. Walter drank Bordeaux and buttermilk.

Oona couldn't sip wine while the Stork's female photographers wandered about with their Speed Graphics. So she had an eggnog without the cognac and would steal a sip of wine from Walter's glass whenever the Speed Graphics weren't around.

Sonny swabbed his chicken burger in mustard, and Walter watched every swab.

'You'll ruin your appetite, kid,' Walter said. 'Mustard isn't good for the sinuses – or the soul.'

No one was immune to Walter's wrath, except perhaps Costello. But even Mr Frank, powerful as he was, didn't want to wind up a 'lasty' in one of Walter's columns – it was the kiss of death, to be the very last item in Winchell's rat-tat-tat. Sonny could imagine his own obit in 'On Broadway.' *A certain snot-nosed scribbler with the initials J.D.S. was declared unphffft by his draft board for having one ball too little or one too many.*

Phffft was Walter's favorite word. It defined the end of something, the ultimate split. A marriage or a friendship could *phffft*, and so could your life or your career. But Walter used that word with an éclat all his own. He took one bite of his chicken hamburger, and as he passed a finger across his throat, like a man sentencing another man to the guillotine, he whispered, *'Phfffft.'*

Then he snarled at Mr B, 'Summon Bruno.'

All action froze at Table 50 until a huge man in a toque that looked like an enormous white mushroom lumbered up the stairs next to the bar – the kitchen was in the bowels of the club.

Bruno, who'd been Mr B's chef for years, was even taller than Sonny, and reached the chandeliers in his magnificent hat. El Morocco wanted to steal him away, but he was devoted to Sherm. Still, he ignored all the maharajas at Table 50, including Frank

Costello, Walter, and Mr B, and bowed to Oona, with that white mushroom still covering his scalp.

'How are you, *ma belle*?'

She glanced at him with her dark eyes. 'I'm in perfect shape, Bruno, but Uncle Walt is having a fit, and God knows why.'

And now the chef deigned to notice Walter with a flick of his brows. 'What's wrong, WW.?'

'Everything,' Winchell said, his voice much more timid in the presence of that toque. 'Your assistant didn't grind the chicken in my burger. It tastes like oatmeal.'

Bruno removed a Lucky Strike from a silver case and stood there until Mr B found his cigarette lighter and prepared the flame. Then he sucked on his Lucky and blew smoke rings at Walter Winchell.

'Would I have a sous-chef prepare the chicken burgers at Table Fifty? I ground the chicken with my own two hands.'

Walter was still suspicious. 'Did you use the same kosher butcher?'

'That butcher is on strike. Someone bombed the premises.'

'*Phffft*,' Walter said without a whisper. 'Then the tale is told. My burger is *treif*. I can always tell.'

'Not exactly,' Bruno said. 'Mr Frank helped us find a butcher at a different location. And that butcher is certified by rabbinical law. But if you aren't happy, WW., I can have the busboys clear the table and serve you something else. Let's say roast of veal à la Sonja Henie.'

'Never mind,' Walter said. 'We can't interrupt a meal, just like that. But next time, I wanna be warned.'

'I'll have a note sent up from the kitchen,' Bruno said. 'I promise.' And he winked at Oona. 'Who's this handsome young chap at your side? I've never seen him at the Stork.'

'He's my favorite suitor, Sonny Salinger.'

Bruno laughed. 'How many do you have?'

'*Dozens*,' she said, defiant in front of that lopsided white hat. 'But

Sonny tops them all. Sonny takes me to museums – and took me to the Stanley once to see a Soviet film.'

'Which Soviet film, *ma belle*?'

Oona's arm curled out like a delicious snake. 'Oh, there were knights with steel on their noses, and they all fell into the ice...'

'*Alexander Nevsky*,' Hem said, like a film scholar with a midwestern squall. 'It was Eisenstein's epic nod to Stalin. The prince of Novgorod destroys the Teutonic invaders in a decisive battle on the ice – I've watched that battle scene ten times. I memorized every shot.'

'Hemmy, what are you talking about?' Walter grumbled.

'Nothing,' Hemingway said as he dug his fork into the sweet potato pie.

Bruno returned to his dungeon downstairs and left Table 50 to its feast of kosher chicken burgers. Sonny could have been sitting at a monk's table. None of the camera girls came around. Everyone chewed in silence. Walter's skin was pink under the chandeliers, like an irascible cherub. Sonny had come to a madhouse – filled with movie stars. He noticed Peter Lorre and Akim Tamiroff sitting at a corner banquette. He noticed Merle Oberon, watched her like a scavenger, as if he could feel her contours, grill into her flesh. He'd joined the drama club, Mask and Spur, at Valley Forge Military Academy. He played all the women's roles in a company of male cadets. He was Juliet to a weak-chinned Romeo; he was Desdemona and Lady Macbeth, his face smeared with charcoal. He was also manager of the fencing team and a member of the French club. He wrote plays and stories with the help of a flashlight under his blanket after the bugler's bedtime call. His mother sent him clippings of his favorite movie stars while he sat in rural Pennsylvania among the other cadets and imagined himself as Errol Flynn and Gary Cooper.

Sonny had dreamt of a Hollywood career during his days at Mask and Spur, though his father considered acting a bum's profession and wanted Sonny to follow him into the importing of cheese and Polish ham. Sonny acquiesced – a little, promising to learn at least two foreign languages. He spent nine months abroad after graduation, mostly in Vienna, where he lived with the Tinkelmans, in the Jewish quarter. He had a tiny room in their maze-like apartment on Dorotheergasse, and was smitten by the Tinkelmans' blond daughter, Lisalein, who was already promised to another man, a student rabbi selected by her father.

Lisa had translucent skin that glowed in the dark. She read Rilke, and was a terrible flirt. She wouldn't meet with Sonny outside her father's flat, and their rendezvous were a few stolen minutes in the maid's closet, where they'd kiss while Lisa left Sonny to fumble in the great enigma of her undergarments, with their endless snaps and ribbons. They'd communicate with notes hidden under a pillow, or inside Sonny's shoe. It exhausted him, this romance without a future and barely a present tense.

He fled to Paris on a third-class ticket, arrived at the Gare de l'Est, with its blinding dome of light, like a religious awakening, took the Métro to the Panthéon, registered at the first fleabag hotel he could find, and prowled the streets like a panther, Hemingway's panther; Sonny was searching for his own apprenticeship – in Paris. He slid along the slippery stones of the rue Mouffetard, with a chunk of bread and blue cheese in his fist, settled in a café on the Contrescarpe, and wrote. He could never be a purveyor of cheese and ham, like his father. He'd have to sacrifice Hollywood and an acting career. He'd been a scribbler at Valley Forge, since he was seventeen, with that flashlight under the blankets. And here he was at the Stork, among all the celebs, with Hemingway right across from him. Hem's eyes were fluttering; his hands shook, as if he were about to have a seizure.

Sonny realized that Hem had his own insane streak, like Walter. Hem was sick of Walter's company, sick of having to pretend that he was at some royal table. But he wouldn't excuse himself – that wasn't a maneuver he admired. He was filled with tauromania. He wrote and lived like a matador.

'Walter, what would happen if there was a whirlwind, and you lost every ghostwriter and press agent and gossiper in Manhattan? You'd freeze to death. You'd have to go off the air, and your column wouldn't be worth shit.'

'Watch your mouth,' said the mob's prime minister with his silver hair. 'We have a schoolgirl at the table.'

'My apologies to Miss Oona,' Hem said. But his eyes still fluttered. 'I was addressing the douchebag.'

Walter took another bite of his chicken burger. 'Hemmy, you don't want to tangle with me. You're not in my league, and you never were. I don't need ghosts. *Phffft!* And you're gone.'

'Yeah,' Hemingway said. 'I read you, Walter – *religiously.* I'm one of your biggest fans. You haven't been so kind to Oona and her friends – you call them "debutramps".'

Spittle appeared on Walter's lower lip. 'I never wrote an unkind word about Oona O'Neill in my life.'

The matador had a crooked smile, attacking with his own invisible lance. 'What about that lasty of yours from a few weeks ago? I can repeat it word for word, Walter, word for word. "*What luscious debutramp arrives at the Stork night after night and keeps her own wardrobe in Mr B's personal closet? Is she or is she not one of the O'Neills?*"'

Walter lost his pink complexion. 'I never said that… Oona, he's lying.'

'It doesn't matter, Uncle Walt.'

'Hemmy, you can go back to your table now – class dismissed.'

The matador crossed his arms and rocked in a chair quilted with satin. 'Wouldn't dream of it, Uncle Walt. I'm having a wallop of a time.'

'I'm warning you,' the columnist said.

Oona rose out of her chair like a sixteen-year-old goddess with her own festivity of flesh and interrupted Walter's counterattack. 'Jerry, let's dance.'

Walter was alarmed. He didn't enjoy being abandoned by one of his protégées in the middle of a battle. He couldn't thrive without an audience. Oona was ungrateful, a spoiled brat, like all the other little society sluts.

'Wait,' he squealed. 'You haven't finished your burger.'

But Sonny escorted her out of the Stork's inner sanctum, and they passed through the plebeian glass door of the main dining room, where all the 'civilians' ate, drank, danced, and gossiped without a glimpse of Merle Oberon and Akim Tamiroff. It was an L-shaped room, with a terrific din that bounced off the mirrors and chandeliers. From time to time, Mr B would make his appearance, and signal to the waiter that a certain diplomat at Table 5 was to have a magnum of Piper-Heidsieck on the house. Otherwise he didn't mingle with the civilians unless there happened to be a brawl. Then he would assume the icy air of a bootlegger and banish the guilty parties from his club for life. But he could sense that Oona would create a stir. She was in all the papers and fashion magazines, thanks to Sherman Billingsley and his roving camera girls. Men and women were riveted to her looks. A cub reporter had sneaked into Brearley and photographed Oona in her gym suit with a pair of hips that were like pliable knife blades. No prep school girl should have flowered like that – it was almost an assault on the nerves.

So Mr B signaled for the society band to scat, and in an instant it was replaced on the tiny bandstand by Lenny's Latin Rialtos. The citizens, who danced between courses, could catch the Rialtos' rhythms like a regular heartbeat; it was a kind of tourist rhumba, where the dancers never missed a step. But Oona was different. Oona was trouble.

Often she danced alone, and she forced the Rialtos to quicken their pace, or they couldn't keep time to the flurry of her hips. Oona was their enchantress, and she came out onto the floor with Sonny Salinger, expecting to teach him a few tricks. But he seized her with alacrity, and she spun around him like a spindle on a silken thread. While she swayed, Sonny's hips held to a tight line, forcing her into a pattern of alternating currents, very fast and very slow.

'Jerry,' she whispered, barely able to catch her breath. The maracas were always one beat behind. The Rialtos could only find Sonny's rhythm with a constant tapping of their toes. Soon there were no other dancers. The civilians couldn't keep up with the clack of Oona's heels. They returned to their tables and watched a rhumba that was beyond their own measure.

'Jerry, gee whiz, when we were at the museum, I didn't –'

'Quiet, Oona,' he said, 'or you'll fall.'

'Never would have figured that you could dance like that.'

And as she stumbled, Sonny gathered her up in his arms and returned her faltering body to the rhythms he had imposed upon the Rialtos and their rattler on the bandstand.

'Where'd you learn?'

He held her motionless for an instant; the rattles stopped. 'I have an older sister. Been doing the rhumba since I was five – with her and my mom.'

'Alexander Nevsky,' she muttered in Sonny's arms. 'Ice.'

And that's when Sonny felt a persistent tap on his shoulder. It was the king of Table 50, the shyster himself, a head shorter than Sonny in his lieutenant commander's uniform.

'Big Ears, can I borrow Oona for a sec? I'd like to show the civilians what the rhumba is really like – à la Walter Winchell.'

Sonny could have defied Winchell, sent him flying across the dance floor, but he would have hurt Oona, wrecked his own chances with her. He was crazy about this Brearley bombshell, possessed by her, lost in her wake. He wanted to marry Miss Oona O'Neill. But his own father had compared a short-story writer to a rag merchant. 'Sonny, your margin is very slim. An editor dies, or catches bronchitis, and you're out on the street.'

So Sonny acquiesced and let Winchell clasp Oona with his childlike fingers. And he was startled by the columnist's gusto. Winchell was a natural song and dance man. He took over the room with every stab of his hips. Oona was nothing more than his accomplice. He swayed with her, clutched her hand, and the Rialtos held to his heartless rhythm. Her exquisite beauty remained in the background somehow, divorced from the synchronized patter of his tiny feet. Winchell was the rhumba artist. Soon he let her hand slip, and performed a solo. Sonny could never have imagined this squat little guy as such a spark plug – a rooster without the wattles. The citizens couldn't stop clapping. 'Walter, Walter.' And suddenly all the swaying stopped. He took Sonny aside, left Oona flat in the middle of a rhumba.

'I can give you a hundred a week,' Walter said.

Sonny stared at him, utterly bewildered.

'You can be my ghost,' Walter said. 'I saw the look in Hemmy's eyes – he recognizes talent.'

'Hemingway hasn't read a word I've written.'

'Don't be such a snob,' Walter said. 'I'm not asking you to kibbitz, or find new material – you'll polish whatever I have in the box.'

'Like your own personal Spinoza,' Sonny said.

'Call it whatever you like, Big Ears – a ghost is a ghost. You'll never starve.'

'I'm not starving now,' Sonny said.

He returned to Oona and picked up where he had left off in his own Manhattan-style rhumba, learnt on the living room rug with his mother and sister as his dancing partners, while his father, Solomon – or Sol – Salinger, who was almost as handsome and tall as Sonny, in pearl gray suspenders and onyx cufflinks, would mock his whole family, mimic every single one, and mutter, 'What a bunch of troopers. My very own vaudeville act.'

It was Sonny who was the real target of his attack, Sonny who wouldn't follow him into imported ham and cheese and earn a proper living, but kept on writing stories, scratch by scratch, as 'the Park Avenue bohemian.'

Sonny hated Sol – no, he didn't hate his dad, just couldn't bear to be in the same room with him. So the Stork Club was a kind of solace, with its cornucopia of ashtrays that seemed to disappear

right off the tables, its magical crop of movie stars in the Cub
Room, the accident of meeting 'Hemmy,' the wordsmith matador
he admired most when he himself started to write. Winchell was
another matter – the guy he had to tolerate, like a pet rodent. But
here he was with Oona, at the Stork, in a room full of mirrors,
and once Winchell stopped dancing, his aura seemed to fade,
and it was his dark-eyed 'debutramp' who flashed wall-to-wall,
her image multiplying and mutating in the glass as her voluptu-
u-u-u-u-ous body rippled, until Sonny seized her hand, led her
past Walter Winchell, past the cloakroom, where he collected
her cashmere coat, past Mr B's gold chain, and right out of the
Stork.

2

THEY WERE IN LA GUARDIA LAND NOW, and the mayor, who
also served as the overlord of civil defense, believed in a
perpetually dark town, where streetlamps left a stuttering haze
after the nearest Con Ed plant had been taken partially off the
grid, while searchlights on the tallest rooftops, roaring with their
own generators, tried to flag a rogue Messerschmitt that might
suddenly appear in the blue-black sky in some mythical air raid.
Sonny realized that the mayor was out of his mind. That mythical
Messerschmitt would have had to refuel and refuel again and again
on its voyage from a secret airstrip in occupied territory. But the
Little Flower reigned in Manhattan, and *his* madness was law.

Sherman Billingsley's club was only five blocks from the
suite that Oona occupied with her mother at the Hotel Weylin.
But Cinderella needed her carriage. So Sonny hailed a Checker
cab. They sat in a backseat as big as a forest, and kissed like a

couple of lunatics, the cabbie spying on them in the mirror, his tongue wagging against his teeth. Oona was always passionate in a Checker cab. Sonny fumbled under her coat, while she sat with her legs in his lap and dug her hand under his shirt like a friendly Messerschmitt.

They arrived at the Weylin in less than four minutes. Sonny was in a daze from his proximity to Oona's flesh. Whatever she wore was like a mysterious sheath that sheltered her from the eyes and hands of overeager boys and men. She hadn't slept with a single one of them, though she was drawn to Sonny's brooding looks. *My Heathcliff*, she told herself, *my Manhattan Gypsy*.

There were recruiting posters all over the place – in storefronts, on fire escapes, and right near the rumpled green canopy of the Weylin. It was invariably Uncle Sam, in a red foulard and a top hat with a blue ribbon that featured a white star, while he pointed a finger at whoever passed in front of his stern gaze. And Sonny thought he was going bonkers, because he could have sworn that Uncle Sam said:

> *SONNY SALINGER*
> *I WANT YOU*
> *ENLIST NOW*

He went through the Weylin's revolving door with Oona and into a lobby filled with broken floor tiles, settees and love seats with worn threads, and lamps with missing bulbs. The lobby was deserted except for the night manager, who stood behind his wire cage with a lurid grin.

'Evening, Miss Oona. Will the young gentleman be accompanying you upstairs? Shall I ring madame?'

'That won't be necessary, Charles,' she told him. It was well past midnight, the Cinderella hour.

Then she whispered in her suitor's ear. 'Oh, Jerry, you know what will happen. We'll fool around and...'

Sonny's throat was raw with desire. 'I'll only stay a couple of minutes, I promise.'

She laughed, and her forehead sizzled with its own electric light. 'You said *five* minutes the last time, and you stayed two hours. You woke Mama out of her beauty rest. She was wearing one of those silly masks that covered all her creams, and she said, "Oona dear, what the devil are you doing behind the couch?" I had to keep you under my muskrat coat until Mama stumbled back to her room... Jerry, I couldn't go through that again. I'd have a heart attack. I'll be leaving for California the minute I graduate; you know that.'

'Then you've given up on the idea of Vassar.'

He could have visited her at Poughkeepsie, stolen her from her dorm, this dark-eyed Cinderella of his. Poughkeepsie was close enough for him to plot – and plan, even propose, once he could afford a ring.

'And what did college do for you, my little Ernest Hemingway? You've flunked out of more schools than I can count... No, I intend to become an actress, and that's final.'

'I'm not Hemingway,' he had to mutter. 'And you won't have Uncle Walt to help guide your career out on the coast.'

Somehow he'd gotten into the hotel's rickety elevator with her.

'There are plenty of Uncle Walts. I found one, and I'll find another. And he'll still mention me – from time to time.'

The night elevator man, who wore a rumpled uniform that reeked of sweat, steered Oona and her beau up to the sixth floor. He opened the accordion-like gate and let them out of the car.

'You can't come in,' she said.

Sonny pressed Oona against the wall while he gnawed at her.

'Jesus, Jerry, I'm not a rabbit. You cannot eat my face.'

Oona was giggling now. She opened the door with a kind of skeleton key and dragged Sonny inside. They stood in the dark. It was the Weylin, with its army of cockroaches and mice. The hotel had become a haven for prostitutes and bookmakers. Gangsters rented out entire floors and bankrolled Friday-night craps games that floated from suite to suite. Crusty old men in their seventies and eighties, who had long resided at the hotel, left carnations and boxes of Godiva chocolates on the doormat for Oona's Mama, Agnes Boulton, who also had high cheekbones and was still a celebrated beauty. There were love letters, too, sometimes twenty pages long, like white petals buried in ink.

This scatter – letters, carnations, and rotting boxes of Godiva – was everywhere.

Agnes couldn't seem to collect the boxes or throw the carnations and white petals into the trash. Sonny kept gnawing at Oona. A light was snapped on. Agnes Boulton stood there without a stitch, her own Lady Godiva in the veiled light of a corner lamp, at the very edge of the foyer. Sonny tried not to stare, but she could have been Oona's older sister.

'Aggie, I'd like to marry your daughter,' Sonny blurted.

Agnes Boulton had met Sonny several times. They'd had hot chocolate at Rumpelmayer's, chicken pie at Schrafft's. Agnes was also a writer, and had sold her first story at sixteen. She wrote for pulp magazines, like *Blue Book* and *Argosy*, and none of her tales could tantalize Sonny – there was nothing but static between the words, and the words themselves were composed of tinsel. He couldn't tell her that, of course.

Finally, with one rhythmical sweep, Agnes Boulton put on the sheerest nightgown Sonny had ever seen, a nightgown that didn't bother to hide her nipples or her narrow hips.

'Sonny darling,' she said, with a brogue she must have picked up from the Provincetown Players, 'my little Oona is sixteen.'

'Mama,' Oona said, 'I'm taller than you are.'

'Never mind. Will you have your nuptials while you're studying for your final exams? It's out of the question.'

'I know it's out of the question,' Oona said. 'Still, Sonny is *my* business.'

Agnes Boulton had a crying fit right in the foyer. 'What would your father say!'

'Who could tell?' she snarled, with a wrinkled nose that couldn't impair her beauty. 'I didn't think I had one.'

'You mustn't say that,' Agnes Boulton moaned, 'not in front of this boy. We are a family – the O'Neills.'

She pointed to the posters of Eugene O'Neill's plays on the foyer walls – she carried them with her from hotel to hotel. Sonny liked the poster of Paul Robeson in *The Emperor Jones*, wearing a bone white uniform, with his arms stretching out to some strange infinity.

'Mother,' Oona said, 'live in your mausoleum. Your husband has one wife too many.'

'Child,' Agnes Boulton said, 'that's cruel, very cruel.'

'No, it's not. I'm in the same scenario as you... Now say good night to my fiancé and go back to bed.'

Agnes Boulton was crying again, and Oona had to lend her a handkerchief. 'He's not your fiancé.'

Agnes wandered back into her bedroom in her bare feet, while Oona dug her tongue into Sonny's mouth for an instant; it felt like a violent wet bird that paralyzed him with rapture as she shoved him out the door.

'That was a gas, telling Mama that you wanted to marry me.'

'But it's true,' Sonny had to insist.

Her nose wrinkled again. 'Are you deaf, darling boy? Will we have a postal marriage? I'll be out in California.'

Sonny was silent in that slatternly corridor with its peeling wallpaper. 'But you might come back,' he muttered.

'To this dump?' she said. 'Not a chance... Oh, I couldn't give you up, Sonny, not when you can do the rhumba like that. My God, I almost peed in my pants. And Uncle Walt is fond of you. He thinks you can take over his column while he's on vacation. Now go! I'll meet you at the Stork.'

Sonny pretended to smile. 'No more museums, no more Russian movies?'

'Who has the time?'

'But when, Oona, when will we meet?'

'Golly,' she said, ruminating with a scratch of her jawbone. 'I have midterms, and a lot of commitments to Uncle Walt and Mr B. It's not that simple being Debutante of the Year at the Stork. I'll leave a note in your mailbox, like I always do.'

She wrapped Sonny inside the wings of her coat, and while old men wandered about in their pajamas, she ground her left hip against his groin, licked his earlobe with a salty tongue, said, 'I'm taken with you, Sonny Salinger, I really am, and that's the problem. But you're a luxury I can't afford – not until I'm an established movie star.'

Then Oona freed him from her own embrace and hopscotched across the corridor to her mother's door.

3

IT WAS WELL PAST THREE by the time Sonny walked home from the Weylin. He kept seeing posters of Uncle Sam in the same red foulard and top hat.

SONNY SALINGER
WE WANT YOU

The night doorman had to let him in, or Sonny could never have gotten inside his father's citadel at 1133 Park Avenue.

'Good morning, young Mr Salinger.'

The doorman took him upstairs in 1133's unadorned elevator car.

The Salingers never locked their front door, even when they went to the Plaza in Daytona for weeks at a time. So Sonny walked into the apartment with all the quiet grace of a cat burglar. His mother and father sat like sentinels in the sunken living room, wearing identical silk gowns – Sol and Miriam, née Marie. Sol had been a traveling salesman from Chicago, a tall, handsome devil, fond of Arrow shirts, who found her on a farm in Iowa, an Irish beauty with red hair, and he ran off with her. They operated a nickelodeon in Chicago – Marie became Miriam to appease his parents, though she never really converted to Judaism. The nickelodeon failed. He stumbled into import/export, was soon a success, managing J. S. Hoffman & Company's eastern branch – Sol Salinger, Manhattan's lord of unkosher cheese and ham.

'Look who we have here,' Sol said, 'the bon vivant himself.' His ears were as large and fully flowered as his son's. They both had the same olive skin. 'Where the hell were you? Your mother was worried.'

'I was at the Stork Club – with Walter Winchell.'

'That bum. He sends his poison darts wherever he can. The guy doesn't miss.'

'Winchell wants me to write for him,' Sonny said. 'To be his ghost.'

Sol broke into one of his demonic laughing fits, and Miriam had to pummel his back. 'You poor schmuck,' Sol said, tears of rage in his eyes. 'Winchell wants you to wipe his ass.'

'Solly,' Miriam said. 'You shouldn't use such language.' Her hair was as red as it had ever been, even if she had to dye it at the roots.

'I found the girl I want to live with for the rest of my life,' Sonny said.

'Who?' Sol asked. 'Sophie Tucker or Ethel Barrymore?'

'No,' Sonny said. 'It's Eugene O'Neill's daughter.'

'You mean the little shiksa who waits downstairs for you and leaves notes with the doorman? Why doesn't she come upstairs like a decent girl and introduce herself to your parents?'

'Dad, she doesn't have a minute to spare. She goes to Brearley. Oona leaves notes for me after class. That's how we meet.'

Sol suffered another laughing spell. 'She's a slut,' he said, 'Brearley or no Brearley. Boy oh boy, I've seen pictures of her in the *Mirror* with her boobs on the table.'

Miriam had to pummel his back again. 'Solly, that's not fair. She's a child, and photographers take advantage of her. You shouldn't be so disrespectful. Apologize to Sonny.'

'Apologize for what? Your precious boy, who scribbles at home like a little rabbi, is in love with a debutante who likes to flaunt her looks. Christ, a war is going on. The Krauts and the Nips are knocking the crap out of us. We haven't had one victory, not one. Roosevelt is having conniptions. And our Sonny decides to become a troubadour.'

'Stop it, Sol,' Miriam said, her temples pulsing under that crown of red hair. They were like a comedy act, with Sonny as their stooge. She swiped a cigarette from a gold box on the glass coffee table beside their divan, a Pall Mall, lit it with trembling fingers, and said, 'Show him the paper.'

'What paper?'

'That letter,' she said, 'from the president of the United States.'

Sol handed him a wrinkled letter – it was Sonny's draft notice. He'd been reclassified, and was suddenly deemed fit for service. His slight heart murmur no longer mattered to Uncle Sam now that the military was in disarray.

ORDER OF INDUCTION
To Jerome David Salinger
GREETINGS...

A tangle of emotions whipped right through Sonny – euphoria, fear, vertigo, and a rumbling anger against Sol.

'Dad, that letter was addressed to me. You had no right to open it.'

'I didn't,' Sol pleaded. 'Your mother did.'

Miriam clawed at her heart, with the cigarette still in her mouth.

'We were frightened, Sonny – so *official*. With the president's own seal. We worried they might deport you.'

'Deport me for what? Publishing short stories?'

'Sonny,' Sol said, 'don't be such a smart-ass. Why would Roosevelt write to you when you were classified as unfit for service?'

'Dad, that letter wasn't *really* from Roosevelt. My draft board just borrowed his name. I'm on a goddamn list. And my number came up – it was like a spin of the wheel. Call me lucky – or unlucky.'

'Go figure,' Sol said. 'We have an Einstein in the house. He has every sort of theorem in his big fat brain. But a feast is required – dinner at Lüchow's. How many sons do I have, and how often do they get inducted?'

'I'd rather go to Schrafft's,' Miriam said, with a vacant, terrified look.

'Come on,' Sol said. 'Schrafft's is for widows and maiden aunts.'

'But I could be a widow... if Sonny is stolen from me.'

Now Sol covered his eyes and rocked back and forth, back and forth. 'Miriam, what are you saying? There are no widows here.' And he tried to escort his wife into the bedroom, the belt of his gown trailing on the carpet. But Miriam broke free and wrapped her arms around Sonny.

'I won't let that malingerer Roosevelt have him.'

Sol was bewildered. 'Miriam, are you a mental? Why do you call FDR a malingerer?'

'Because he stole my boy, and never bothered to prepare for this war.'

Sonny had to remove his mother's arms from around his neck. She nearly tottered, and he had to hold her up, but he wasn't thinking of Miriam or Sol, or Uncle Sam, or his induction notice, really a calling card to Fort Dix, in the heartland of New Jersey – with its endless airstrips, firing ranges, and marshlands, where an inductee like Jerome David Salinger might get lost and never be found again. Sonny didn't give a damn. He didn't even care about surviving the war. He was preoccupied with one thing alone – his interrupted romance with Oona O'Neill.

4

ONA WAS IN A FOREST, and she wore nothing but a fisherman's net. And right in the middle of the forest was Table 50, but it didn't have any chairs, except one. There were mirrors hanging from the tree trunks. A man sat down, seized the chair for himself. Oona didn't recognize him at first. He was wearing a white toque, like Bruno, Mr B's chef, but it wasn't Bruno, wasn't Bruno at all. There were deep red gouges on his cheeks, as if his face had been set on fire with a torch. It was Uncle Walt, without his usual truculence. He was shivering in his tiny kingdom at Table 50, in the forest. And then she realized that the forest itself was on a river of ice. Knights with steel on their noses stood behind the trees, like the ones from *Alexander Nevsky*. But these knights hadn't come to battle. They watched Uncle Walt.

A bell rang and dragged Oona from her dream. It was the house phone. She cursed, got out of bed in her flannel gown, crossed the living room in a slight daze, and picked up the phone. The night manager was on the line.

'Christ, Charles, do ya know what time it is?'

'Sure, Little Mum, it's five-oh-six A.M. on the dot. And you have a young gentleman downstairs. He's quite persistent. He won't leave. I could summon the house dick. But I wouldn't want to create a scandal. I believe he's wearing pajamas under his top-coat. It's most irregular.'

'Did he offer you a name?'

'Yes, Little Mum. "Sherman Billingsley".'

Oona giggled to herself. 'Show him up, Charles.'

'I will, Little Mum, I most certainly will. I believe it's the same young gentleman who accompanied you a bit earlier.'

'Charles,' she said, 'I know damn well who it is – my fiancé. I lost him for a couple of hours.'

She hung up the house phone and waited for Sonny near the door. He knocked once, timidly, like some trickster summoned to the dean's office at a second-rate college. She opened the door, and there he was – Sonny in a topcoat and pajamas, a fedora perched over one eye.

'My pirate,' she said, 'my very own pirate – in his pajamas. Well, come on in.'

They tiptoed across a vast territory of furniture and tottering towers of Godiva chocolates and entered Oona's bedroom. It was mostly barren except for a framed photo beside her bed of Oona and her father on a beach, taken when she was one or two. She was sitting on his shoulders, and the playwright had a mischievous smile beneath his mustache.

'Well, Sonny, that's quite chivalrous, to visit me *twice* the very same night. Charles almost sent for the house detective.'

'I didn't have a choice,' he said with a measure of pain. 'You're in the middle of exams, and the next time you leave a message with my doorman, I'll be gone.'

Oona could barely tell what was on his mind – perhaps he was stuck somewhere inside one of his own stories.

'Well, where will ya be?'

'At Fort Dix.'

She looked at his draft notice, which he had carried with him in its original envelope. 'I thought…'

'Oona, I was lying in bed, in my pajamas, smoking one of mother's Pall Malls, and I realized I might never see you again. So I came over – on a whim. No, it was more than a whim. I had to see you.'

'Private Sherman Billingsley in his pajamas.'

She shucked off his topcoat and pulled him down onto her narrow bed. She wasn't wearing her undies, and the torturous lines of a garter belt. He tried not to peek at her nipples and pubic hair that rose up through the wrinkles of her flannel gown. 'Poor little civilian soldier,' she said as she batted off his fedora, clutched him by his big ears, and placed him near the taunt outline of her left nipple.

And Sonny began to suckle like some kind of satyr. He didn't even attempt to remove her nightgown. She had to protect her status as the alluring ice queen of Table 50 – Sonny knew that. She moaned like a little girl and kept clutching his ears. A good part of her gown was covered with spittle.

'Sonny,' she whispered, 'you'd better stop.'

He hiked up her gown to the middle of her thighs and caressed her calves. She shivered, and shoved him away.

'Oona, what if Uncle Sam grabs me and I vanish into the void?'

'I have a solution,' she said.

She guided his hand under her gown again, as if it belonged to a blind man, and let it rove against the silk between her legs – for a second. It was Sonny who was shivering now. This moment, he realized, the touch of Oona's silk on his fingertips, would remain with him – a live, electric wound. She had the erotic power of a sixteen-year-old witch.

'You can't stay here, Sonny, in my bed. Mama will kill us, even if she admires you. She's read all your stories, and underlines every other word in green ink.'

'Why?'

'To cannibalize your gifts, I suppose. She steals from *everybody*.'

So he put on his topcoat over the pajamas, looking like some ridiculous cavalier. Oona would grieve, mourn his absence at Table 50, especially to Uncle Walt.

'I'll write,' he said.

'You'd better!'

And then she began to sob. 'I'll miss you, Sonny Salinger. I never had a beau who went away – just like that.'

She heard a crackling sound in her mother's bedroom. She threw Sonny out the door, licked both his eyelids like a feline on the prowl, whispered, 'Don't forget me,' and rushed back inside.

Agnes Boulton stumbled about in her sleeping mask. 'Is there a problem, dear?'

'No, Mother. Charles rang us. He said there was a prowler on the premises. But it was a false alarm. Go back to bed!'

Oona returned to her bedroom. She didn't want to dream of a forest with mirrors hanging from the tree trunks and knights with steel on their noses. None of her beaux ever dropped her or ran away to war. She had to remind herself that Sonny's draft notice wasn't a slap in the face. She panicked, as if she were still in that forest of mirrors. Sonny's doorman had become her letter box. But what if Sonny was sent to some camp in the interior, and the doorman didn't know his latest address?

He'd left his fedora – it sat on her bed. She put on the hat and gazed at herself in the mirror.

She saluted the face she saw. Then she tossed the hat across the room, curled up, and went back to bed. She didn't dream of knights with steel noses. She didn't dream at all.

PART ONE

Slapton Sands

April–May 1944

1

'S AL-IN-GER!'

The young corporal had raced up the winding stairs of the castle and stood against the stone wall to catch his breath. He was looking for Sonny, the granddad of his regiment, billeted with a bunch of nineteen-year-olds.

'Sergeant, New York is calling. Come quick. You don't want to lose the connection, sir.'

'Corporal Benson, you don't have to keep saying *sir* to a non-commissioned officer. You might wound your larynx.'

'I understand, sir, but come quick. Captain gives me hell if someone misses a call.'

Sonny followed the young corporal down the winding stairs – it was the remains of a medieval castle with murder holes for archers. He imagined these archers as the elite foot soldiers and snipers of their own era, sworn to the earls of Devon or some other panoply of gangster princes. A single archer could command the terrain in front of the castle from one hole and couldn't be touched or attacked.

The telephone sat in an alcove in the old dungeon that was now an underground canteen. The canteen was deserted except for a few Red Cross nurses who sat in a far corner, eating fish and chips in their fancy blue uniforms. Some wore officers' caps; others wore coronets. They preferred captains and colonels, but the prettiest of them, Lieutenant Veronica Hamm, sensed that Sonny had a higher standing than most other staff sergeants. Yankee colonels kept clear of him, and she wondered why.

A few volunteers from the Red Cross Motor Corps entered the canteen in their fancy shoulder straps and black leather boots. They considered themselves the lords of the canteen. With them was Captain Norbert Whittle in his Oxford gray tunic. He was commandant of the entire fleet of ambulances in South Devon. Short and blond, with bristling blue eyes and a scar that ran down one cheek, he abhorred this Yankee invasion of *his* countryside. And he couldn't understand why a staff sergeant like Sonny had his own quarters at Tiverton Castle.

'How are you, Yank? Having some fun with the natives? I've kept my eye on you. Chatting up young girls in knickers at a coffee bar near Angel Hill? Shame on you.'

The nurses laughed and licked their fingers. 'Ain't he a naughty one,' said Lieutenant Hamm. 'Sergeant Salinger, you have five girls at this table. Don't you want to chat us up? You might not get another chance.'

Sonny had little interest in Lieutenant Hamm; she was the Red Cross's own Veronica Lake, a femme fatale with a dreamy, cross-eyed look and a grab bag of tricks. He had another kind of calamity to consider. He would have to brace himself for his mother's call. She phoned him religiously once a week through the Devon exchange, sent him woolen socks and articles about Hollywood stars – Miriam was the Hedda Hopper of Manhattan. Sonny had to learn from his own mother the rituals of Oona's romance with that miserable satyr, Charlie Chaplin, who was *three* times her age; she married him last June, the moment she turned eighteen. She'd gone out to Hollywood, while he was shunted from base to base, fort to fort, and no matter how hard Sonny petitioned, he couldn't get past the barrier of OCS, as a potential officer candidate. Some of his persistence concerned Oona. He had wanted to descend upon Hollywood as a second lieutenant during one of his furloughs. He wrote her letters that were impassioned love songs, often twice a day, and soon she stopped replying. It was the satyr's fault.

He marched past the commandant and his little bump of Motor Corps boys and picked up a telephone receiver as black as the stone-like buttons on the commandant's blouse.

'Sergeant Jerome David Salinger,' the operator sang, 'New York calling. Your party is on the line.'

Sonny thanked the overseas operator and heard a click.

'Mom, bless you for the socks. I have the warmest feet of any soldier boy in Devon.'

But there was silence at the other end of the line and not that usual whimper of 'Hello, hello, hello.'

He heard a sniffle, then a sob.

'Mother, is something wrong? I miss your Hollywood reports. Is Dad ill? Has he had problems moving over to the domestic ham and cheese market?'

He could hear a sudden chirp. 'Jerry, it's me.'

No one called him Jerry now. *Jerry* was another name for the Germans.

The left side of his face froze. His tongue was trapped.

'I just couldn't have all that bitterness,' Oona said. 'Some of the stuff you wrote me about Charlie – after our marriage, monstrous things. They didn't sound like the Sonny I knew.'

His face unfroze and all his tattered logic returned. 'You aren't in Hollywood. The operator said New York...'

He listened to the little teasing laugh he loved so much. 'Sonny, I'm at Table Fifty – with Uncle Walt.'

'Big Ears,' Walter Winchell cackled into the phone, 'I told ya to work for me. I'm considered *essential* to the United States. You could have sat out the war.'

'But I like it here in Devon. I don't have to watch you dance. Can you please put Oona back on the line?'

'Mrs Chaplin, you mean.'

'Yeah,' Sonny said. 'Mrs Charlie Chaplin.' He was furious. The Stork Club had stolen Oona from him. She wouldn't have become Debutante of the Year without the Stork, would have been just another girl from Brearley, who wasn't photographed with Winchell and didn't wear skin creams in women's magazines. She would have stayed in Manhattan, with Sonny perhaps…

He had written awful things after her marriage, had made obscene drawings of Oona and the satyr – a shriveled old man with a swollen prick – and sent them to her, out of desperation as much as spite. He admired *Modern Times* and Chaplin's other classics, had followed the Little Tramp from film to film – until Chaplin cast a spell over his girl.

'Oona, are you still there? I shouldn't have sent you those letters. But you didn't write, and all I got from my mother were Cinderella stories.' And then he blurted like a little boy, 'Love you, Oona, always did.'

The sobbing grew violent. 'Jerry, please don't say that. We were comrades, good friends.'

'Comrades,' he spat into the phone, remembering the touch of her silken hairs like some instrument flying out of a murder hole at a castle in Devon.

'I was attracted to you, Jerry, but you heard Uncle Walt. I'm a married woman.'

'Then why did you call?' He was a member of CIC, the Counter Intelligence Corps, had trained in Maryland and with a British team in Derbyshire, knew every trick of espionage and interrogation, could rip out a man's jaw with a pair of hooked fingers, gut him with the prongs of a fork. Oona shouldn't have been able to find Sergeant Salinger. He was considered a ghost with an armband, a pistol, and a gold badge, a CIC agent attached to the Twelfth Infantry of the Fourth Division. He'd given out his number to Miriam and Sol, no one else.

'Jeez,' Oona said. 'I was at the Stork, and –'

'But how did you get this number?'

'From Uncle Walt. He called up some general, and I don't know, here we are. I wanted to say I'm sorry. I took advantage – a little. All the other girls at Brearley were jealous that I had a beau like you, with your Gypsy eyes. You met me outside of school like –'

'Your own private prince.'

'Exactly,' she said. 'But it just wasn't in the cards. I didn't lie. I told ya I was going out to Hollywood, and that I wanted to be an actress.'

'But you're not an actress now.'

'That's my fate… I heard from your doorman that you were overseas.'

'You went to Park Avenue?'

'The way I always did,' she said. 'I thought of the Stanley, and that battle on the ice, and I wanted to wish –'

The line went dead. He'd thought of her incessantly, maddeningly, for two whole years, wanted to murder her, kiss her, marry her, and she found the ghost of Tiverton Castle in a few minutes with the help of Uncle Walt. The overseas operator returned. 'Sorry, Sergeant Salinger.'

'Oona,' he shouted. He wanted to hold her there forever on that tenuous, crackling string. Her voice excited him, soothed him. He forgot all about her marriage to the satyr. He'd romance her at the Stork with the gifts of a counterintelligence agent – the wonder and secrecy of words, with their brittle truths and scabrous lies. All his feelings had become compromised since he'd entered CIC. The only scabbard and shield he had left were the stories he published in *Collier's* and *The Saturday Evening Post* about soldiers and civilians who wandered through some strange battlefield like lost children.

'Oona, I could hop on a plane. I don't care. We could meet at Table Fifty, do the rhumba…'

He heard a sob that was all too familiar. 'Hop on what? Sonny darling, are you insane? That little gold digger is gone from your life – gone.'

A deep shiver went right through him like a jolt from the Buck Rogers ray gun he remembered as a boy. The overseas operator had lost Oona and returned with Sonny's mom.

'Did you get my last package?'

'Yeah,' he whispered, cupping a hand over the receiver so that the commandant and his cohorts couldn't listen.

'Darling, I can't hear you.'

'Mom, I have enough socks to get me through the war.'

'Then don't be stingy,' she said. 'Share what you have with your buddies.'

'I don't have buddies, Mom. I live in a tower – alone.'

'Is that what you do in Devon?' she asked. 'Then why are you there?'

'I can't talk about my training, Mom. You know that.'

'Sure, sure,' she said in an operatic voice. 'Sonny Salinger, America's top secret. Your father wants to say hello.'

And he went through that numbing ritual, the terrifying space between words, like hot coals tossed at him, one by one – that's what he always had with Sol.

'We – miss – you, son.'

He was frightened of his father's raw emotion. He couldn't respond. 'Dad, how's ham and cheese?'

'Business – is – slow,' Sol said. 'We've had to take a beating. Cut our headquarters in half.'

'Say, Salinger,' Captain Whittle shouted, 'don't hog the line. We have one telephone at the castle, you know. We all want a little piece of the pudding.'

Sonny ignored him.

'You Yanks,' the commandant said, performing for his entourage, 'you come here and think you have the entire show.'

'Dad,' Sonny said like a CIC man, 'the market will come back, you'll see.'

He said good-bye to Miriam and Sol and put back the receiver. He couldn't strike the commandant of the Motor Corps in front of a dozen witnesses. He would have been ripped from the ranks of CIC, and sentenced to sit out the war. But the commandant was seething about the little gambol at the phone. He stood in Sonny's way.

'We don't want you at the castle, Yank.'

He tore the telephone right out of its socket in the wall, grinning like a jackanapes. 'Now you'll have to have your little tête-à-têtes at some call box on Blundell's Road.'

Sonny's jaw was rippling.

'Look at him, lads,' the commandant chortled. 'He'd love to scalp me, he would. He's as wild as a Red Indian.'

Sonny barreled past the commandant and marched out of the castle with the same ripple in his jaw.

2

TIVERTON, A LITTLE TOWN IN DEVON that had gone to the dogs until the Fourth Division arrived with its general staff, usurped several buildings on the cobbled stones of Barrington Street, grabbed the ruins of Tiverton Castle for itself, and established its headquarters with armed guards, but without much secrecy, at a manor house on a greensward at the very edge of town. Now Tiverton hummed with the noise and currency of GIs, staff officers, and Red Cross personnel. The town sat at the ford of two rivers, but there was such a scarcity of river traffic that Tiverton might have disappeared without the Fourth Division. And it fell upon Sonny and several other CIC agents to keep townsfolk and members of the Fourth apart. Officers and their bodyguards could sit in cafés or tearooms and buy vegetables and tins of deviled ham from the greengrocer on William Street, but they were discouraged from having long chats, which might provide some clue about where and when the Allies intended to strike. Sonny himself could wander about. The CIC had free rein over Tiverton. His own unofficial headquarters was a café on Gold Street, the Blue Mermaid – the name must have come from some imaginary creature that had risen out of the river Exe. She was pictured in the window of the café with a blue mouth and a blue tail, and somehow this goddess reminded Sonny of Oona O'Neill, at least the Oona he recalled, as her lips turned blue in the cold. The café had different-colored stones on its outer wall, like a solid, compacted rainbow.

Many schoolgirls congregated at the café, and Sonny must have seemed exotic to them wearing his red-and-black CIC armband, like some royal chamberlain or military man who could oblige a general to cut off a conversation with a greengrocer. The schoolgirls ravished him with questions. But he never spoke about the war. Not one of these girls was as voluptu-u-u-u-ous as Oona in her Brearley uniform. They did the boogie-woogie to their own musical beat, in their flats and high socks. They called him 'Billy the Kid.'

'Do you have a bride in the States, Billy?'

'No,' he nodded.

'Then you must be on the prowl,' said the prettiest of the schoolgirls.

'Someday perhaps. But you get very cautious once your heart is broken.'

And they all wanted to hear about Billy the Kid's broken heart.

The owner of the café got them to scat and they went off like a tiny legion to the café across the street.

'They are very cheeky, Sergeant. Might I refill your cup?'

Sonny thanked the owner, Ralph, who was in his fifties, and couldn't become a crusader in this war.

'A bit of ersatz cream and sugar, Sergeant? And what about a lemon tart, made by the wife's own lovely hand?'

Sonny sat there with a notebook. He'd started a novel about a prep school boy who went on the prowl and never returned to school. He'd taken a course at Columbia with the country's foremost literary editor, Whit Burnett, who had published two of his stories in a prominent quarterly, and had encouraged him to write a novel. But Sonny preferred to sprint across narrow terrain, and go on to the next narrow terrain and the next; still, he went down several rabbit holes in his novel and was left with a useless clot of words. And while he sat at the Blue Mermaid with his notebook and his untouched tart, Corporal Benson appeared.

'Sorry to disturb you, sir, but you're wanted at the castle.'

'Wanted by whom?'

'It's all hush-hush, sir. I think it's a bit of treason.'

3

THE RUINS RESEMBLED A FORTRESS that had been eaten alive, sucked apart from its own interior, since half the towers still stood, with barred windows, brazen mortar and brick. There were no sentries about, amid this little twitch of treason. Sonny climbed up to the southeast tower and was never challenged once – the tower served as an interrogation room. Both his arms were tingling. Inside, he found one of his mentors, Colonel Byron Rose, headmaster of Sonny's training school in Derbyshire. Byron had several broken knuckles. He'd survived a horrific fire at Dunkirk and had blisters under both eyes that had all the decorative swirls of a mask. With him was the little commandant of the Red Cross Motor Corps and Nurse Hamm, handcuffed to a single chair that couldn't accommodate them and their buttocks – the chair shivered under their weight. The room itself was barren except for a lamp and that shivering chair. The captain had red bumps under both eyes. Sonny went to clean the snot and blood that ran down the nurse's nostrils.

'Don't,' Byron said in a menacing whisper. He handed Sonny a sketchbook. 'What do ye see, lad?'

Sonny was puzzled. 'I see my regiment on maneuvers – somewhere in the hills of Devon.'

'Now turn the page.'

There were other sketches of the same riflemen in full battle gear, done in charcoal. Sonny himself was among them.

'Has Derbyshire examined the drawings?' he asked.

'Yes – *infinitely*.'

'And what have your cryptos uncovered?'

'Not a clue,' Byron said with scorn. 'But that's not the issue. The commandant of *our* Motor Corps out on a lark, sketching *your* boys? Come on, Salinger, isn't that a rotten kettle of fish?'

Sonny was still confused. 'The terrain is barely identifiable, sir.'

'That's the whole point. We're massing for a big push. And Mr Ambulance here and his whore are providing proof of that push. Did ye know that they met with Jerry before the war?'

'It was a Red Cross conference – in Berlin,' Captain Whittle said.

Bryon wrapped him once with the full force of his knuckles, and the chair toppled over. Whittle and Nurse Hamm landed on the stone floor all in a tangle, while Byron hovered over them like a mountainous hawk.

'Did I ask you to speak, old son?'

'No, sir, you did not,' Whittle said, his nose running like Nurse Hamm's.

Byron took out a file from an enormous cardboard sleeve, shuffled several photographs, and revealed them to his captives.

'Do ye recognize any of these chaps?'

'Yes,' Nurse Hamm said with a whistling sound. 'They were part of the German delegation.'

'And members of German military intelligence – Abwehr agents posing as Red Cross maharajas. Did they attempt to recruit you, offer some silver and gold?'

Nurse Hamm stared into his mean little eyes, and they frightened and bewildered her. 'Money was never discussed. We exchanged addresses… and then we had the blitz.'

'I'm talking about *another* blitz,' Byron said. 'Captain, did you prepare your pictures for our German friends?'

'No,' the commandant insisted. 'I would never do that. They're for my portfolio.'

'Look at him! Our local Toulouse-Lautrec. And what about Lieutenant Hamm? How long have you been shagging her, old son? We have you both on our lists, gadding about like lovebirds. Is she your contact with Jerry and the Abwehr?'

Sonny looked inside the cardboard sleeve. The first three Abwehr agents were dead. The fourth had been blinded on the Eastern Front, and was convalescing at a soldiers' home in Mannheim, permanently removed from the war.

'Salinger,' Byron said, 'take over the interrogation. Slap them, and slap them hard. We can't afford any slipups. Time is precious.'

Sonny had to accommodate this half-mad colonel, who could have demoted him and left him to rot in Devon.

He stepped on Whittle's hand.

'I like that, lad,' Byron said, 'I like that a lot.'

Then Sonny kneeled over Captain Whittle. 'Are you arrogant – or just dumb?'

'I can't follow you,' Whittle muttered, whipping his head back and forth.

'Why would you draw pictures of a regiment on secret maneuvers?'

'It's my passion,' he said. 'The boys love my sketches.'

Sonny stepped on Whittle's hand again, ground it into the stone floor. 'You shared this passion of yours with members of the division?'

'Yes,' Whittle cried.

'Salinger,' Byron muttered, 'ye think the pair of 'em have been raising carrier pigeons? I mean, lovebirds with malignant information about all our moves.'

'I doubt it, Colonel. Your own team would have stumbled upon their pigeon coops. And the Abwehr agents they met are all out of commission. We'll impound the sketchbooks, sir. That's punishment enough.'

'And give them another licking.'

'The moment you leave.'

Byron saluted Sonny. 'Very well, Agent Salinger.' And he bolted from the tower before Sonny could return his salute. Sonny had to shout after him, 'The key, sir, to the handcuffs.'

'Salinger,' Byron called as he continued down the winding stairs, 'use your initiative, man. Didn't Derbyshire teach you a bundle of tricks?'

Sonny leaned over the captives and unlocked their handcuffs with two twists of his pocketknife. Then he helped the commandant and Nurse Hamm to their feet.

'That was beastly,' the commandant snarled. 'You shouldn't have stepped on my hand.'

'Next time I'll step on your face,' Sonny told him.

'Norbert, leave the Yank alone,' Nurse Hamm said, wiping her nose with a stitch of toilet paper that was as precious as sugar and lard. 'The Yank saved your life. There was nothing but deviltry in that colonel's eyes.'

'I'd still like my sketchbooks back.'

'Captain,' Sonny said, 'you can reclaim them *after* the war.'

'That's reassuring. Half of Europe is one big fort. Jerry has his own damn seawall, impregnable at every point. And we'll come across the Channel like ducks at a carnival. Every single duck will fall.'

Nurse Hamm slapped the commandant's face. 'Stuff it, Norbert.'

The commandant raised his bruised hand to strike her, let it glide in midair for a moment, and vanished without his sketchbooks. Sonny stood there alone in the CIC interrogation room with the Limeys' own Veronica Lake. She was no femme fatale, just a nurse in wartime, who happened to look like an American movie star.

Her body began to pulsate like some bewitched thing. 'That awful man from your spy school,' she murmured, 'that awful man.' Sonny clutched her in his arms until the pulsations stopped. She had the bittersweet aroma in her hair of shampoo from the Fourth Division's shelves.

'That maniac didn't have to humiliate us like that,' she said.

'He could have made a very long run to headquarters with those sketchbooks and had your fiancé dismissed.'

'Norbert's not my fiancé,' she said, and left Sonny in the tower with that toppled chair.

4

THEY AVOIDED HIM AFTER THAT ENCOUNTER, whispered in his presence. He was Sergeant Salinger, the secret agent in their midst. An electrician arrived from headquarters and had the telephone at the castle repaired, while Sonny wandered the cobblestone streets in his GI windbreaker, pecked away with two fingers on his army-issue Corona in his tower room, or else sat at the Blue Mermaid. The Limeys didn't like him any better than the general staff's own intelligence team. Members of the CIC were like the Comanche of the Fourth Division – outcasts and intruders they didn't quite understand. Sonny and his fellow agents served as scouts in Tiverton, ever watchful. He had the authority to arrest a general. He also had the best digs in town.

His regiment touted him as an author published in *The Saturday Evening Post*, but he didn't have a single friend. His superiors knew how valuable Sonny would be once the invasion force landed. Sonny could speak with the locals. Soldiers of the CIC would be the first to enter a captured French village. They would root out collaborators, chat with the mayor and chief of police, determine who could be relied on and who had to be shot. They would find quarters for the general staff and for themselves. But their methods remained a mystery. And that's why they were so mistrusted.

Suddenly, the entire coastal area near Slapton Sands was evacuated – tiny villages became ghost towns overnight – many of the evacuees found shelter further inland at farms and hotels. The Admiralty put their belongings in storage, but local farmers had to sell their cows and pigs to slaughterhouses at a savage price and sacrifice their own crops. Other evacuees, who couldn't seem to find quarters, were bused to a hastily built compound of Quonset huts near Tiverton Castle, on the banks of the river Exe. The compound was run by the Red Cross and policed by Sonny and his driver, Corporal Benson. The evacuees were farmers and fishermen mostly, with their own little clans, plus some pensioners and widows who'd never seen much of the world beyond the red slate of the Sands. The buses they'd arrived in had blackout curtains. Not one of them knew why they were here – a wartime emergency, they'd been told by a marine corporal who visited their cottages one afternoon and presented them with a small pile of military scrip like a sinister Santa Claus.

They couldn't leave the compound unless they fell ill and were carried off on a stretcher to one of the division's own hospitals, also a series of Quonset huts, with an armed guard right beside their bed. Their only sin, it seems, was having lived near the Sands – a wild, lonely beach in South Devon.

And now Sonny and his fellow CIC agents were summoned to Slapton Sands. A few stragglers had been spotted in the vicinity, beachcombers perhaps, farmers who wanted to have a last look at their cabbage fields, or villagers who never left and had managed to slip through the fingers of evacuation officers. Sonny and Corporal Benson sat in one of the same grim buses with blackout curtains that had brought the evacuees to their compound in Tiverton. All the agents carried .45s in a suede holster. Some of them had trained together at Fort Holabird, outside Baltimore, and in Derbyshire, but there was very little camaraderie on that bus – their training had left them with a core of suspicion, even among themselves. And that bus ride, without a morsel of sunlight, made them twice as somber. Not one of these merry men looked into another lad's eyes. They stared off into the distance, as if those around them weren't quite real.

The ride was interminable in that gray bus with its flickering lightbulbs. The CIC commander assigned to the Fourth was with them, a man Sonny had never seen before and might never see again; these commanders were constantly shifted about, since the Fourth itself feared them and their agents, and they were often promoted and demoted in the same instant sweep. He called himself Captain Blunt, but that could have been one of his many aliases. He was a tall skeleton of a man with long fingers. He had a swagger stick, like a British colonial officer; it was a curious baton in his bony hands. He would poke some agent in the ribs with the stick if that agent veered from the path Blunt had chosen for him. He claimed to have been a mathematics professor at Cornell – if so, he was sort of a prodigy, since he didn't seem much older than many of his agents. He also had one lazy, wandering eye. 'Salinger, I've read your stuff in the *Post*. Command might want you to keep a daybook, a diary, of our fishing expedition at the Sands.'

'I'm not much of a diarist, sir. And are we really on a fishing expedition?'

'Yes, we're trolling for recreants. And it's of vital importance. The Sands have to be swept clean of any human debris.'

Beachcombers had become human debris at Slapton Sands. That was the jargon of counterintel.

The captain remained quiet for the rest of the trip. Even in that curtained-off amphibious tomb, Sonny could hear the constant racket of seagulls and taste the pungent salt of the sea. The bus stopped in the middle of the Sands at low tide, and while the captain's Comanche climbed down in their combat boots, one of the agents asked, 'Sir, what happens after we find this debris?'

'Arrest them,' the captain said.

'And should they resist arrest, sir?'

'Simple. Shoot the shit out of every last son of a bitch.'

'But they're civilians, sir, caught up in our sweep.'

'They're clandestines,' the captain said, 'who have no business being here. We'll bury them in the shrub.'

'Is that official, sir?'

'Nothing's official, Agent Sullivan. You're CIC.'

Sonny stared at Captain Blunt with a mordant smile. 'Does that go into the Slapton Sands diary, sir?'

'Of course. No one has clearance to read that book – it will sit on a shelf until doomsday.'

'Like the rest of my writing,' Sonny said.

'Nonsense. I'm one of your biggest fans. We're all expecting great things from you.' Then the captain used his swagger stick to cut an imaginary X across Sonny's heart. 'But if you ever write a novel about us, Salinger, we'll fix you – and have the pages burned, one by one.'

'That's reassuring,' Sonny said, with the first scattered pages of a novel in his kit. 'But I'd rather not be buried with all the debris.'

'A wise choice,' the captain said, poking Sonny's arm with the same swagger stick.

It was a curious beach, cluttered with barbed wire and batteries of antiaircraft guns, as if waiting for an invisible German armada to arrive from across the Channel. There was a paucity of sand on Slapton Sands. Sonny found spent shells among the pebbles and sheets of red slate. They passed one tiny village after another, every one with a church that had somehow lost its steeple. The Admiralty presided over a little kingdom of ruins, with rats running along the cobbles.

Blunt sent various agents into the different corners of Slapton Sands. The agents worked in little teams. The captain himself tagged along with Sonny and Corporal Benson, who, as Sonny's driver, was somehow attached to CIC; he had an armband but not a gold badge. He was nineteen and grew up on a farm in Pennsylvania, near Amish country. He idolized Sonny and had volunteered to be his driver. Like the others, he had a .45 in a suede holster.

Sonny could hear that numbing slosh of the sea, but they went inland, into the bramble, away from the Sands. The scrub seemed endless, like a maze of stalks and twisted leaves. Blunt kept whacking at the leaves with his swagger stick and created a tiny storm around him. Within ten minutes of maneuvering, their faces were all scratched. Corporal Benson found a hut hidden in the bramble.

They all ducked into the low, narrow doorway.

There was a boy with matted hair inside the hut, squatting on the earthen floor, hugging his knees and shivering.

'Ah, our first specimen,' the captain said, wavering close to the boy with his swagger stick.

'Don't hurt him,' Sonny said. 'Can't you see? The boy's starving.'

Sonny took a Hershey bar out of his kit and gave it to the wild boy, who gobbled it up, wrapper and all.

'That's not in the regulations,' Blunt said. 'He's hiding in an evacuated area. He belongs to the Fourth Division, dead or alive. And we can't dawdle here. We have to cover the entire perimeter.'

'He might be a mute, sir,' Sonny said. 'Some kind of outcast.'

'That still doesn't give him the privilege of staying here.'

Sonny motioned to the boy, gave him his own windbreaker to wear, and the boy followed the three soldiers out of the hut.

'He's your responsibility, Sergeant,' Blunt said.

They went deeper into this land of hedgerows, marched along a lagoon sodden with red clay. There were no other huts. The captain's compass didn't seem to work. It was the wild boy who led them out of the bramble.

Sonny heard the report of a pistol – it sounded like a muffled crack of thunder.

God help us and this crazy mission.

Blunt blew his whistle. All the other teams of agents suddenly appeared on Slapton Sands. Several of them had their own cargo of human debris — a crippled fisherman who had hidden in his boat, a deranged woman who had pranced out of a tiny cottage on the shore, a gaggle of beachcombers who had decided to claim this evacuated area for themselves, a farmer who was captured near his prize cabbages.

The teams assembled in front of the bus with their prey.

'Any casualties?' Blunt asked. 'We heard a shot.'

'It was nothing, sir,' said Special Agent Sullivan, the senior member of the crew. 'I fired into the air and stopped one of these buffoons in his tracks.'

'And you covered every inch of the perimeter? Another crew will be here tomorrow, and if they find any human debris, we'll spend the rest of the war scrubbing the toilets at Collipriest House.'

They climbed aboard that bus of black windows and drove from Slapton Sands, with the water churning in the Channel like layers of molten lead.

5

THE BOYS OF SONNY'S REGIMENT were encamped behind a fence near headquarters. They had their own hospital, their own canteen, and movie palace in one of the Quonset huts. They weren't supposed to mingle with the population of Tiverton, but the generals couldn't keep them cooped up forever. They were given an occasional pass to wander into town, but there was always a very strict curfew, enforced by Sonny himself. They flocked to the Tivoli, a movie theater on Fore Street, in the heart of Tiverton. The Tivoli wasn't much more than a storefront near a lingerie shop and a pub that served Bass ale. It was often a soldier's prime destination in the middle of the afternoon, at half a crown a ticket. These boys couldn't have a sweetheart in Devon, or they might have landed in the brig. So Sonny had to shine his flashlight in the Tivoli's darkened shell. And if he did happen upon a corporal smooching with a salesclerk from the lingerie shop, he wrote out a chit, and sent the corporal back to Collipriest House. That chit remained in Sonny's pocket. He wouldn't ruin a corporal's career. But he did warn the salesclerk.

'You'll have to keep away from the Yanks, miss.'

She'd dressed up for her date in the dark. She wore her finest velveteen blouse, and she was fuming. 'Oh, you're a smart one, dearie. You're a duck. What will ye do – arrest me?'

He admired her dander. 'No, but I might have to arrest your Yank if it ever happens again.'

And Sonny never had much trouble after a warning like that. Still, the townsfolk were curious about soldiers who seemed to be hiding in plain sight. Half of Tiverton would wander over to Collipriest House and watch the boys play baseball from their side of the fence. It had become an elaborate ritual, with the boys wearing ragtag uniforms, with bats, balls, gloves, and cleats delivered from the Brooklyn Dodgers or the Boston Braves. There were constant battles among the players of 'Yankee cricket,' as it was known in Tiverton, as if this strife on a dusty field could relieve a little bit of restlessness about the uncertainty of their fate.

Meanwhile, Sonny patrolled the perimeters in a jeep, with Corporal Benson at the wheel. It was strange to see a staff sergeant with his own driver, but there he was in his windbreaker. He had gifts to deliver from the base commander – a gigantic tin of genuine army-issue coffee beans to the café on Gold Street that served ersatz coffee made of ground acorns and dandelion leaves until Sergeant Salinger came along.

The owner of the Blue Mermaid was delirious. 'Sergeant, why me?'

'Ah, Mr Ralph, would I snub my favorite café in town? The Fourth would like to show its appreciation to the citizens of Tiverton for welcoming us. But you can't charge tuppence extra for a cup of the real thing, or it's the last can you'll ever get from the division.'

And off they went to a row of tin huts on the Bolham Road that looked like a random chicken coop and served as a camp for Italian prisoners of war; it was guarded by a couple of retired British marines, and Sonny brought a bundle of loot from Collipriest House – ham sandwiches, Hershey bars, and V packs of Camels, with four cigarettes in each tiny cardboard container. The V packs were quite valuable and had become a kind of black-market currency on and off the base. But Sonny never hoarded his V packs. He dispensed whatever loot he had to the marine guards and prisoners of war. He sensed the rampant boredom at the camp, and using his pull with the CIC, he connived to have Army engineers at the base build a bocce court for the prisoners. Their leader, Sub-Lieutenant Lorenzo Tropea, knew enough English to converse with Sonny.

'Cavaliere Salinger, we are much, much grateful.'

This sublieutenant was an unusual sort of soldier. He'd never carried a gun in his life. A rare-book dealer in Milan, he was plucked out of his shop one morning by a fascist gang and sent to serve as a bookkeeper in Mussolini's section of the Afrika Korps. Captured at El Alamein, he sat out the rest of the war inside a chicken coop in Devon. Lorenzo had one irresistible passion – the life and art of Ernesto Hemingway. And no matter how hard Sonny tried, he couldn't keep Lorenzo off that subject. The sublieutenant would close his eyes and wail like a lovesick boy, '*Sergente*, please, please tell me again.'

'I'll never bring you another V-pack, *Sottotenente*.'

'What do I care about Hershey bars and cigarettes? Tell me again,' Lorenzo begged, his eyes still shut.

'I told you a hundred times. I met the maestro once – at the Stork Club.'

It pained Sonny to summon up his moment at Table 50 with Oona, like a riveting claw in his back that wouldn't heal.

'Was he dolorous?'

'Dolorous about what?' Sonny asked.

'After the Pulitzer Prize was ripped from his hands. That's what it said in the papers. *Doloroso*. He cried like a baby.'

Sonny couldn't bear that repeated repertoire. 'Hem didn't cry at Table Fifty.'

He saluted Lorenzo and ran from that little land of chicken wire. He drove up Castle Street to the compound of Quonset huts where the evacuees from Slapton Sands were housed. The Red Cross looked after their wants. He saw Lieutenant Hamm bandaging a fisherman's arm and feeding him barley soup. Sonny had come to visit that wild boy he'd found in the scrub. The boy was wandering about in army fatigues – he seemed lost in this compound. He wasn't mute after all.

'It ain't be fittin',' the boy said. Others called him 'Silent Tom.' The nurses must have bathed him and washed his hair. He looked like a sulking angel in baggy trousers.

'Oi had me a home, and oi intends to return to it.'

'Tom,' Sonny said, 'they'll shoot you down like a dog. These are invasion plans. None of us counts. But I'll tell you what. Tomorrow, if I can, I'll take you for a ride in my jeep. We'll tour Tiverton together.'

The wild boy frowned. 'Tiverton, he says. What be Tiverton to the Sands? A pot of the nasty. Oi can see the French coast on a windy day with a magnifyin' glass. You'll never get across, you Yanks, not when Jerry's Atlantic Wall is waitin' for ye with turrets – 'tis a castle without an end.'

And Silent Tom went off to the latrine, hiking up his trousers – like Chaplin's Tramp.

6

SONNY WAS UP IN HIS TOWER, pecking away with two fingers, writing a novel that seemed to lurch backward with every line, move into invisibility, as if whatever he wrote could erase itself, when he got a call from command. Sottotenente Tropea had escaped from the chicken coop on the Bolham Road in his prison pajamas. He knew the Limeys and their Home Guard would cripple Lorenzo, so Sonny had to get to him first. He summoned Corporal Benson, and they rode in the jeep with their CIC siren at full blast, as a warning to any intruders. They passed under the crumbling arch that wool merchants had erected on Gold Street a good while ago – when wool owned the world – and parked outside the Blue Mermaid, with blackout slits on their headlights. Sonny ran into the café, just as two of 'Dad's Soldiers' were trying to arrest Lorenzo. They had clubs and hammers, and must have been sixty years old – there was bedlam in their eyes. They were walloping Lorenzo into the linoleum of the Blue Mermaid until Sonny arrived. The massacre ended as Sonny strode into the path of their hammers. They were a mite cautious around Sonny's armband and gold badge, emblems they didn't quite fathom. Both of Dad's Soldiers had blackened teeth.

'Look here, mate, he's a fugitive. He might have interfered with some young miss, and…'

'Well,' Sonny said, 'shall we call Collipriest House and untangle this mess?'

'No need to get snotty,' said the senior member of the Home Guard. And they both took off with their clubs and hammers.

Lorenzo limped back to his window table, as if Dad's Soldiers and their hammers had been some illusion, an illusion of blood, and he continued reading *The Sun Also Rises* in his prison pajamas while he drank Arabian coffee from the gigantic tin can Sonny had brought to the Mermaid – it was Sonny who had given Lorenzo an overseas pocket edition of Hem's novel. He had fixed the *sottotenente* up with a permanent library of pocketbooks.

'You know what would have happened once Dad's Soldiers had you *permanently* in their hands. You'd have a broken head and a one-way ticket to Wormwood Scrubs as a menace to society. Can you imagine what those convicts at the Scrubs would do to a prisoner of war?'

'I don't care,' Lorenzo said, holding up *The Sun Also Rises* as his shield. 'I'll have had my cup of coffee with a bit of sun in my eyes. I'm not going back to that chicken coop.'

'*Sottotenente*, after we cross, whenever that is, I'll get you Hemingway's signature.'

Lorenzo was deeply suspicious. 'Don't you dare tempt me with your tricks.'

'It's not a trick,' Sonny said. 'Hemingway wouldn't miss the show. Wherever we are, he'll be there, too. The War Department wouldn't have him, but he'll wear a correspondent's clothes and carry credentials.'

'And you'll tell him about me, a prisoner of war who loves his every word.'

'I will.'

And Sonny escorted Lorenzo back to the Bolham Road. But when he returned to the castle, the bus with blackout curtains was already assembled, like some participant of a mass deportation. *Slapton Sands.* Sonny knew secrets he had never been told but had to intuit for himself. There would be no more baseball games behind the fence at Collipriest House. All the players were gone. The division's tents and Quonset huts were deserted. The base had disappeared. A few stranded captains had been left behind – they rumbled about like buffoons in battle fatigues, clutching messages that tore in the wind.

7

HIS MEMORY FELL. ALL THAT pertained to this phantom exercise was like a farrago in his skull. He did recall climbing off the bus and stepping onto red gravel and shards of red slate, his CIC commander, Captain Blunt, swiping the air with his swagger stick. 'Carry on, Salinger. Don't stand there like a dummy.' But he did stand there. Perhaps it was the fractured nature of the CIC, men and boys who soldiered other soldiers but didn't quite know how to soldier themselves. Or it was the nervousness of it all, the great unknown.

Ike himself had arrived from Salisbury on Bayonet, his armored coach and sleeping car, to watch the war games. The Limeys were suspicious of a general who had never had a field command. Ike had been an operations officer, had moved men and matériel around like so many chess pieces on his private board. Half the Limey generals believed that an amphibious attack against the Atlantic Wall was a 'butcher's bill' that would lead to wholesale slaughter, and they grumbled against Ike and his war games. But there's the rub. The whole damn Admiralty had a red face because of the cock-up surrounding Exercise Tiger, where His Majesty's fleet was meant to play Fritz on Slapton Sands, firing live ammunition at members of the Fourth to simulate an actual cross-Channel invasion, while someone somewhere had neglected to tell these Yanks where the live ammunition would land. It was Sonny who had to count the dead.

His Majesty's offshore guns were meant to fire above a certain 'white line,' way over the ears and eyebrows of boys who hit the Sands in their battle packs, but weren't made aware of such esoteric details; they strove across that invisible 'white line' and were smashed to pieces, their heads and limbs colliding like little earthquakes. Some made it across that blue-red hail of fire and arrived at the hedgerows, while the wounded were carted away in ambulances that bore no insignia, and the dead were cared for by a special squad of gravedigger engineers. That's what tore at Sonny, right into his kishkes, as Sol Salinger would say. The dead didn't really exist. The gravediggers ripped away their dog tags and piled these unidentifiable soldiers in their battle gear, as if they were handling so much freight. And into an enormous pit they went behind an abandoned farm near the Sands, piled upon one another, with Captain Blunt at the grave site.

'Count, you son of a bitch,' the captain screamed at Sonny.

'Sir, they'll disappear – just like that.'

'That's the general idea, Salinger; we're in the middle of an invasion.'

'A mock invasion,' Sonny said.

'Do – you – want – us – to – fail?' the captain screamed. 'Ike will suffer – count!'

'Ninety-seven, ninety-eight, ninety-nine,' Sonny recited, and wrote in his diary. He stopped at 105, while these military morticians began to cover the grave with the red gravel and red earth of Slapton Sands. They collected the helmets and dog tags and wandered off with the efficiency of postal clerks. But the grave wasn't deep enough, and Sonny saw several fingers, bootlaces, and strands of hair.

He picked up one of the mortician's shovels and covered the fingers and laces with clumps of red earth.

'That's not your job, Salinger. The wind and rain will do the rest.'

'What is my job, sir?'

'To certify that we were never here. You are to cover up every mark we leave behind.'

'But there are naval guns firing right at us, sir.'

'That's Force U,' the captain said. 'And Force U doesn't exist.'

'U' was the code name for Utah Beach, one of five landing points of the future Allied invasion, but Sonny was told none of this at the time. Slapton Sands had been selected because its gravel, its hedgerows, and its hidden lagoon bore a startling likeness to Utah Beach. And Force U was a secret training exercise to have the Fourth Division master the 'dance steps' of an assault on Utah Beach.

But the cock-up had only begun. After the first wave of attacks on the Sands, a convoy of assault ships, or LSTs, carrying soldiers, sailors, engineers, and amphibious tanks and trucks sailed from Plymouth into Lyme Bay to simulate a Channel crossing – and then follow the Fourth onto that beach of red gravel. This convoy of eight assault ships, with the code name T-4, was assigned a pair of destroyer escorts from His Majesty's fleet. But one destroyer failed to show. And the area around Lyme Bay was crawling with German barracudas, or *Schnellboote* – speedboats from a base in Cherbourg. A flotilla of nine barracudas stumbled upon T-4, and mistaking it for a convoy on a simple training mission, it tore into T-4 with its guns and torpedoes, and returned to Cherbourg, not wanting to confront a sea filled with Great Britain's own barracudas.

There'd been a cock-up in radio frequencies, and His Majesty's fleet lost all contact with the convoy, even as fires ripped across the LSTs and two of the assault ships sank.

That's what Sonny had gleaned from the dispatches he read. He could no longer tell what was real about Force U and what was manufactured. The *Schnellboote* from Cherbourg could have been one more fanciful tale. Perhaps a rogue Corsair had fired upon its own convoy. But Sonny could feel a strange tug at his soul, and that's when his mind swirled about. Somehow he was on one of the targeted ships, stranded in an oil-slicked sea, with runnels of fire in the water. He was with his own regiment, or another. Dead bodies wandered about in their Mae Wests right under his nose. Sonny didn't have to count. Mae Wests were everywhere. He could recite what his instructors had told him at Fort Holabird – you couldn't survive in that damn sea for very long no matter how many Mae Wests you wore. You would perish of deep bone chill marked by a precipitous drop in temperature. And so he clung to whatever he could on that sinking ship – the edge of a useless life raft that had been frozen or rusted into place, a charred beam across the fantail, a helmet glued to the deck with congealed blood – while red and green tracers from some *Schnellboot* whizzed past Sonny and set one of his sleeves on fire, and a lone gunnery officer on his perch was shooting at some shadow in the water that constantly shifted. It took Sonny a while to notice that *this* gunnery officer didn't have any eyes and ears, that he was a limpid, looming skeleton in battle fatigues, the only other figure on board this LST.

Sonny blinked once, and the eyeless skeleton was gone. So was the sinking ship. He was at a field hospital in South Devon, somewhere between Tiverton and the Sands, glancing at another skeleton. Captain Blunt stood near him in a British helmet with a cheek guard.

'Look alert, will you, man?'

Sonny realized that he was carrying an Ml carbine with a bayonet. So were other CIC agents, including Corporal Benson.

'What happened?' Sonny asked.

'Salinger, are you alive or dead?' And then Blunt whispered, 'There was a cock-up, on land and sea. And we are here at this field unit to erase as much of it as we can.'

Nurses were running about, and he recognized Lieutenant Hamm, with her entire Red Cross crew in their coronets and veils, with blood on their hospital smocks.

He waved to her and then asked Blunt, 'Is the exercise over, sir?'

This lean skeleton of a CIC commander glared at him. 'It's never over until we reach the Far Shore.'

Another code name, for the beachhead across the Channel – the Far Shore, like some treacherous Hallelujah Land. But this makeshift ward with a tottering operation table could have been a butcher shop – blood flew like globs of phlegm and spittle. The surgeons didn't wear masks. One surgeon rasped in Sonny's ear, 'Do something! We were ordered to treat these lads as if we were veterinarians. But a damn dog hospital would give better service.'

Sonny couldn't say a word. He stood with his bayonet and a fixed stare.

The Red Cross Motor Corps arrived without their usual swagger. They'd been shuttling wounded soldiers in ambulances that were little better than tin boxes on wheels, shuttling them from different landing spots to a makeshift hospital in an apple orchard that wasn't even on the map. They didn't have a moment of respite, a moment to wipe the blood off their Oxford gray tunics. They gulped wormy water from the same canteen. They swept soldiers with missing arms and legs right off a mock battlefield, in the midst of a fake attack, and also took soldiers and sailors with severe burns off the battered LSTs. The scar on the commandant's cheek began to twitch – Captain Norbert Whittle, whose sin was to draw sketches of Sonny's regiment.

'Salinger, I can't even say one word to a chap, or accept a letter to his sweetheart. What is this bloody business?'

The Far Shore, Sonny wanted to say. *The Far Shore*.

8

THERE WAS A CORTEGE OF JEEPS outside Collipriest House again. The Fourth had returned to Tiverton. Its generals strolled into the front parlor in waist-high olive drab jackets that the supreme commander himself wore. It hadn't become standard issue yet, but Ike loved to thrust his fists into the open side pockets of his new wool jacket. And these generals did the same. Their fists were always in their pockets.

The Fourth had to be replenished. Additional troops arrived. Sonny did have an unofficial count of the dead at Slapton Sands: 747. But that number appeared nowhere except in his diary. He still had his room in the castle tower. He still had his driver. He still had his jeep. But *nothing* was the same. It was as if he had suffered from deep bone chill and had survived somehow. His teeth were chattering and it was well into May. His mother wrote that Oona was pregnant and expected to have her first child with the satyr in July. Sonny started to write Oona but couldn't finish. The letter sat on his desk with the pages of his novel that were moving backward, like a crab. He had little appetite, but he sat in the underground canteen with the Red Cross nurses, who had labored ceaselessly in that field hospital after the cock-up at Slapton Sands. They couldn't utter a word about the endless tracery of bandages, or the lads who had died in their arms with such a grip on their elbows, it took a pair of doctors to break that death lock. All their chatter was coded now, with a touch of horror in their high-pitched voices.

'Be a lamb, will you, Salinger, and deliver a few Hershey bars to the old-timers in their huts? We're short this month, and we wouldn't want the geezers to suffer. They've lost their farms.'

'But they'll get them back, Lieutenant Hamm.'

She purled her eyes at Sonny. 'After that *incident*? They'll be lucky if their farmhouses still stand. You saw the craters.'

'There were no craters,' Sonny said.

'That's right. No craters at all.'

'But I'll deliver the Hersheys,' he said.

'Don't you look smart today.'

He, too, had a short woolen jacket with slash side pockets, a gift from his CIC commander, who'd been presented with a dozen prototypes of Ike's jacket for his agents. He had the Hershey bars, but he couldn't seem to go near the evacuee huts. They stank of chicken shit, he told himself. There were no chickens in the Quonset huts. He didn't want to be reminded of all the blood and red gravel and that secret grave full of soldiers.

Slapton Sands.

He got into the jeep with Corporal Benson, who didn't have an Eisenhower jacket of his own. But it was strange. Every soldier in Tiverton, it seems, saluted Sonny. He looked like a general in that jacket, Ike with big ears.

'Where to, sir?'

He could have gone to the Blue Mermaid or visited Sottotenente Tropea at the tiny Italian prison camp, but he wasn't in the mood for companionship.

'The Tivoli,' he said.

The corporal groaned. 'Aw, Sergeant, are we going to see *Meet Me in St. Louis* for the seventh fucking time?'

The Fourth received the earliest cuts of every film from MGM – these cuts were pure gold. The films arrived overseas in the generals' private pouch. Somehow, Sonny had been put in charge, Sonny selected the films. And since the Tivoli was starved for new releases, he would often wink at the general staff and let the town theater borrow the Fourth's own fare.

'*Meet Me in St. Louis,*' the corporal muttered to himself while he drove from the castle. 'Sergeant, there isn't any justice. Margaret O'Brien is the biggest star in the world, and she's six years old.'

'Seven,' Sonny insisted. He knew the birthdays of every star, shared them with his mother.

'And who's the second-biggest?' the corporal asked, sounding like a quizmaster.

'Lassie.'

'That's my whole point, sir. A fucking Collie dominates Hollywood – and a little girl with a missing tooth.'

'It's wartime,' Sonny said. 'Audiences love loyal dogs and little girls who know how to cry.'

There wasn't much traffic in Tiverton, as petrol was so scarce. The corporal parked right in front of the Tivoli. He wouldn't go inside. 'I've had enough of Margaret O'Brien, sir.'

The cashier wouldn't allow Sonny to buy a ticket. 'We couldn't stay open without you, Sergeant Salinger.'

He plunged into the dark. He wasn't in search of soldiers and their renegade sweethearts. He didn't even watch the flickering shadows on the Tivoli's front wall. The dialogue comforted him when he didn't have to pay attention to the words. He didn't have to listen to the screams inside his head. He'd been going to the movies since he was four, most often with his sister, Doris, a divorcée who was six years older, and a buyer for Bloomingdale's – Doris was a big deal. But Doris never loved the dark. Movies were a punishment she had to endure to keep her little brother occupied. Sol paid her a quarter to watch over Sonny, while he sat there, sucking up all the lost souls on the screen.

He could *smell* the projector, *feel* the filament of light come out of the little cave in the rear wall. He could breathe so much better in that stale air. But the screams wouldn't stop, not even in his private fort – at the Tivoli. He was washed right back onto that sinking LST, with the Klaxon in his ears, the warping cry that meant he had to abandon ship, with all its weaponry. He couldn't remember climbing aboard at Plymouth. Who had sent him out to sea? He had no battle gear or life preserver. He was the lone survivor on an assault ship that didn't have a single other passenger. Here he was, captain and first mate, cook, stoker, gunnery chief, helmsman, and engineer. He didn't have to pilot this tub. He was bulletproof, like the heroes he could wake from all the Tivolis of his childhood. Rin Tin Tin and the Royal Whisperer. It was the age of silent serials, 1925 or '26. The Whisperer kept a cape bunched around his shoulders. He was a casualty of the First War, and limped about on a wooden leg. He had an uncanny knack for catching criminals. The Whisperer always worked alone. There was no need of captions or subtitles. The audience never learned what this peg leg whispered into a police captain's ear, or what his talent was all about. And that's what intrigued Sonny. The Whisperer whispered one or twice, and the lord of crime was undone. It held a boy, seized his imagination, as if the wildest gifts could come from nowhere. And that's what seized him now, at the Tivoli: Sergeant Salinger on a sinking ship. He could hear the cries of soldiers in the Channel waters. And still, he steered without a steering wheel. He had a destination. The Far Shore.

He felt a tug at his shoulder. Corporal Benson was crouching in the aisle. 'Sir, you've been sitting here for seven hours. The manager doesn't know what to do. The projectionist is gone. The house is empty. You sat right past the last show. But you're the grand pasha at the Tivoli. They could never have had July Garland and Margaret O'Brien without you, sir.'

'Corporal, I was ruminating,' Sonny said. 'I'm always refreshed after a long sit in the dark.' He had a sudden flash of boys with dark blue skin being raked out of the water with a huge fishing net.

He scampered out of his seat and followed Corporal Benson up the aisle with a pronounced limp, just like the Royal Whisperer, another lad with a peg leg.

PART TWO

The Far Shore

June 1944

1

H E LEAPT OUT OF THE LANDING CRAFT into a wallop of water, flailing a bit, like a bat lost in a storm. Sonny had a life preserver that was almost a strangulation cord, plus a combat pack on his shoulders that pounded as the water pounded. He couldn't afford to get his manuscripts wet. He had the melody of words inside his skull as he could hear the terrible whine of bullets all around him. A dogface fell and disappeared into the undertow, then resurfaced with one of his fingers shorn off. Despite that rush of blood, there was a calm that Sonny hadn't anticipated. Utah seemed half-deserted, with ripples of barbed wire and steel spikes in the sand. Sonny hadn't arrived with the first assault wave, but the second. Nor had he arrived with his own regiment. The CIC had come to reconnoiter, to act as scouts and interrogate any captured collaborators, but there were no collaborators on Uncle Red, Utah's remote southern sector.

Frogmen were already on the beach, dismantling trip mines and the explosives attached to concrete barriers – triangular pyramids that cluttered the sand. Amphibious tanks shed their canvas skirts that had helped keep them afloat. They ripped through the wire and battered the masonry seawall that extended right across Uncle Red. These 'swim tanks' had come dancing out of the water from the bellies of their mother ships. There was hardly a pillbox to be found in this *peaceful* patch of Utah, and the Shermans crushed whatever pillboxes and machine-gun nests were still alive, though they couldn't completely dislodge the Krauts from their concrete encasements along the dunes.

Most of the calm around Sonny had come from a miscue. The combat mission's control boat had led its landing crafts astray; washed south by the currents, the first and second assault teams had rushed through the water almost a mile from their planned destination, onto a beach that still had *some* 'incoming mail' from Kraut artillery in the dunes and a whole lot of 'outgoing mail' from B-26 Marauders that flew sortie after sortie over the Kraut tunnels and bunkers, leaving an epic cloud of dust and smoke in their wake.

Uncle Red was cleared within an hour. Dogfaces, frogmen, and boys from the CIC could have been on their own private lagoon, accompanied by the constant grind of amphibious tanks, rain whipping into their faces from the force of the wind, and the distant illumination of their own destroyers – lightning bolts that hovered over the water.

Standing near the shoreline, directing traffic in that haze of dust and smoke, was Theodore Roosevelt, Jr., deputy commander of the Fourth Division, and the lone general who'd arrived with the first wave. At fifty-six, he was the oldest boy on the beach. Wounded in the First War, he had to hop about with a cane. The sand kept shifting around him, as if he'd stepped out of a mirage, like a magnificent toad in his goggles.

He had a pinched face, and his helmet seemed much too large for his head. He seemed aware that Sonny was with the CIC.

'Well, we don't have too many captured Krauts for you to interrogate. Carry on, Mr Salinger. We have to clear off Uncle Red. Our paratroopers landed in the middle of the night. Those boys are stuck in the interior. We have to find them before they get scalped.'

And the general went back into the haze.

Sonny felt stranded for a moment, like a beachcomber in the midst of battle. Then he recognized Corporal Benson and Captain Blunt, who'd arrived on the same landing craft with several other

CIC agents, but without his swagger stick. It must have disappeared in the undertow.

'Sarge, we made it, Sarge,' the corporal gloated. 'I could kiss the ground. We made it to Normandy. It was a piece of cake.'

'Quiet,' Sonny said, 'before you get your ass blown off.'

He could no longer tell if Blunt was their commander or not; that's how mysterious – and fluid – everything was in the CIC. Blunt had lost that crack discipline to lead a cadre of agents. His eyes bulged within the sockets of his skeletal face. Blunt no longer had his bearings. Sonny had to grab him by the elbow. 'This way, sir.'

'Don't touch me,' the captain spat like an asp. 'I don't like to be touched. Who the heck are you, anyway?'

'One of your own, sir. Sergeant Salinger. We're still attached to the Twelfth.'

The captain muttered to himself. His combat boots seemed stuck in the sand, as if he were moving across an endless slab of wet concrete. Sonny didn't have much of a choice. He had to drag his own captain along the dunes.

'Sarge,' the corporal whispered, 'we could leave him here. The medics will find him.'

'Shut up,' Sonny said. 'Cap belongs with us.'

The corporal pounded his chest. 'He's no captain. Look at him! He's a loony. Leave him here.'

'Corporal,' Sonny said, 'if you're derelict, I'll leave *you* behind. And you'll become like one of the ghosts we caught on Slapton Sands. Help me, dammit!'

And so they dragged him along until they found the scattered bits of their own regiment, boys who had arrived on the beach long after the first and second wave and weren't really comfortable around the CIC. The lieutenant in charge of the nearest rifle platoon looked at Sonny askance. But Sonny had established his own relation to the Fourth while he'd been at Tiverton Castle.

'We have to get off these dunes, sir. There are mines near

the machine-gun nests. We're still too much of a target.'

'And go where?' the lieutenant asked. Sonny could tell from the glaze in his eyes that this was no civilian soldier swallowed up in the draft. First Lieutenant Thomas Oliver III had graduated from the Military College of South Carolina, otherwise known as the Citadel. He was a 'squirrel shooter' – a southern boy with hollow cheeks and clipped blond hair. He couldn't hide his disdain of the CIC. 'Sergeant, can't you tell? The Krauts have flooded the marshlands and left us with one open causeway. We'll have every sniper in the area on our tail if we walk that line… And who's this skull you brought along for the ride?'

'Our commander,' Sonny said.

'Commander of what?'

'Counter Intelligence, Fourth Division.'

'Unbelievable,' the first lieutenant muttered, slapping the pistol butt at his side. 'Don't you masterminds at CIC have *any* human beings?'

Blunt woke from his torpor. His body stiffened. He didn't need Sonny's support. 'Lieutenant, you'll order your men to wade through that marsh.'

Lieutenant Oliver saluted the walking skeleton. 'Yes, sir. Sorry I insulted you, sir.'

And the Twelfth persevered. The minute the dogfaces approached that one available exit off the dunes, they had Screaming Meemies in their ears – *Nebelwerfer*, mortar rockets that arrived with a relentless wail. Sonny didn't dare fasten the chin straps of his helmet. The force of a Screaming Meemie could rip his neck off under a fastened strap. Yet no war games in the world could have prepared him for that sound – it clung to you like a banshee, bit into your bones. The dunes quaked under him with each deafening whistle of a Meemie. The dogfaces ran toward that strange lagoon, wider than a mile. And now Sonny realized why Slapton Sands had been chosen for Exercise Tiger; it had its own rough terrain, its own lagoon – Slapton Ley. But this flooded farmland was much more insidious than a still-water lake in South Devon. It was no country creek – it had been bulldozed and mined and strung from end to end with trip wire as sharp as a razor. Some of the boys had tossed away their life preservers once they crossed the seawall. They hadn't expected an artificial lake on the far side of Uncle Red. You could move along in three feet of brackish water and then fall into a hole ten feet high. And then there was a diving expedition to pull that dogface out of the deep. Still, several dogfaces drowned, lost in that infernal web of wire.

Sonny was vigilant; Sonny maneuvered, as if he were reading a map with each step he took. The corporal, he realized, could take care of himself. But Blunt drifted in and out of a dream. And Sonny felt responsible for this ruthless captain who might have been relieved of his command while they were in the midst of crossing the Channel. It didn't seem to matter now. The CIC was suddenly like some forgotten nimbus. They were all dogfaces on this lagoon that Kraut demolition engineers might have flooded with inflammable material. But Sonny didn't see any fires on the lake, not one rifleman lit up like a burning tree. Still, he held up Blunt by the straps of his battle gear.

'Let go of me,' the captain said. 'I can walk. I'm not an infant.'

And then Blunt would sink under the surface, and Sonny had to pull and pull to bring him back, while sniper bullets created ripples all across the lake, or spun a rifleman around and left him to lie in this wet German cradle.

There was no reprieve, not a second to reconnoiter and taste the wind. They had to cross this lagoon, or fall back onto Uncle Red. Sonny peed in his pants. They all did. And while they waded, with wires ripping into their combat boots, the Meemies wailed. And when a Meemie crashed into the water, starting up a minor hurricane, with dogfaces flying into the air like rag dolls, every sort of paraphernalia struck the water – helmets, Hershey bars, and human limbs. Sonny had a crushing vertigo, as the limbs floated past him like little barks, buoyed by the currents and the salt in the lake. The Krauts wanted to leave them stranded in this flood, finish this assault on the first day. Their lagoon seemed to have its own infernal horizon, as if it commanded the whole of Normandy.

First Lieutenant Oliver, twenty-three years old and fresh out of the Citadel, barked at his platoon, more of a soldier than Sonny would ever be. Sonny wanted to survive, not carve his name into the Norman coast as the daredevil of occupied France.

'Move along, Private. You're floundering. The Krauts would love to catch us bare-assed in their little sea… Sergeant Salinger, you can't hold on to that skull of a captain forever, even if he is with Counter Intel.'

Sonny didn't want to contradict this southern cowboy from the Citadel.

'We'll need him, sir, once we're out of this morass. He's a fucker when it comes to interrogating saboteurs.'

'Salinger, do you see any saboteurs on this lake?'

'No, sir.'

'Then drop him, son. That's an order.'

Sonny continued to clutch Captain Blunt by his straps.

'Did you hear me, Salinger?'

'I did, sir. But I'm CIC.'

The lieutenant cursed and waded over to *his* captain. They whispered in the water. Then the lieutenant returned.

'We'll settle this some other time, Salinger. But you're on my shit list, remember that.'

'I will, sir.'

His feet were feeling numb, despite the razor cuts in his boots. They had to cross this flooded farmland, cross it as fast as they could. But they were like ducks in a pond, catching sniper fire. The Krauts were hiding somewhere, away from the marsh. It took three hours to cross, maybe even five. There was no such creature as dry land. And then it all stopped, as weirdly as it began. The wetlands turned to stone. They'd come to a tiny village called Sainte-Mère-Ménilmontant, or something close to that. It hardly deserved to be on a map, with its fifty inhabitants, until the Krauts arrived and turned Sainte-Mère into a little camp for their *Soldaten* who occupied the bunkers and machine-gun nests of Hitler's fabled Atlantic Wall. That wall seemed very sparse. Sonny had found little else but abandoned bunkers and a few machine-gun nests on Uncle Red.

Sainte-Mère might have been near a drop zone for the Eighty-second Airborne. But Sonny didn't see a single sign of paratroopers, not one spot of blood on the cobblestones, nor one bullet hole, nothing except a church with a crooked spire.

Lieutenant Oliver was prepared to storm the village and occupy every house and garden.

'Sorry, sir,' Sonny said. 'You'll have to wait here until we have a long look.'

'That's preposterous,' the lieutenant said. 'I won't stand for it.'

'You will,' Sonny said. 'It's our priority – CIC.'

'Then what are my boys supposed to do?'

'Camp on the cobblestones – until we tour the village.'

Sainte-Mère had a single tarred and cobbled street that traveled down a slope from one end of the village to the other. It had a bakery with pretzels in the window, a butcher shop laden with a variety of smoked sausages, a church with Nazi banners flying from its crooked spire, and several brick and stone houses with swastikas pinned to the garden walls. There was also an unmanned guardhouse and antiaircraft gun. The Krauts had fled this village. Only one of the houses, the most luxurious, with bright yellow awnings and a metal gate, was occupied. The Krauts had left their chief clerk and paymaster behind. He wasn't a military man. He'd been a grocer in civilian life – Hans Schloss. Corporal Benson and Sonny were puzzled by his role as the little king of a fake Tyrolean village in occupied France. But Captain Blunt wasn't puzzled at all.

After the paymaster introduced himself and offered everyone some schnapps, Blunt seized him by the collar and slapped his face.

'Herr Schloss, why are you still here?' Blunt asked in the melodious German of a stage actor. Sonny would have stumbled along in any interrogation, wouldn't have found the right mode of attack.

The grocer insisted on answering Blunt in English.

'What value would I have? Only another mouth to feed.'

'But I'm not sure I care about your little welcoming committee,' Blunt told him. 'What happened to the Eighty-second?'

The grocer squinted. 'I don't understand you, Herr Kapitän?'

'The paratroopers,' Blunt said. 'They must have come here. There must have been a struggle.'

'Ah,' the grocer said. 'The sky soldiers. They landed in *another* village, not far from us.'

'You saw them?'

'Yes, yes,' said Herr Schloss, 'all the silk… Have some schnapps.'

Blunt sniffed the schnapps without drinking it and dragged the grocer out of his little dream castle. They broke into another stone castle and the captain tried to shove Herr Schloss into a little closet with a toilet seat.

'No, Herr Kapitän, I do not have to move my bowels.'

'Sit, I said.'

The little grocer turned very pale. 'I cannot, *Mein Herr*. We would all explode.'

Blunt smiled for the first time Sonny could remember. 'Ah, now the fun begins. How much of this toy town is booby-trapped?'

'All of it,' the grocer said with a triumphant smirk.

Blunt should have been pleased, but he wasn't. 'And still they left you behind. They knew you would suffer once we discovered your tricks. You could have run, and yet you stayed. *Why*?'

The grocer puffed out his chest. 'They needed a *Schauspieler*, or it wouldn't have worked.'

'And they elected you,' Blunt said.

'Of course. I am a civilian – a paymaster. And civilians cannot be shot.'

Blunt slapped him again. 'Where are your German friends, the ones who disappeared from their bunkers on Utah Beach like invisible men and mined this town?'

'I have no knowledge of this, Herr Kapitän. Why would they inform a clerk?'

'Ah, but if I tell my colonel that you're a captain in the SS, he'll make you sit on that toilet seat… or shoot you in the head.'

'But that would be a lie,' the grocer said with the same smirk. 'I am not with the SS.'

'Well, suppose I lie.'

'Your superiors, they would not believe you.'

Blunt turned to Sonny. 'Sergeant, how long would it take you to produce forged documents that would give Herr Schloss the status of an SS captain?'

'An hour, sir,' Sonny said, 'with a proper lamp.'

It was another lie, of course. He didn't have the materials.

'You are insane,' the grocer said. 'All of you.'

'Herr Schloss,' Blunt said, 'where are your German friends?'

'In the *bocage*,' the grocer said. 'Waiting for you.'

It was Norman country, with field after field of hedgerows at the bottom of the village. These hedgerows were practically impenetrable – walls of earth and stone, held together by twisted roots that had been there for centuries. They could be seven feet tall, with Kraut machine gunners hiding behind each hedge.

Blunt dragged Herr Schloss out to Lieutenant Oliver, who was still waiting with his riflemen on the cobblestones of Sainte-Mère. 'Shoot the little son of a bitch. He's a Nazi spy.'

'But I can't just…'

Herr Schloss shivered and got down on his knees. 'I am not a spy. I am a clerk, a paymaster, *bitte*.'

'Where are the other villagers? Your captain got rid of every one, including the village priest, and replaced them with Krauts. So you could have your boiled potatoes and schnitzel while they guarded the coast. And then they all disappeared… You wanna stay alive?'

'Yes, yes, *Mein Herr*.'

'Then you'll take us on a walking tour of this village and show us where every mine is placed, with every trip wire, or you'll end up with your Heinie ass on one of your own trick toilet seats.'

And so they toured this fake Tyrolean village with Herr Schloss as a walking minesweeper, and with Lieutenant Oliver and the Twelfth's demolition team. Herr Schloss was shrewd enough to sense that he'd found a real protector – this graduate of the Citadel.

'Herr Oberleutnant,' he muttered, 'I am of some use, yes?'

'You're doing fine, son,' Oliver said, though Schloss was more than twice his age.

The demolition team dismantled the triggers attached to every toilet seat. And while they were touring the village, one idle dog-face reached through the broken glass of the bakery window and plucked out his prize – a gigantic pretzel. He gnawed at it, wouldn't share his plunder. His face turned brackish green. He grew dizzy, stumbled across the cobblestones, his mouth full of bile.

'Medic,' another dogface shouted, 'medic – it's an emergency.'

The first dogface fell to the ground, while his whole body trembled, like someone having a seizure. And then the trembling stopped.

A medic arrived. He crouched over the dogface and couldn't find his pulse.

'We'll have to bag him,' the medic said, sniffing the half-gnawed pretzel.

'What happened?' the second dogface asked.

'Cyanide, I guess. Why'd he go near the window?'

Captain Blunt arrived with Herr Schloss, the lieutenant, and his demolition team. Blunt didn't waver for a second. He took out his Colt .45 and shot the little grocer in the head, the wind whipping blood into the lieutenant's eyes. Oliver stood there with his mouth agape.

'Salinger,' Blunt called.

Sonny arrived with Corporal Benson.

'Saboteur, Salinger. Mark it down.'

And that's when Sonny had a revelation, as that crooked church spire appeared with a sudden pull in front of his eyes. 'Airborne,' he mumbled. 'A paratrooper got battered by the wind and landed in this village. His silk hooked onto some lump of metal, and the Krauts shot him down like a dog. I'm sure of it. That damn grocer must have hid the body somewhere – I'll bet Herr Schloss really was a captain in the SS.'

It was Corporal Benson who found a dead paratrooper in the nave of the church, embalmed in silk. The boy's boots were gone, and the blood on his face had hardened into a red beard.

'Holy moly,' Lieutenant Oliver said. 'Salinger, you're all right. It was the SS.'

2

THE BOYS FROM GRAVES REGISTRATION buried the fallen paratrooper in the churchyard of Sainte-Mère with a little marker, while the regimental chaplain delivered a sermon.

'Here he lies, one of our mighty sons who sacrificed himself...'

Sonny couldn't bear to listen. The chaplain's speech had nothing to do with that sky soldier and what he might have felt hanging from a spire that bent under his weight in a village of swastikas and red flags. The chaplain swept away all the dignity, all the fear, all the strangeness of the boy's last moments.

Meanwhile, the Twelfth used the dead grocer's castle as its headquarters and canteen, but its commanders remained in a quandary. They couldn't unriddle the *bocage* – field after field of Norman hedgerows that would have to be taken from the Krauts one field at a time. Lieutenant Oliver had been promoted to company commander on his first day in Normandy, and now he wanted Sonny and the skeletal captain from Counter Intel on his own assault team of riflemen.

A ghostly quiet descended upon Sainte-Mère. Boys of the Eighty-second Airborne had landed in the *bocage* and couldn't punch their way out of that earthen nightmare. And it was the Twelfth's job to 'rescue' the paratroopers from hostile territory and move deeper into the Norman countryside with the Eighty-second. But its strategists couldn't come up with a master plan, not in that wild, unpredictable growth.

It took Oliver's squirrel shooters half a day to cover the first hundred yards. Krauts in green summer wool would rise right out of the *bocage* with their bayonets and machine pistols. Without any collaborators to collect, Sonny dove into the fray with his Ml. He saw the mad, wolfish hunger in the eyes of Krauts he was meant to kill. It was savagery in slow motion – men snarling, biting, shooting, and ripping at one another in a strange rhythmic dance he could hardly believe was happening.

These must have been the former guardians of the bunkers and tunnels on Uncle Red, who'd taken over Sainte-Mère and might have murdered the village priest, and who poisoned the pretzels in the bakery window, booby-trapped *every* toilet seat, and took potshots at that lad from the Eighty-second, with his silk caught on the crooked spire. They were ferocious under their wide helmets, their faces contorted into hideous masks. They yelped and cursed the *Amerikanische Schweinehunde*, even as some of them lay near the hedgerows, licking their wounds. And still neither side appeared capable of seizing ground, of capturing that stone-filled farmer's field. The struggle could have gone on forever, ending any notion of an Allied juggernaut across Normandy, and the great American gamble to reach the Rhine before winter.

The struggle concluded as capriciously as it began, with the Krauts vanishing into another field and leaving their wounded behind. But the Twelfth had witnessed the carnage of these soldiers from Sainte-Mère, who had butchered boys of the Eighty-second dangling in the treetops; several Krauts had 'surrendered' on Uncle Red, while machine gunners standing behind them ripped into the regiment… and then ran into the dunes without a sign that they had ever existed.

Lieutenant Oliver sang a Christian song and shot the wounded Krauts as graciously as he could.

'Can't be helped, Salinger. *No Prisoners*. That's our battle cry – and the motto of the Fourth.'

'Since when?'

'Since we landed on Utah… and they tricked us with that false surrender on the beach.'

Sonny was also a trickster. That's what the CIC was all about: enticing information from collaborators, spies, and potential saboteurs. And now Sonny, with his rabbinical beliefs concerning the human spirit and the holiness of mankind, nourished on Park Avenue, with Miriam Salinger at his side, had become a hunter and killer of men with his Ml and his Colt. And he still had to watch over Captain Blunt while he broke through the *bocage* with his fellow dogfaces, where he encountered the next German ambush and the next. Where did all these Krauts come from? Every last homicidal maniac in Normandy couldn't have been billeted in an obscure French village with German delicacies in the window – a bit of homeland away from home, a stage set to draw the Americans in and have them sit on wired-up toilet seats.

Sonny couldn't help but feel that this curious battleground on shifting parcels of land was much more fickle than Hitler's Atlantic Wall or a transplanted Tyrolean village. An entire German regiment had arrived out of nowhere, or must have been waiting, waiting in the hedgerows.

General Roosevelt limped like a scarecrow from company to company with his Colt in one hand and his cane in the other. 'Boys, we can't leave the Eighty-second stranded. We have to marry up.'

But how could Sergeant Salinger and Company E marry up

with sky soldiers who couldn't be found? The dogfaces rushed deeper and deeper into this labyrinth of hedgerows, wondering if they had wandered precipitously into their own burial ground. Sonny wrestled in some forgotten field with a German boy who couldn't have been more than sixteen, with blond eyebrows and a wisp of a beard.

I can't kill this kid.

The young soldier lunged at him with his bayonet, and Sonny knocked the bayonet out of the kid's hand, told him in German to please do them all a fucking favor and find another field and another war. The kid howled once and disappeared into the foliage. And that's when Sonny saw this insidious commando – or forest creature – with a blackened face, who was wearing German pantaloons and a GI field jacket, and went about in bare feet.

'Hey, you,' the creature said, his scalp camouflaged with twigs, 'stop right there, and be quick about it. Who the fuck are the Andrews Sisters and what are their first names?'

'They're balladeers,' Sonny said. 'Patty, LaVerne, and Maxene…'

The commando persisted. 'Who's the prettiest one?'

'That depends,' Sonny said. 'Patty is much prettier, but I prefer Maxene… Who the hell are you?'

'I ain't finished yet. Who played shortstop with Joltin' Joe in '41 and '42?'

Sonny was reluctant to answer. 'The Scooter, Phil Rizzuto.'

'You're all right, kid,' the commando said, introducing himself as Captain Phil Clare of the Eighty-second, while he proceeded to explain the odyssey of his jump into Normandy. Landed miles from his drop zone, he said. Clare was captured by a Kraut patrol but managed to elude those boys.

'Is that why you're wearing Kraut pants?'

That was another skirmish. The captain had to survive on wits alone. He lost his boots in an ambush. He was second in command of his battalion, he said. And while he sat on his haunches, other paratroopers with blackened faces showed up with a pair of Kraut boots for their captain. They had metal crickets that served as a signaling device for the Eighty-second.

Sonny hadn't met soldiers like these before. Never mind the charcoal and the crickets. They were scalp hunters, and hadn't come to the Far Shore to seize territory, but to kill Krauts. They kept their own box score and counted every kill. They weren't uncertain in the *bocage*. And Sonny realized that the Twelfth hadn't arrived at this spot to rescue airborne infantry. It was the scalp hunters who'd come to lead the dogfaces out of the morass.

They had a string of ears attached to their cartridge belts, Kraut ears caked with blood. It seemed ghoulish. Captain Clare could recall the circumstances of every ear he'd collected.

'The first one,' he said. 'That was a beaut.'

'I'd rather not hear about it,' Sonny said.

'You CIC boys,' Clare said. 'You're devils. You dismantle a guy, mutilate his mind and soul, and you consider that okay.'

'But we're not torturers,' Sonny said.

Clare scratched his chin. 'What do ya mean? We kill a guy before we cut.'

And the colloquium ended right there. Sonny couldn't match Clare's logic, nor his stealth. The sky soldiers sang out their credo as they marched across the roughened terrain.

Who are you?
The Eighty-two
Airborne, Airborne

That screed served notice that the Krauts weren't simply battling riflemen from across the Channel, but scalp hunters who kept trophies of their kills. The Krauts had their own scalp hunters, Sonny supposed, men drawn to that screed, fighter to fighter. But it didn't last very long. The Kraut machine gunners dwindled. There were fewer and fewer surprise attacks. If they found some loner in German wool, Clare dismissed him with a wave of his hand, like some medieval king. Sonny didn't realize it at first, but the battle of the hedgerows had ended. No one, it seemed, wanted to engage these scalp hunters. Hitler's elite had withdrawn to Cherbourg.

General Roosevelt sat in a portable chair that his aides had settled on a hill near the very last field at the mouth of that maze. He was lauding the Twelfth to Captain Clare.

'We married up and got you out of this mess, didn't we, Captain?'

'You sure did.'

Clare admired this gimp of a general who'd gone into the hedgerows with his boys, clutching a cane. He might have fallen without that stick in his hand. And yet he seemed to have little fear. His raincoat was riven with bullet holes. He'd shot at Krauts between the hedgerows.

His eyes were bloodshot, and his left hand started to shake. He should have been invalided out of the war. Yet here he was, on this clandestine battlefield, where whole companies of Krauts lurked behind hedgerow after hedgerow… until the sky soldiers swarmed down upon them with their own brand of thunder.

Roosevelt saw the string of ears on the captain's ammo belt. 'What's that, Captain Cowboy?'

'An amulet, sir.'

The general smiled. 'Sergeant Salinger, you ought to arrest this man. He's been practicing a kind of cannibalism.'

'Amulets are beyond the pale of my jurisdiction, sir,' Sonny said, jousting with the general.

'Well, make a note of it,' Roosevelt said, rising from his chair with one great shiver and limping off a battlefield with the bodies of German soldiers strewn about like ragged harlequins with missing ears. He had a constant crook in one shoulder, like a hunchback, and he was burdened with a dreadful pallor. He had no business being here.

'Should I help you, sir?' Sonny asked.

'I'm fine, soldier,' Roosevelt said with a wince. 'Thank you.'

He got through the hedgerows with his cane as a kind of baton.

But he tripped and fell, this broken little man who was the Fourth's first and last general in the field. Sonny picked up the brigadier and carried him in his arms, like a child. Roosevelt couldn't have weighed more than 120 pounds. Sonny fed him water from his canteen. 'Slow gulps, sir, or you'll cough up whatever you swallow.'

'Salinger,' the brigadier said, 'are you my nurse now?'

'No, sir.'

Roosevelt struggled out of Sonny's arms and continued to hop along. 'But I thank you kindly, soldier.'

Sonny knew he wouldn't last. His heart gave soon after he entered a little Norman village in a captured Kraut truck that he used as his personal caravan – none of the medics could revive him. He'd just been promoted to a two-star general and never lived to learn about the promotion. Roosevelt had paraded through Normandy sick as a dog and still he persevered, a two-star general limping after his boys from the grave.

Sometimes, once or twice, Sonny could feel the wetness of a whisper behind him, a telltale touch of air that belonged to General Roosevelt in his ill-fitting helmet, strapped on at a crooked angle. He wasn't the Fourth's mascot or regimental ghost. He marched; he sat down on a wall to catch his breath. And then he vanished, just like that, and the boys had to fight without their fallen deputy commander, the only general who had been with them on Uncle Red.

PART THREE

Cherbourg

June 1944

1

THE LITTLE HOUSE WOULDN'T STOP ROCKING. Rails fell off the garden wall. Shingles splintered. The crumbling chimney sounded like rats dancing on the tilted tiles of a rotten roof as the bombardment of Cherbourg continued with its own fierce noise, which was like a dissonant, half-crazed rhumba that Sonny might have danced to at the Stork with Oona O'Neill. He had a sudden whiff of her perfume, and nearly stumbled.

They were ten miles or so from Cherbourg, interrogating the local chieftain of the French fascist militia, whom several washerwomen had cornered and captured in this very house, which belonged to the chieftain's *petite amie*, a fascist postal worker. The chieftain, Jean-Marie Merlot, was twenty-two, and wore a borrowed Gestapo uniform and a beret. The washerwomen had scratched his cheeks and broken the fingers of his left hand. Sonny appraised him as a supercilious young devil who had profited from the war. His nose was stuffed with mucus. He cupped his broken fingers in the palm of his left hand and blew on them from time to time.

Sonny and Corporal Benson had their own jeep again, parked behind the little house. The bombardment of Cherbourg had been going on for days. The Krauts had erected their makeshift castle, Fortress Cherbourg, a ring of battlements around the harbor, like a winding staircase with metal teeth. They also had minefields, racks of barbed wire, ditches, and subterranean tunnels on the landward side, surrounded by hills with another ring of battlements, and Sonny was forlorn that he wasn't with his regiment and the men of the 82nd and the 101st, insane cavaliers, like Captain Clare.

The Allies couldn't keep their tanks and trucks and jeeps supplied with petrol without capturing the port of Cherbourg. And yet Sonny was stuck here in Rauville-la-Bigot with a member of the *milice*, a beret over one eye. Jean-Marie had been the lord and master of this village until a day ago — mayor, sheriff, shylock, and executioner. He and his thugs had occupied the Hôtel de Ville and had their own private café and bordello, Le Chien Méchant. But he was a wiser thug than most. He hadn't interfered in the daily commerce of Rauville-la-Bigot, hadn't demanded tribute. He strutted around in his Gestapo uniform and grabbed a few dim-witted farmer boys as slave laborers and had them shipped to Germany. He hadn't been paid a sou by his masters in Berlin. He inspired fear and deep distrust, but most of his tasks were ceremonial. He fêted Gestapo captains from Cherbourg. He had fascist parades.

Sonny was convinced that this smug militiaman had been inside the makeshift fortress, and would be vain enough to offer him some vital clues that might help the Allies seize Cherbourg and its prize harbor.

Captain Blunt wasn't with him and the corporal in Rauville-la-Bigot. Blunt was closer to the German lines, interrogating Krauts who had surrendered during the constant pounding by the Allies. The lamps in Jean-Marie's little office blinked on and off. The floorboards rumbled beneath them.

'*Petit*,' Sonny said, 'I think you had better talk, and talk fast.'

'But you are *spions*, all of you. You have no legitimacy. I will talk to General Eisenhower, only to him.'

'Ah,' Sonny said, 'I suspect the general will not take this scenic route. And I could deliver you to members of the maquis. They will not be so kind to you.'

The fascist chieftain sneered. 'I had them all shot long before you arrived. You will not find Resistance fighters in Rauville-la-Bigot. And why should I worry about de Gaulle? He wears diapers, I have been told.'

'But he could strangle you with those same diapers, whether he wears them or not.'

Jean-Marie kept sneering. 'First he would have to come to France. And he is much too afraid, my little friend.'

This boy gangster's vanity was still the key to his uncovering. Sonny would have to peel him like an onion to find that first layer of raw skin.

'What if we stood you near Le Chien Méchant? The villagers would toss stones at you.'

'I'll survive,' he said. 'They wouldn't dare touch my uniform.'

Sonny smiled. 'Get undressed.'

Jean-Marie looked at him as if he were a lunatic. 'What are you talking about? The colors I wear are sacred.'

This chieftain, this murderer, began to twitch. 'In Paris, people survive on rutabagas – everyone, rich and poor alike. Their teeth fall out. But here we have eggs.' His face lit with some eerie dreamlike color. 'And it's all on account of my armband… I keep our baker in business. Our café would have shut down years ago.'

'Bravo,' Sonny said. 'Every housewife and widow must earn a bonus taking off her garter belt for some Gestapo officer with a wanderlust. What's your cut?'

Jean-Marie was indignant. 'Cut? I have no cut. I live like a monk – in my uniform. I keep Rauville-la-Bigot alive.'

'Then why did the washerwomen who work at the Hôtel de Ville break your hand and put you under house arrest?' Corporal Benson asked.

'They're ungrateful,' he said.

'Get undressed,' Sonny insisted.

'Wait, wait,' Jean-Marie said. 'I am not unreasonable, Sergeant Salinger. I will tell you all I know and get to keep my armband.' He was very smug. 'The fortress cannot be breached. It has eighty-eights and mortars at all five levels. You will not be able to penetrate its walls with your bombs and cannons. It is futile, this American assault. The commandant can move his men from tunnel to tunnel and mount his own attack at the fortress's weakest point.'

'How many soldiers are inside that castle?' Sonny asked.

'Ninety thousand – a hundred, perhaps,' Jean-Marie muttered with a tentative smile.

Sonny grabbed him by the shoulders. A hundred thousand soldiers could have held Normandy for another month. 'You've never been inside Fortress Cherbourg, have you? Not even once.'

Jean-Marie looked at the curled tongues of his shoes. He seemed bereft, half alive, despite the regalia of his Gestapo ornaments. 'Why should they trust a boy from Rauville-la-Bigot? I could have been a counterspy, like you.'

'Yet you killed for them. You wore their uniform.'

'That means nothing to the *boche*,' he said, his chin withdrawn. He'd been a nuisance as a boy, the village pest. He never finished school, was reprimanded and beaten by his father, a farmer who could not even till his own soil. Jean-Marie was among the first to welcome the Krauts after they arrived in Rauville-la-Bigot. He was given his own revolver. He organized the *milice*. He executed the mayor and all the teachers who had mocked his delinquent manner and his mediocre knowledge of history and French folklore. He'd never heard of Charlemagne, Molière, or Montaigne. And yet his very ignorance appealed to Sonny. Still, he and the corporal undressed Jean-Marie and sent him naked out the door.

They heard the clamor in a minute, as he was kicked and buffeted about, dragged across the dirt and stones by women in kerchiefs and men without molars in their sunken mouths. 'Enough,' Sonny said, and retrieved the young assassin as villagers bowed to this tall American soldier with his sergeant's stripes.

'Sorry,' Sonny sang in French. 'We need this piece of shit.'

And that's when Blunt arrived in a jeep with Oliver, who was a major now, in charge of his own battalion. The Krauts had barricaded themselves in the streets near the harbor, and the major had to uproot them house by house, liberating hostages trapped in the cellars – infants, women, and palsied old men with bulging eyes. The major fed these hostages K packs of peanuts and Hershey bars. The Twelfth had already lost half its boys since the landing on Uncle Red, and had to rely on raw recruits.

'Well,' Blunt asked, 'did you learn much from this fascist fuck?'

'He's never been near Fortress Cherbourg,' Sonny said.

'Then give him back to the village. Everyone suffered under his rule.'

'Can't,' Sonny said. 'They'll tear him to shreds.'

'He deserves it,' Blunt said.

'I won't have him executed by a mob.'

'Fine,' Blunt said, tossing a blanket around the boy assassin and shoving him into the back of the jeep. 'We'll look after him, Salinger. I'll be his guardian angel.'

The boy's *petite amie*, Mauricette, came toward the jeep with her swaggering hips, like the maiden queen of the village. She was the cashier at Le Chien Méchant. She wore burning red lipstick and a rose with wilted petals in her hair.

'*Chouchou*,' the boy said, his back hunched under the blanket, 'save me from these American gangsters.'

Chouchou lunged forward with a dramatic sweep of her shoulders and spat in the boy's face. The villagers saluted her and cheered. 'Capitaine Mauricette.'

Blunt started to drive off, and Sonny had to race after him. 'Sir, what now?'

'Salinger, you go on to the next village and do the same thing. You find the son of a bitch in charge and interrogate him.'

'And after that?'

'You go on to the next – until you get to Cherbourg.'

And Sonny was left with Corporal Benson in a village that the Americans had just liberated. But the inhabitants of Rauville-la-Bigot couldn't seem to look into his eyes, even with all the American flags draped against the windows and the treasure trove of Hershey bars he and the corporal had distributed from the back of their jeep. His uniform with its chevrons intimidated them. He could have been one more occupier with a few enticing gifts. Hadn't the general staff of the Twelfth ripped off the Nazi banners from the Hôtel de Ville and arrived with all their maps? Senior officers seized the very best offices for themselves. Clerks had to huddle in the basement. All the other *milice* had fled, but Jean-Marie had remained, a king without his kingdom, until Blunt had spirited him into some dark void. Sonny doubted he would ever see that boy with the beret again.

2

EACH VILLAGE WAS A LITTLE CLOSER to the railroad line that led to Cherbourg. The rails buckled and the earth flew around them in the middle of the bombardment a few miles away. Sonny watched a squadron of P-47s fly above him like the body of a brazen bird that ripped apart and came together again with a groan. The Krauts had abandoned Montquebec, left their tanks and eighty-eight-mm guns behind. There were no fascists flitting about, no collaborators, no Krauts in civilian clothes. Villagers came out of their cellars to greet them. The corporal wondered how they had survived.

'On rutabagas,' said the mayor's wife, 'and on whatever rations the *boche* provided.'

'A bit of carrot stew,' said the village priest. His cassock was a little too fresh and shiny in a time of war and dissolution; there wasn't a single stain on his black skirts.

'And the French Gestapo?' Sonny asked.

'They vanished the morning you appeared on the beaches,' said the mayor's wife, without the slightest tremor in her voice.

'But the *boche* much have been here in Montquebec,' Sonny

had to insist. 'They ran without their artillery.'

'Because of your lightning attack,' she said.

There were only a few pinches of lightning. The Twelfth was shoved back a little every time it pushed off. The regiment had to slug it out in the hedgerows and all along the railroad line, with its half-hidden Kraut machine-gun nests.

Something seemed strange to Sonny, *irregular.* There was no rubble in the streets. And the clothes of these villagers were a little too neat. There was no sign of starvation, no jowls, not one gaunt neck. The women's nails were polished. The men were fat.

'Where's the rest of the village?' Sonny asked.

'They're still in the cellars,' said the priest. 'They're frightened. But come, we've prepared a meal for you.'

Sonny smiled to himself. He and the corporal entered a little red house that had escaped the Allied bombardment, like the rest of this enchanted village. A wicker table had been set for Sonny and the corporal with napkin rings, candles, and a marvelous crust of country bread. The priest served them carrot stew with a ladle. Sonny could sniff coriander. He got up from the table. He wasn't in the mood to breathe arsenic in the coriander.

'*Père*, you sit. We'll serve you.'

'But you are our guests, my child.'

'Still,' Sonny said, 'I insist.'

The priest shrugged his shoulders and sat in Sonny's place. His gray eyes twinkled as he wolfed down the stew. 'What a pity,' he said. 'You're missing a delicious meal… We saved and saved for a moment like this. We wanted to do our little part and protect our protectors. You must be famished.'

It was like a bizarre cartoon: a village without a swirl of dust or a crooked steeple. Had the Twelfth overlooked Montquebec on its drive along the coast? And yet here were Sonny and the corporal as an interrogation team.

'Something stinks,' the corporal whispered.

'Agreed,' Sonny said. He put his .45 on the wicker table. '

qui êtes vous? You're not from this village, and you're no priest. You have a farmer's hands, full of bumps.'

This fraud in the shiny cassock began to shiver. 'We're not *collabos*,' he said. 'We ran a small hotel near Rocheville. The *boche* took it over. We had little choice. We served them until they left.'

'Then why didn't you stay where you were?'

'We were tainted – as Nazi-lovers. We fed whoever we could. We rescued a British aviator. But we're not with the maquis. We have no status.'

'And that coriander,' Sonny said, 'came from your hotel.'

'Yes,' said the fake priest. 'It was in our pantry. The *boche* could requisition whatever they wanted. They demanded four-star meals at a seaside hotel. They wanted to take our entire équipe with them to Paris. So we ran away.'

'And disguised yourself as a priest. But why Montquebec?'

'Because it was deserted,' said the pastry chef, who had pretended to be the mayor's wife.

'But where are the *real* villagers of Montquebec?' asked Corporal Benson.

'It's a great mystery,' said this priest, who'd been the majordomo at the hotel. And Sonny's mind took flight. He imagined all these dissemblers in some new short story. That was the gift of a CIC man. Sonny was a born dissembler.

'And what happens if these villagers come back?'

'*Alors*,' said the priest. 'We will celebrate – and fight. Perhaps they will not forgive us for the little hotel we had. All the marmalade… and the butter we ate from a tub.'

Sonny couldn't leave this little tribe of mountebanks here, in the middle of so much war traffic. He had the MPs carry them off to an internment camp, while he went looking for other lost souls.

3

THREE WEEKS INTO THE WAR, and they already had a nickname – *le Gestapo Américain*. They had to interrogate like wild dogs, since it was harder and harder to tell the difference between *collabos*, who hid behind the medals they had collected from some earlier war, and villagers who had suffered throughout the occupation. Sonny made more and more arrests the closer they got to Cherbourg. No one seemed willing to talk, not even the owners of bicycle shops. And because they had so little time, they would borrow the commandant's office at local Gestapo headquarters, with the Führer's picture removed from the wall. They avoided cellars and torture rooms in their interrogations. Yet this tall American still inspired a certain kind of dread.

Once inside Gestapo headquarters, wives informed on their own husbands; the mayor, who'd been mum, plucked out a list of *unreliables*.

'I cannot say with certainty, monsieur. But these are the ones you should watch.'

It made Sonny ill. He had to sit in the Nazi commandant's chair until the MPs arrived with their van. And then he vanished to yet another village. Suddenly, all the interrogations stopped. The commandant of Fortress Cherbourg had surrendered. But he could not control the little outposts on the hills overlooking Cherbourg, and pockets around the railroad tracks, or at the Hôtel de Ville, where a handful of Krauts were dug in.

Sonny and the corporal entered Cherbourg in a bone-chilling calm. Weary of snipers as they were, they bounced across the rue de la Bretonnière, finding only a dead horse in the street, attached to a broken battle wagon. They arrived at the Hôtel de Ville, where Major Oliver strutted about with the riflemen of E Company. He had a tank with a flamethrower at his command. A fire roared within the Hôtel de Ville, with thick balls of black smoke billowing from every window. But Oliver was the chief of his own fire brigade. He positioned the nozzle of the flamethrower at the charred walls and windows of the Hôtel de Ville.

'Sir,' Sonny whispered, 'shouldn't you wait? There are a few rebel soldiers inside. They can't last forever.'

Oliver stared him down. 'Salinger, stay out of this. You're strictly CIC. Did you see any white flags?'

'No, sir.'

There wasn't any need of a white flag. The German soldiers leapt out the windows, one by one, wearing blankets that resembled fiery rags around their shoulders. They could have been creatures from another world. The medics arrived. Sonny stared at one of the soldiers, whose eye sockets were gone. All the flesh had been sucked from his face. Yet his blackened teeth revealed a jarring smile, like an angel soaring into the unknown.

PART FOUR

The Commandant of the Ritz

August 1944

1

No one could have predicted the velocity of the Allies – their breakout from Normandy and sweep across France. German panzer divisions were racing back across the Rhine like ragged columns of ants, and the Ninth Air Force had practically knocked the Luftwaffe out of the sky. Ike and his generals wanted to sidestep Paris. They would have had to deal with a whole German garrison – and supplying grub to over two million Parisians would have been a logistical nightmare. But Ike didn't have much of a choice. The Froggies were peeling off from the Allied juggernaut and moving toward Paris on their own, under General Leclerc, who was in command of the Second Armored Division. And the Twelfth had been elected to liberate Paris alongside Leclerc.

It was sort of an inconvenience for Sonny. He couldn't stop beside a country road and peck away at his Holden Caulfield novel on an army-issue Corona. He had to accompany his regiment. Still, there was a great deal of confusion. Leclerc drove up the avenue d'Orléans in a Sherman tank, wearing both a kepi and an American blouse. His entire command must have seemed like a bunch of unicorns in foreign dress. Parisians blocked the avenue, grasping at some of these soldiers in their black berets, climbing onto the tanks, tearing buttons off a soldier's blouse as magical souvenirs.

But Sonny was given an unbearable burden. Captain Blunt sat in the back of Sonny's jeep as they were entering Paris from the southwest, at the porte d'Italie.

'You'll have to arrest Hemingway,' he said. 'Correspondents

aren't allowed to carry firearms. He's collected a rogue's regiment. "Papa's Irregulars," he calls them.'

Sonny had heard a similar tale. Hem gathered a band of stragglers around him at Rambouillet – dogfaces who were stranded from their own outfits, other correspondents, a private cook, photographers, cameramen, military historians, and such, a motley crew of soldiers, civilians, and Resistance fighters, equipped with submachine guns and hand grenades.

'A whole regiment? That's unlikely.'

'Does it really matter, Salinger?' the captain said. 'He's a menace, that old man. He ought to be in an insane asylum. He's shot his way to the place Vendôme and *liberated* the Ritz. But there was nothing to liberate. The Luftwaffe left weeks ago with some of the Ritz's treasure. That crazy has captured a haunted house.'

Göring had occupied the Imperial Suite and filled half the hotel with his fellow officers. There was every sort of rumor about him, clandestine reports that Ike's intelligence team had gotten from a chambermaid who risked her life for the Allies. He wore ermine nightgowns and one earring, she said, and danced with waiters in the dining room. He had a jar filled with precious stones in his suite, and jeweled slippers with high heels. He was a morphine addict who stayed up half the night, staring at his emeralds and rubies. But he disappeared from Paris and the Ritz with his high command, his emeralds, and works of 'decadent' art he had robbed from rich collectors. There were no more Germans at the Ritz.

'And suppose I find Hemingway? Do you really want me to arrest him? He's an icon. We'll be laughed at – worse. All the wire services will pick it up. We'll be in the doghouse, not him.'

'I don't care,' Blunt said. 'I want that rogue's regiment to disband… I've got to get to the avenue Foch. I'll find my own way.'

The CIC had usurped 84, avenue Foch, the posh headquarters of the SS and all its counterintelligence branches, in the luxurious sixteenth arrondissement. It was the most notorious 'hotel' in Paris. It seems that whatever guest was invited to 84 seldom came out again. Sonny had to wonder why the CIC always occupied the former establishments of the Gestapo and the SS, no matter what town they were in. Perhaps it was convenience, or something a little more sinister than that. Secret agents clung to the territory of other secret agents.

'Good-bye, kiddies. And don't get lost. Bring me Hemingway's scalp.'

The captain leapt off the jeep and was immediately swallowed up by a little mob of Parisians who kissed him and carried him into a corner bistro, where another mob waited to kiss him. Meanwhile, Sonny and Corporal Benson rode behind a half-track, a 'Dirty Gertie,' filled with dogfaces, some of them with delirious little boys and lovely Parisian girls on their laps.

'*Les GIs,*' the girls screamed, '*les GIs,*' as they kicked out their legs like cancan dancers.

There were still snipers on the rooftops. Sonny watched them climb among the chimney pots with their long rifles. The German commandant had surrendered the city from his sumptuous quarters at the Hôtel Meurice. But a general in claret-striped pants couldn't control every pillbox and machine-gun nest, every maverick sniper stationed on the roofs. He was powerless. Parisians ran into the Meurice and nearly kicked him to death. And the constant crackle of gunfire mingled with the sound of celebrants. Paris was still under siege. Sonny's own unit had to dismantle a machine-gun nest dug right into the place d'Italie. Celebrants danced around the hailstorm of bullets that left flying splinters of glass and a shower of little stones off the façades of buildings. And in the midst of that hailstorm, a dozen girls with shaved skulls and bare breasts marched along the boulevard Vincent-Auriol, with a female member of the maquis behind them, carrying a submachine gun. Some of the girls couldn't have been older than thirteen. They all had swastikas painted in blue on their breasts. They must have belonged to some brothel that serviced the *boche*. Parisians tossed bags of excrement at them like firebombs.

The fighting stopped for a moment as these young girls with bald heads passed in front of the little German fort dug into the ground. Sonny was seized with a sadness he couldn't control. He didn't want the girls to be harmed, no matter what their sins were, no matter how hard they were mocked and poked by the Parisians.

The German soldiers surrendered.

Sonny didn't want to catch a glimpse of their fate. He had his driver swerve around the half-track and into the heart of Paris.

2

HE DREADED THE RITZ. IT reminded Sonny of the Stork, with its cacophony of myths. He imagined Chaplin must have stayed here once upon a time in the Imperial Suite. It had been a playground for celebrities until the Germans arrived and took over half the hotel. The Ritz had its own neutrality. It was a haven for *collabos*, like Coco Chanel and somber-eyed Arletty, the most beautiful woman in the world. He'd seen her in *Le Jour Se Lève* a dozen times. His mother had sent him clippings of Arletty and her beau, a young German lieutenant in the Luftwaffe, who had lived with her at the hotel.

Sonny and Corporal Benson, with their CIC armbands intact, stood under a white awning shaped like a cupola, at the entrance of the Ritz. A soldier wearing the motley uniform of a cavalry recon outfit blocked Sonny's path with a submachine gun cradled in his arms.

'No tourists allowed,' the soldier barked.

Sonny stared him down. 'Well, we're here to see Hem.'

'What for?'

'To arrest him,' Sonny said.

The soldier livened considerably. He put down his submachine gun and removed an enormous walkie-talkie from the pocket of his pants. 'Crooner to the commandant, do you read me?'

The radio crackled and Sonny heard Hem's scratchy voice. 'What's up, Crooner?'

'Sir, we have two live ones at the gate. They've come to arrest you.'

There was a slight pause and then another crackle. 'Send 'em up.'

And so Sonny entered the Ritz, a hotel without a lobby or a lounge, to discourage curiosity seekers and uninvited guests without cash in their pockets. Paintings had been plucked from the walls. The mirrors had stark blue veins in them. The hotel's tiny elevator rattled in its cage. It was piloted up to the third floor by another soldier in a cavalry recon uniform. They went down a corridor to room 31. The chandeliers rocked over their heads and could have come crashing down on Sonny and the corporal with their unpolished vertebrae and creaky stems. Sonny ducked and didn't have to knock. The door was open. There was a scatter of men inside, woolly men with mustaches. They seemed out of place among the pink lampshades, the doilies, the gilded mirrors, and antique furniture. One of these Irregulars sat cross-legged near the door, cooking coffee on a camp stove. The others were cleaning their submachine guns with towels from some raided linen closet. They had hand grenades clipped to their belts. With them was Papa Hemingway with an enormous paunch. He could have been Falstaff rather than the rich, muscular writer with a panther's sleek moves that Sonny had met at the Stork.

Hem had ballooned out. He couldn't even hide his belly button under his half-open blouse. Sonny was crippled by that first glance. This bravado wasn't even close to the Hemingway that Sonny had once adored, that monk-like young man in multiple sweatshirts, scratching poetry into little blue booklets in some unheated Paris café. That writer had gone utterly underground, and a self-proclaimed officer emerged, the commandant of the Ritz.

'Papa,' asked a Resistance fighter among the Irregulars, *'on peut fusiller tous les deux?'*

'Not today,' said the commandant. 'We don't have firing squads at the Ritz.'

'D'accord, mon capitaine.'

Hem stared at Sonny's sergeant stripes and his CIC armband. 'Who sent you? General Patton or the provost?' Then he stared a second time, squinting with his weak eyes. 'Hey, kid, haven't we met?'

'At the Stork,' Sonny said.

All the scratchiness in Hem's voice was gone. He chortled like Falstaff, another soldier-clown in search of a mission.

'I remember. It was at that skunk's table. W-a-l-t-e-r Winchell. You were with Oona O'Neill. What a gorgeous gal!' Hem caressed the stubble on his chin with a blistered hand. 'Sonny Salinger. I've seen your stories in the *Post*. Damn good. Read your profile. You prefer to write in foxholes.'

Sonny felt embarrassed. 'I never said that. It's pure baloney… from *The Saturday Evening Post*. The bastards changed my titles. They wouldn't let me keep "Death of a Dogface".'

Falstaff chuckled again. 'Can't have the word *death* in a title, not at the *Post*. Wouldn't be kosher… Who's your accomplice?'

Corporal Benson introduced himself. 'Proud to meet you, Papa.'

Sonny had noticed a kiosk near the hotel's front desk. It must have been where German officers parked their pistols and ceremonial swords before going up to their rooms. And here was Hemingway with an entire arsenal. The enormous brass bed with its pink coverlet was piled with hand grenades and revolvers.

'Papa,' the corporal asked, 'did you notice any German officers hiding in the attic?'

And that's when Hemingway began to talk in a kind of telegraphese he must have used with his Irregulars. It was one more bit of swagger. 'Swept the place clean. Not a Kraut in sight.

And not much of a staff. Had to serve ourselves lunch in Le Petit Jardin. Lucky we brought our rations, or we might have starved.'

The Ritz was half-deserted when Hemingway arrived with his band. The waiters didn't even have their white shirts. The manager had fled somewhere. And his assistant wasn't prepared to accommodate new guests. So Papa stormed the palace, and it was now his headquarters, in the same hotel where Marcel Proust had once wandered about, preparing to flirt with the hotel's young waiters.

'Papa,' Sonny said, 'you'll have to give up the guns and the grenades.'

And Falstaff's face suddenly darkened. He'd come to a war zone as a correspondent from *Collier's,* and gathered his own troops in Rambouillet. It was hard to keep a pistol or a submachine gun out of his hands. He dubbed himself a captain of his own scruffy militia, in borrowed uniforms and with borrowed guns, and beat Leclerc and Sonny's regiment to Paris. And Sonny knew that Falstaff would remain in Paris, exiled at the Ritz. Who would dare dislodge him? The generals couldn't afford to tangle with Papa Hemingway. It was much too risky. They'd rather box him in. And so this *libération* had become his tomb. He was locked in a palace on the place Vendôme. And Sonny could sense Papa's wistfulness.

'Where do you go next?' Papa asked.

'To Le Sphinx.'

It was Paris' most celebrated brothel. It had its own private clientele. Until last month, you could meet Picasso and members of the German high command at Le Sphinx. The girls were very haughty there, Sonny had been told. They didn't have to sleep with a man. They could pick and choose their own objects of desire. A dwarf, a busboy, or another girl. That was the hallmark of the Sphinx, and made it so different from any other brothel. *Les poules* were in command.

Sonny had aroused Papa's interest. 'And who are you going to arrest, Sergeant Salinger?' Papa asked, squinting at Sonny's chevrons for a second time. CIC agents weren't usually supposed to display their rank. But it was part of Sonny's disguise – Sergeant Salinger.

'I can't disclose that,' Sonny said. 'It's privileged information.'

'Lemme guess. Boldy.'

The baron de Boeldieu, or Boldy, was a celebrated collaborator. He could be seen with officers of the SS on the avenue Foch, at auction houses, or at the Sphinx, which had become his preferred haunt. He'd rescued several rich Jews, smuggled them out of Paris, and had given up the hiding places of others. He lived his life on some extraordinary whim. He'd betrayed his friends and shielded his enemies. He was incurably unreliable. He could have rushed across the Rhine with the Krauts. Göring would have let him sit out the rest of the war at Carinhall, his extravagant estate outside Berlin, in a forest filled with peacocks. But whimsical as ever, he remained at Le Sphinx.

'Papa,' Sonny said with a masked smile, 'is he a friend of yours?'

'I had dinner with him once – at the Ritz. Don't judge him too harshly. He's saved a lot of souls.'

'And watched others suffer – if my dossier is correct… Ah, but I have a favor to ask.' Sonny removed a GI pocket edition of Papa's short stories from a coveted place in his Eisenhower jacket. 'It's for Sottotenente Lorenzo Tropea.'

'Do I know him?' Papa asked.

'Yes, in a way. He's in an Italian prisoner of war camp at Tiverton. And he's devoted to your work. He thinks of little else. He knows your early tales by heart. His English is as good as mine – perhaps even better, since it's precious to him.'

Papa smiled. 'If you say so, Sergeant.' He dedicated the book with a pencil stub, in a slow and deliberate scrawl, and returned it to Sonny. 'Now, are you going to arrest me or not?'

'That would be criminal of us,' Sonny said. 'Right, Corporal?'

The corporal hesitated for a moment. 'Right,' he finally said. 'Absolutely criminal.'

The corporal felt a shiver run right through him. He would tell all his buddies back home that he had met Ernest Hemingway at the Ritz.

'Have you read my stories, son?' Papa asked.

The corporal panicked. 'I…'

'He isn't much of a reader,' Sonny said. 'But I've recited your stories to him – like songs.' And Sonny began to recite from 'Soldier's Home,' about a boy who returns from the First War and can't seem to adjust to civilian life. The boy's name was Krebs. But the words didn't please Papa Hemingway, didn't please him at all. And Sonny had to stop in the middle of a sentence, as Papa grimaced, looked like a crazy man, rather than an Irregular at the Ritz.

'What's wrong?' Sonny asked.

'Wrote that story in one sitting,' Papa said. 'Didn't have to change a word. It's a young man's arrogance.'

'No,' Sonny said. 'It's a gift.'

Papa's lip curled and began to tremble. 'If you say so, Sergeant.' He looked like a guy who'd just been lobotomized. But that current of madness disappeared. And he was the commandant again, with his Irregulars. War had become a kind of romance to Papa, a quixotic quest, with bandoliers and invented fables and flags, while it was nothing but pillage to Sonny, the soiling of a landscape, all the unheroic horror and static silences that Hem himself had once written about.

'Sergeant, the boy who wrote that story had shrapnel in his ass and thighs – I still do. But it was *another* war, a kinder war in a way, though the killing was just as brutal. I don't have the stamina to sit in cafés. I saw myself as a priest on a holy mission. That holiness is gone. What am I, Sergeant?'

Sonny was silent. He couldn't say the words.

'No better than a luxurious prisoner of war. Patton *and* the provost won't let me fight. So we had our little run. And I'll enjoy my stay at the Ritz. Now go and catch Boldy if you can.'

3

THEY TOOK THE SIDE STREETS, which had fewer tanks and Dirty Gerties, and not one German outpost. Benson had to drive at a crawl, as men and women danced in front of the jeep. But they arrived at the Latin Quarter, where Hem had lived on the rue Cardinal-Lemoine with his redheaded wife and his little boy, Bumby, without heat and hot water, and refashioned American literature with a few short stories, like 'Soldier's Home.' That Hemingway had been replaced by the commandant of the Ritz, a fusilier rather than the father of a brand-new idiom, a piercing flatland of sentences without a single adjective or adverb. Sonny sought the same simplicity, at least some of it. He also admired the lushness of Scott Fitzgerald. *Gatsby* was his favorite book. But Fitzgerald was also gone – and forgotten.

A little gang of *clodos* had assembled on the sidewalk of Cardinal-Lemoine with their bottles of rotgut whiskey. Some of them wore the discarded uniforms of Nazi officers, with the twin lightning bolts of the SS. Sonny knew that these tramps weren't collaborators, just unlucky souls. He didn't want them torn to pieces by members of the resistance. He got out of the jeep and made the *clodos* strip to their underwear.

'*Vite,*' he said, '*vite, vite!*'

While the *clodos* hopped and danced, Sonny took their tailored uniforms, dug them into a trash barrel, and set the uniforms on fire with his Zippo lighter. He watched the cloth, silk and wool, crackle, hypnotized by the flames, caught in their swirl, as if the fire and their fumes had the power to enchant – and to wound. The corporal had to nudge him.

'Boldy, remember? Le Sphinx. He could be planning a trip to China, Sarge.'

Sonny shook himself out of his trance. They could still hear the crack of gunfire from some lone-wolf sniper as their jeep stalled for a second on the cobblestones.

Down the Mouffetard they went, a market street without any markets. The Mouffetard had become a winding road of empty stalls. The Krauts had grabbed every crop within a hundred miles of Paris so that the officers of the high command could have their vegetables and beef at the Crillon and the Lutetia, at Maxim's and Le Tour d'Argent – Sonny had been to none of these places.

The vendors stood beside their empty stalls and saluted Sonny and the corporal. Some of them and their wives and children waved miniature American flags. Sonny didn't feel much like a liberator. He'd come to arrest and interrogate *collabos*, like the baron de Boeldieu, who'd profited from the war and had committed treason while headquartered at Le Sphinx...

Finally they reached the boulevard Edgar-Quinet and found a slot in front of the brothel, which looked like a fortress with its barred windows and nondescript façade. There was a medallion of a sphinx dressed like a pharaoh on the front wall. Otherwise, Sonny might have fled right past it. He knocked on the front door. No one answered. Sonny knocked again, louder this time.

'Open up. We're on a military mission.'

The door opened with a terrific screech. A dwarf stood near the entrance with a truculence that Sonny had never encountered. He wore a red uniform with bandoliers and a cartridge belt, and had a Luger under that belt. 'Madame Marlun isn't here,' the dwarf snarled, half in English, half in French. He had a beautiful mouth, despite the venom that he spat.

'I'm Pierre,' he said. 'Le Sphinx is not open for business, not in such disastrous times. You can see for yourselves, every girl is gone. And Madame is indisposed. I doubt she'll ever be back.'

The bar and the sofas in the salon had been covered with drop cloths. There were frescos on the wall of pharaohs wearing black masks. That was the only mark of opulence at Le Sphinx. Sonny had to step on shards of glass strewn everywhere, like a macabre minefield.

'I'm here to see the baron,' he said.

The dwarf smiled. 'Is he expecting you?'

'That doesn't really matter. I have official documents.'

'But it might matter to him,' the dwarf said. 'Come with me – both of you.'

They followed the dwarf behind a red curtain, went through a curious maze lit with a pink light – Sonny couldn't have retraced his steps. This truculent dwarf had led him into a labyrinth. They entered a darkened room. The dwarf himself screwed a bulb into a socket, and Sonny found himself in the company of another militia, like Papa's Irregulars. But these Irregulars were all *poules*.

The dwarf had lied to him. Le Sphinx's girls hadn't disappeared from the premises. They stood around a golden chair, carrying every sort of armament. One of them kneeled in front of a bazooka that could have knocked Sonny and the corporal through the Sphinx's front wall.

The baron de Boeldieu sat on his golden chair with his legs crossed. This wasn't his office; it was his throne room. He was much younger than Sonny had imagined – in his mid-thirties perhaps. He had a singularly handsome face, with an aquiline nose, high cheeks, and purplish eyes in the dim light of the dwarf's bulb. He was wearing a silk shirt, a foulard, and a velvet suit, like some *maquereau*, or master pimp.

Sonny introduced himself, 'Sergeant Salinger, CIC. ...Boeldieu, Papa sends his regards.'

'But that's not why you're here,' the baron said in a silken voice; his English didn't have the slightest hint of a foreign accent. 'And who's this boy?'

'My driver,' Sonny said.

'That's peculiar. How many other sergeants have their own drivers? You've come to arrest me.'

Damn Captain Blunt and his nonchalant orders – arrest this one and that one, Papa at the Ritz and a *maquereau* in a velvet suit. Sonny wanted to leave the Sphinx alive, and he had to deal with that militia behind the baron's throne. And so he bargained as best he could. 'I need some information. And you're a perfect repository.'

'Why is that?' the baron asked.

'Because you've played both sides to perfection.'

'Talk, talk, talk,' said one of the *poules*, who had silver hair. 'Talk will get us nowhere. It's time for an execution – a double execution, if you ask me.'

'Raymonde, don't be so impetuous. Give the sergeant and his companion a chance to plead for their lives.'

Sonny had to rely on all the conniving, sinister, meddlesome little gods of the CIC to get him out of this mess. Still, it comforted him to have Papa's inscribed stories in his pocket, almost like a talisman, the stories he would mail to Sottotenente Tropea if he ever survived Le Sphinx.

'Boldy, my sudden disappearance won't help you one bit. Other agents will come. Le Sphinx has been marked. And so are you.'

'Ah, but I don't intend to stay here forever,' the baron said.

'Why not… if we make a deal?'

'And what kind of deal can I make with the Americans? You'll sing like a canary to save your life.'

'I don't have to sing,' Sonny said. 'It should be obvious to you.'

The baron clapped his hands. His fingers were long and thin. 'Bravo. What a performance. I'm safe here, Sergeant. All I have to do is survive this ridiculous day, and then we're gone, with new identities…'

'Shame on you,' Sonny said. 'They'll track your ass wherever you go. You're a fugitive. But there's no reason to leave. You can stay at Le Sphinx in your golden chair... Business as usual.'

The baron leaned toward Sonny. 'And whom do I have to betray?'

'No one,' Sonny said, improvising as fast as he could while the corporal shivered at his side.

'Will I get assurances? From General Patton?... I don't believe your lies. Why would the Americans help me?'

'Because we have no other conduit to the black market. And we have to feed a starving town. You can unblock the traffic of merchandise and produce. No one else can. You're the *caïd*.'

Sonny was thinking of *Pépé le Moko*, a film with Jean Gabin, who was the *caïd* of the casbah – the king of crime – in Algiers. Pépé was safe as long as he kept to the walls of the casbah. And Le Sphinx was Boldy's casbah... while the Krauts occupied Paris.

'*Caïd*,' the baron muttered. 'That's true. But de Gaulle is back, and I'll get the guillotine.'

'Can de Gaulle feed Paris?'

'No,' the baron said. 'But he's an uncompromising prick.'

'He'll have to compromise,' Sonny said. 'Does he control the warehouses?'

'I'm not a magician,' the baron said.

'Yes, you are. *Nothing* moves without a nod from you.'

Sonny had enraptured this traitorous king of crime. 'Will I meet with the great Eisenhower?'

Sonny smiled like a jackal. He didn't even have to pounce. 'Boldy, Ike can't be seen with the likes of you.'

'I suppose I'll have to meet with other vermin from your own branch of counterspies and crooks. Have you taken over that German palace of spies on the avenue Foch?'

'Yes. But the Krauts still have a toehold in Paris.'

'A tiny one,' the baron said. 'Let's drink to our success.'

'*Chef*,' said Raymonde, who was savvier than the rest. 'You aren't going to trust this *canaille*, are you? The madmen will come, hang you from a hook, and burn swastikas into our tits. Don't trust him.'

'Why not?' the baron said. 'He might do us a small favor and keep the maquis from the boulevard Edgar-Quinet for a little while longer… Pierrot, what do you say?'

'I agree with Raymonde,' the dwarf said. 'Kill them – right now.'

'And have other visitors? Other armies at our door? The sergeant can help us. He's a genuine trickster.'

The baron opened a bottle of Château Lafite Rothschild that he had stolen from one of the Ritz's secret cellars on the Left Bank, somewhere on the rue Lecourbe. He sniffed the cork and let the bottle breathe for a moment while the dwarf searched for two glasses. Then he poured a glass of Château Lafite for Sonny and himself, and nothing for the corporal, or Pierrot and Raymonde and the rest of his militia.

'*Santé!*' he said.

Sonny's head throbbed with the first sip of wine. He was being outmaneuvered, even while the baron saved his own skin.

'How is the bearded one – Papa?'

'He shaved his beard,' Sonny said. 'And he's holed up at the Ritz for the duration. The provost won't let him travel with a gun, and his army of Irregulars.'

'He'll find a way – he always does… Who told you to arrest me?'

'The order might have come from Patton. I'm just a clerk.'

The baron laughed. 'That's what the Gestapo call themselves. Hitler's clerks. You're not a clerk… They'll have to kill me. I know too much.'

Sonny had to keep dancing in some private landscape while his mind was mottled with Château Lafite. 'But that's your wild card, Baron. That's your letter of transit. You know all the compromises that were made, all the deals. If they harm you, who can tell what will surface, what will pop up?'

The baron tucked on his foulard. 'So I should sit here and wait until they burn off my fingers one at a time.'

'No,' Sonny said. 'Unleash the food supply. Make whatever deals you have to make, and you'll be indispensable.'

'Pierrot,' the baron said, 'I like this *mec*. We'll give him our own *laissez-passer*.'

'*Chef*,' the dwarf said. 'That's foolish. He'll squawk the moment he's free.'

'And what about us?' Raymonde asked, with the red luster of rage in her eyes. 'Don't we have a vote?'

'Vote your head off,' the baron said. 'It's overrated, this voting business... Pierrot, let him take another sip of wine and escort him to the door – with his driver.'

Sonny took a second sip. He mind wandered for a moment and he could swear that he saw Oona among all the *poules*, Oona with pink lipstick and a bandolier of ammunition.

'Jerry,' she said, 'my poor little Jerry of the CIC.'

Where's Chaplin? he wanted to ask. *Where's the Tramp?*

But he couldn't even hold on to that image of her. The trickster had tricked himself.

Pierrot led them out of that labyrinth of rooms. Sonny had to clutch the walls. 'He's foolish, that commander of ours,' Pierrot said. 'He's a child. He believed your bullshit.'

Pierrot unlocked the front door, shoved Sonny and the corporal out onto the boulevard, and locked Le Sphinx again. Sonny stared at that emblem of the sphinx as a man – a pharaoh – on the front wall.

The corporal was shaking. He had to sit at the edge of the sidewalk. 'Jesus, I nearly crapped in my pants. But you bluffed your way out of there, Sarge.'

'It wasn't a bluff,' Sonny said.

'You mean we aren't gonna send for the commandos? What will we say to Captain Blunt?'

'Nothing,' Sonny said. 'Not a word.'

'And Boldy continues his career as the fucking king of crime?'

'He has no career. Someone will finish him. It doesn't have to be us.'

The corporal rose up from the curb, and they both got back into the jeep, with that continual crack of sniper fire in the air.

'Where to now, Sarge? The avenue Foch?'

'No,' Sonny said. 'Fuck the avenue Foch.'

And they drove down the boulevard, into the turmoil of a town that was still caught in the charged dream of its new American Allies and former conquerors, the Krauts.

Sonny couldn't keep awake. Boeldieu must have drugged him with the Château Lafite. He had a nightmare during this afternoon of celebration and random attacks. He found himself at 84, on the avenue Foch, in one of the interrogation rooms. But he wasn't being grilled by the Krauts. The entire setup parodied the Cub Room at the Stork, with its banquettes and little parliament of mirrors, suddenly festooned with swastikas and bloodred Nazi banners. Oona sat in front of him at Table 50. She was the torturer, Sonny could tell, though time had *curled* backward in his favor. She wasn't Mrs Charlie Chaplin of Hollywood. She was wearing her gym suit from Brearley, with the sweep of her bosoms accented by the harsh light of the interrogation lamp.

'Jerry,' she whispered, 'still love me?'

'More than ever.'

Oona leaned over and kissed him on the mouth with a passionate suck of her lips as her tongue roamed like a salamander.

'Then tell us the Allied invasion plans.'

'Oona,' he muttered the moment that salamander fled, 'I ain't Ike.'

And Oona started to peel off her gym suit in a calculated tease to bewilder Sonny and make him confess secrets he didn't have. But he couldn't even summon up the aroma of her armpits, as the rapid report of a machine pistol jolted him out of this Nazi Cub Room. He and Corporal Benson didn't have to bother with any Krauts. A cadre of Free French militia careened around them on the boulevard Edgar-Quinet in a prewar Citroën. There were eight or nine men and women in that little car, with their legs dangling out the windows and a truculent look on their faces. It reminded Sonny of a willful circus troupe.

'Hey, *Amerloques*,' shouted the driver, 'we have work to do. Get out of the way.'

And for a moment Sonny wished he could summon up 84 again, no matter the consequences, and what his fate would be.

PART FIVE

The Green Hell

October – November 1944

1

Papa's stories never got to the *sottotenente*. The parcel was returned to Sonny's regiment with two words stamped on it in blue ink:

ADDRESSEE UNKNOWN

The blue ink baffled Sonny. Had that tiny camp for Italian prisoners of war disappeared from Devon? Had it taken flight on some magic carpet from the Bolham Road in Tiverton to another town? Or had the *sottotenente* gone berserk and been banished to Wormwood Scrubs? How would Sonny ever know?

He was stuck with his regiment in the Hürtgen Forest. There wasn't a glimmer of sun in this 'Green Hell.' The Twelfth endured perpetual darkness in a landscape of tree trunks often a hundred feet high, with foliage that seemed to have no beginning and no end. Sonny had marched into a monstrous fairy tale close to the German border. There wasn't enough space between tree trunks for a tank, a jeep, or a Dirty Gertie to get through, except on the rough forest roads and fire trails, which were all booby-trapped and a sniper's paradise, a perfect 'serenade' for an ambush. Sonny's headquarters was a farmer's hut at the edge of Hürtgen, on the Belgian side of the border.

The Krauts had pillboxes planted everywhere in the foliage, and the forest floor was perilous ground, seeded with land mines known as 'Bouncing Bettys,' that could rip your balls right off. And that's why dogfaces of Sonny's division walked about with their helmets cupped between their legs. But the treetops in Hürtgen were just as vicious. German artillery exploding in a treetop would rain down shards of wood as nasty as razor blades and hot scraps of metal that could dig into a dogface's belly, arms, and back, and ruin him for life.

The Allied advance had been stopped in this fairy-tale forest of Hansel and Gretel. Sonny didn't have one prisoner of war to interrogate, one Belgian Nazi, or fascist banker from Luxembourg. The well was dry. All he had was the constant hoot of night owls. He sat near a hooded hurricane lamp and worked on his Holden Caulfield novel. It was like raising the dead, since he had already established in an earlier tale that Holden Caulfield didn't survive one of the Allied assaults in the Pacific. And then a creature in camouflage green and gray entered the hut with skeletal eyes and a skeletal face. It was Blunt, whom Sonny hadn't seen since Paris. Blunt had navigated the secret corridors of the CIC, and was a lieutenant colonel now, with a light colonel's oak leaf on his shoulder. And Sonny had thought he'd never last, ever since that first day on Utah Beach.

Blunt was staring at the returned packet on Sonny's writing table. 'Salinger, it never even crossed the Channel.'

'What do ya mean? It has "Addressee Unknown" marked all over it.'

'I inked that myself, kid. You're CIC. You can't send a package to a prisoner of war. It could be encrypted.'

Sonny's mouth twitched. 'Encrypted with what? It has Hemingway's signature.'

Blunt laughed with a mouthful of crooked teeth. 'That blusterer with his fake militia? You couldn't even deliver him from the goddamn Ritz.'

'Come on, Colonel. Hem is out of your hair.'

But the skeleton in his camouflage suit wasn't satisfied. 'He's an insult to the CIC… And you had baron de Boeldieu slip away from the Sphinx.'

'Slip away? I'll bet he's still there with his little army of *poules*.'

The skeleton smiled. There wasn't a pinch of fat on his face. 'The baron's with us now. We purchased all his rights and privileges. I can't think of anyone else I'd rather have at my table. We couldn't have fed Paris without Boeldieu.'

'That's grand,' Sonny said. 'How did you enjoy your torture table on the avenue Foch?'

Blunt revealed his crooked teeth again. 'Don't knock it, kid. The SS will soon be working for us.'

Sonny looked up from his manuscript. He wanted to rip off the oak leaf and have Blunt swallow it. 'Is that what this war is all about? A horse race between opposing counterintelligence teams?'

'It would be,' Blunt said, 'if we didn't have the Hürtgen Forest in our fucking way. All our intelligence is crap. We're dug in for the duration. And you won't have this hut much longer. Some general has fancied it for himself and his staff.'

Sonny wore a mask of dismay. 'I didn't know we had any generals in the Hürtgen. I thought they're in Paris with Ike and the rest of the high command.'

'Don't get cute,' Blunt said. 'And give me your *Hemingway*.'

Sonny's mask of bewilderment was genuine now.

'The book, the book – the GI paperback,' said Blunt. 'I'll send it off in one of my own pouches and it will get to your *I*talian prisoner of war.'

The CIC lieutenant colonel plucked the parcel off Sonny's writing table and left the hut, a haunted creature in his camouflage suit. Sonny couldn't get back to his novel. He listened to the owls and pretended that the eerie space between every hoot was the halting rhythm of his sentences. But he still couldn't get back to Holden Caulfield, dead or alive.

2

THE ALLIES HAD TO TAKE ONE TREE AT A TIME, one machine-gun nest, one German bunker. The Krauts had been here before – they withdrew from the forest and then returned. They recognized every inch of the terrain. They were dug in on the hilltops, and could read every one of the Allied positions, even in the thick foliage. It was like a bunch of belligerent boys battling a band of wandering, footloose children. That's what the Twelfth had become in the Hürtgen Forest – children.

Sonny lived in a foxhole now, nearby Corporal Benson and several newbies, since the Twelfth had nothing but raw recruits. Most of the regiment had been wiped out in this Green Hell. Sonny survived because of the woolen socks his mother knit for him every week. The weather had gone fierce by the middle of November. There was a whipping rain that left mountains of mud, and not a single pair of overshoes had arrived from the Quartermaster Corps. Sonny shared whatever woolen socks he had left with the corporal and the newbies in their foxholes.

'Sarge,' the newbies said, 'your mom's a saint.'

'Not at all, but she does knit a mean pair of woolen socks.'

Some of the newbies didn't make it. The constant mortar attacks and flying shrapnel and shards of wood from the treetops drove them half-insane. They sat shivering in Miriam Salinger's socks, their heads under a blanket.

'I can't cut it, Sarge. The pounding never stops.'

Sonny had grown deaf in one ear from the constant barrage, and though he was now his squad leader, he still didn't have the authority to send a dogface back to the rear lines with a bad case of the shivers. There were no more medics in this part of the forest. They'd all been wiped out by enemy fire, since they had to move around a lot, seeking out the wounded and dogfaces who had grown hysterical and had lost their senses under attack. Sonny had to soothe them back to sanity.

'You'll be all right, soldier. Just breathe hard and think of Betty Grable.'

Sonny and the corporal were in a parade of foxholes for misfits. Somehow they had to survive.

'Private Markowitz, you'll do fine.'

He peeked under the blanket and saw the glaze in the boy's eyes. He didn't have much choice. He slapped the private twice, and that glaze vanished.

'If you sit there like that, soldier, you'll die.'

'But I'm scared, Sarge, I'm so scared.'

'We're all scared,' Sonny said. 'This is the Green Hell. The Krauts own this forest. And we have to take it back.'

They'd become a bunch of tree huggers. That was the only way to defend themselves against the flying debris, or else they built a log roof over their foxholes. But the Krauts had their own spotters, and such roofs were easy to find. Major Oliver, the boy wonder from the Citadel, was still commander of E Company. He'd put Sonny in charge of a rifle platoon, since Sonny and Corporal Benson were the only noncoms he had left. He had no medics, no scouts, no artillery forward observer, just dogfaces with swollen feet, their M1s, and a few rifle grenades. And he was always eager to jump off with his ragged riflemen and overrun some Kraut entrenchment. But the problem was that half his boys were retreads, rear-echelon clerks who'd been sent to the front and could barely fire an Ml. And such retreads were utterly unreliable under fire. They were liable to shoot up their own squad. And so Sonny had a double burden – the retreads and the seasoned Krauts, with their own forward observers, who could spot every rifleman in E Company, even in that dense wilderness. They could observe them through the damn needles of the white pines.

Still, Regiment relied on Major Oliver and his company of 'squirrel shooters.' Regiment always had Oliver jump off first in any attack on German bunkers in Hürtgen. But most of the major's squirrel shooters were long gone, victims of some random sniper or shrapnel from a tree burst. And he had to jump off with retreads and raw recruits. Yet he attacked and attacked and attacked. And Sonny had to run across the twisted roots and fallen pinecones and needles, with a canteen flapping at his side and the green four-leaf ivy patch of the Fourth Division on his shoulder.

The major did have one advantage. He was a maestro with a flamethrower that he carried with a bucket strapped to his back. If he could create some kind of diversion, he would crawl behind a Kraut bunker, point his hose with great precision at an orifice in the bunker's log and concrete wall, and let the flames fly from twenty feet or so. The Krauts didn't even have a chance to surrender; that's how fast the flames swept through the bunker.

Soon he was called 'Fireboy.' He went nowhere without that bucket on his back.

Sonny knew he wouldn't survive the Hürtgen if he stayed with Fireboy too long. The major took too many chances, too many risks. He crept right up close to a bunker or pillbox, and was too easy a target with the tank on his back – he looked like a hunchback made of metal. But somehow Sonny did survive, and so did the major, who was very solicitous of all his retreads. He wouldn't banish them to their former rear-echelon posts. And none of them had the least desire to go back. Their own heads were on fire with the madness and bravado of the major's jump-off points. They taught themselves to use their M1s. It was nearly a miracle.

Sonny and the corporal were startled. They didn't have that same facility to inspire. They charged up a hill with these converts to Major Oliver's religion. They captured pillboxes, had their share of prisoners. But Regiment considered them too precious to revert to their former role of rear-echelon interrogators, at least not while they were in the Hürtgen, and belonged to E Company.

The major grieved over every lost retread and had his own burial service, reading passages from the Bible he knew by heart.

Naked came I out of my mother's womb, and naked shall I return thither: the Lord giveth and the Lord hath taken away; blessed be the name of the Lord. Amen.

Fireboy dug the grave himself with his trench shovel after conferring with Graves Registration. He would mark each grave with a soldier's dog tags and helmet crowning the fallen boy's rifle thrust into the thistles and half-frozen soil. Sonny had to observe each religious ceremony with his head bowed and his hands crossed. He couldn't dishonor the dead of E Company. But Lieutenant Colonel Blunt was furious when he saw the grave markers. He removed the dog tags from each grave and thrust them into the pocket of his field jacket.

'Fireboy,' he said, 'do you want the Krauts to steal the dog tags and pounce on us, posing as GIs?'

'Colonel, this is sacrilege,' Oliver said. 'Put 'em back, every fucking dog tag you stole.'

The lieutenant colonel stared at him with all the smug superiority of his rank. 'And do you think Regiment will back you up?'

'I don't care what Regiment says, or Battalion. I'll go to Division Headquarters if I have to.'

Blunt saw how delusional the major was. Or perhaps he understood that Division would back up this marathon flamethrower and the retreads of E Company. He put back every dog tag in its proper place and vanished into a cove of pine trees.

3

THEY NOW BIVOUACKED IN GERMAN TRENCHES covered over with roofs made of logs to shelter them from tree bursts while they slept. They didn't have enough blankets and long coats and insulated boots. When the snow fell and the ground froze, they had to huddle together and dig their canteens under their belts, or their drinking water would have turned to ice. They never had enough ammunition. Often the gun bearers would arrive with blankets and bandoliers in the middle of the night. Whatever roofs the boys of E Company had, they were still exposed. The Screaming Meemies never stopped. The mortars flew at them day and night. The retreads often whimpered in their sleep. The relentless pounding was meant to drive them mad. But Fireboy had his own religious fervor. He would prepare his platoons and jump off at the first whisper of light that meandered through the treetops. And he took one more pillbox, one more Kraut machine gun nestled in a mound of earth, squinting at his flamethrower with the eye of a squirrel shooter. The Krauts tried to kill him more than once. They weren't ignorant of this Fireboy and his insane platoons. But he danced around their sniper bullets and whistling shells. The major was his own radioman. 'Fireboy to Girlie One.' He called in the coordinates while he peered through his binoculars and watched the P-47s arrive in swerving lines and strafe some hillside where the Krauts were entrenched.

'Girlie One to Fireboy. How do you like the music?'

But they were still freezing, and the Krauts intensified their artillery. The major didn't need any medics. He noticed every twitch, every whimper. And when he had to, he'd send a retread back to the rear.

'I want to stay with you, Mr Oliver. It's the only home I got.'

'Aw, come on, Private, you'll clerk a little, have some R & R with those playboys at Regiment, and as soon as you're sick of them, you'll run home to the company. But bring us some blankets.'

'Yes, sir.'

Sonny was startled when Fireboy woke him in the middle of a light barrage.

'Salinger, do you have any of your mother's famous socks? I can't feel my toes.'

'Sure thing, Major.'

Sonny could have traded in socks and collected a fortune. But he didn't believe in bartering. He'd never bartered before.

'Sir, I could massage your toes. It really helps.'

The major removed his own ragged and wet GI-issue socks and put on the socks that Sonny gave him.

'Thank your mother, Sergeant. I'll pray for her… You don't like my Bible readings, do you?'

'I'm sorry, sir. It's hard for me to imagine the kind of Lord who put us in this Green Hell.'

'He didn't put us here, Salinger. The Devil did.'

And Major Oliver must have had the Lord on his side. The next morning, two days before Thanksgiving, a whole bunch of bearers arrived through the pines carrying the company's holiday dinner, since no damn jeep could get through the lines. The cooks had prepared gravy and genuine mashed potatoes and turkey sandwiches on some kind of pumpernickel bread from a bakery in Luxembourg.

'The Lord giveth and the Lord taketh,' Fireboy said. And Sonny didn't argue. He hadn't giveth much, not in this Green Hell. They were alive only because of Fireboy's religious zeal and his surefire accuracy with a flamethrower. The white pines seemed to have a preternatural glow during a dusk that disappeared into the trees.

PART SIX

Luxembourg, High and Low

December 1944

1

ONE DAY EARLY IN DECEMBER, on a rainy afternoon, the Krauts vanished like a horde of gremlins from that Green Hell, with their mines and trip wires. There wasn't a German helmet to be found, with its little apron-like neck guard in the rear. All the bunkers had been pillaged or buried under mounds of clay. The pillboxes looked like dunghills. Every corpse had been removed, every rocket launcher, every cannon, every useless, broken bicycle of the German Bicycle Brigade. It was as if the Krauts had never returned to the forest to hit GI Joe with a merciless surprise attack, or perhaps had never been there at all, and the Twelfth had been ravaged and almost ruined by some invisible force of nature – a walking whirlwind.

It didn't feel right. Major Oliver stomped around with his flamethrower, but Sonny and Corporal Benson had their own bit of luck. They could abandon the major and E Company and move into a little stone house in Luxembourg, beside the walled town of Echternach, where Charlemagne himself had once bivouacked with his army of Franks, a long time ago. It seems that this sector had always been a slaughterhouse, the home of ancient battlefields. But Sonny didn't care. He had a bed to sleep in with a hot-water bottle and an indoor shower where he could rinse off the black soil and grime of a month in the Hürtgen. He'd come to a borderland. Germany was on the other side of the river Sûre, at the very edge of Echternach. Sonny could have marched right across a stone bridge, along the narrow lanes of the rue de la Sûre.

He woke to the bells of the basilica inside the medieval walls of

Charlemagne's little fortress town and to the chants of priests at their morning prayers. The songs revived Sonny and removed that constant cannonade he heard day and night in his one good ear. Hürtgen would remain with him. He knew that – the perpetual darkness and perpetual blood. The Bicycle Brigade with their little lanterns and long-range rifles as they attacked in the middle of the night like pranksters on some infernal Halloween. He wouldn't forget how their rain capes flapped in the wind, and what deadly shots they were; how they could ride and steer across the gnarled ground, plant their mines and aim their guns. You couldn't shoot at them; they didn't leave much of a target. They were too damn quick. You had to run them down, like some tracker or deer slayer. Sonny had bagged only a single bicycle rider during his month in the Hürtgen, had chased him for half a mile. The bicycle rider didn't wear a helmet, but a hunter's cap. He'd killed two members of Sonny's squad while they were asleep – had executed them, really, spilled their brains. And that's why Sonny was so persistent, why he chased and chased. The bicycle rider chortled to himself. It was the rain cape that ruined him. Its rubber gave off a sheen in the bit of moonlight that hovered over the tops of the white pines. And Sonny nicked him in the ear with his Colt .45. The bicycle rider tumbled and fell into a ravine. Sonny left him there…

But now he had these morning songs from the basilica that drifted across the medieval walls to his house on the rue des Ramparts. There was a watchtower in front of Sonny's bedroom window with its murder holes, but he couldn't imagine any Krauts lingering inside. Sonny could peer over the walls. The entire town seemed deserted. He couldn't find a soul near the town hall with its double staircase and dormer windows. The citizens of Echternach must have been frightened of these new invaders with their jeeps and Dirty Gerties. The couple who prepared Sonny's breakfast looked at him with a kind of cautious bewilderment. They were used to a German presence in Echternach. They chatted with him in French and English, though they had a Frankish tongue of their own that was handed down from Charlemagne himself, Sonny imagined. They ran a hotel in the heart of Echternach that must have been a haven for the new Nazi elite.

This *other* house with its arched roof was where they lived, and Sonny discovered photos of the Führer tucked under a blanket in the bedroom closet. The husband and wife were very short, around five feet or so. And Sonny must have seemed like a giant to them, a half-Jewish giant. They both wore identical blue pullovers that smelled of mothballs. He had ham and butter and dark country bread and coffee served in a pewter cup that reminded him of a chalice. It was the best coffee he'd had since the last time he sat down with his mother at Schrafft's over a butterscotch sundae and a shared slice of apple pie.

'Can I be of any further assistance, Herr Sergeant Salinger?' asked the woman, who had much more pluck than the man. She must have been used to invaders half her life. 'You will come and visit us again, after the war, yes? It is nonsense, this war, no?'

The man nudged his wife to be silent about the war.

And Sonny wasn't in the mood to debate with her. 'Yes,' he insisted. 'Total nonsense.'

The woman smiled. She bowed and left with her husband. They must have served coffee to the Wehrmacht these past four years, drank to Hitler's health out of their own pewter chalices. He wouldn't permit them to tarnish his first morning in Echternach, with Corporal Benson in the room below. They'd been out of Hürtgen these past two weeks, and the morning songs from the basilica began to confuse him. Suddenly, oddly, he *felt* the presence of God, as if he were some freakish disciple of Major Oliver's. He couldn't have prayed, nothing like that, or recited from the Book of Job and the Song of Songs. He had no sense at all of an afterlife. Yet that constant cannonade had softened a little, had stopped exploding inside his skull. He drank his coffee and followed all the undulations in the ramparts, and the magical movement of the stones mingled with the morning songs like musical notes.

He had Miriam's socks and a spick-and-span room, even if its last occupant was probably a Kraut.

The rain beat hard on his window. A storm was brewing. The sky had turned black.

He would show a movie this evening; he'd become E Company's projectionist. He would requisition a room in the basement of the town hall. Sonny had his own collection that went with him from war zone to war zone, with a little help from Special Services. He'd show *The Lady Vanishes* or *The 39 Steps*. He was a spy hunter addicted to spy films. Sonny Salinger of the CIC. And just when he was in the mood for a little R & R, he felt that first tremor, like a rubber band that went up and down his spine. Then he heard the crump of artillery, as if it came from some faraway basilica. It drowned the church songs. He still didn't believe what was happening. *The jitters*, he told himself. He blamed it all on the Green Hell – and the lashing wind of a thunderstorm. But thunder couldn't have made the floorboards rise and fall. Plaster chips rained on his head. The chiffonier tottered. And Sonny found himself under the bed, in the company of a terrified white mouse that climbed on his knee and nestled there.

He heard the creak of boots on the boards, then the sound of voices in the windswept street below – German voices. He'd left his holster on the night table with his magazine pouch. A face appeared below the coverlets.

'Sarge, the Krauts are coming.'

'That's impossible. They fled from the Hürtgen. They crossed the Rhine.'

The corporal stared at the mouse. 'Some companion.'

The mouse scuttled into a hole, while Sonny crept out from under the bed.

The whole house began to sway like a rocking horse. 'Sarge, we're fucking under attack.'

Sonny stared out the window. Members of a Kraut Bicycle Brigade stood in front of the house's tiny couple. They must have crossed the Süre downriver, rather than risk an American patrol on Echternach's stone bridge. There were at least fifty riders, all of them with their lanterns and long rifles, and gas masks on the handlebars. Their commander, a young lieutenant in goggles, asked Frau Schmit, the tiny man's wife, if they were harboring any of the American swine from the Fourth Division. She could have easily betrayed Sonny and the corporal. But she didn't. And he had to wonder why.

'Herr Leutnant,' she said with her usual pluck, 'you aren't blind. You could look for yourself.'

The young lieutenant doffed his hunter's cap. 'You have always welcomed us, *meine liebe Frau*. But I will leave a few of my fellows here, in case the *Schweinehunde* happen to arrive. They feed on human flesh.'

The lieutenant left a squad of six bicycle riders near the house and pedaled with the rest of his patrol right into the wind and rain and through the ramparts of Echternach. Sonny could hear the faint report of pistols from inside the walls. He had a bad case of vertigo in this swaying house.

'Sarge,' the corporal said, 'what should we do?'

'Join the fight.'

'But there are six of those sharpshooters outside your windowsill.'

'So?' Sonny said. 'We'll surprise them.'

Then he could hear a curdling scream as members of the Bicycle Brigade rode off with their tunics on fire. Sonny and the corporal ran down the narrow, winding stairs with their Colt .45s. Frau Schmit was on the bottom stair. She clutched Sonny's arm, with absolute terror in her eyes.

'You will take us to America, Herr Sergeant Salinger, yes? I saved your life.'

Major Oliver stood outside with that metal hump on his back and the tube of his flamethrower, like a serpent's tongue. He was alone.

'Fireboy,' Sonny said, 'how'd you get here?'

'By instinct,' the major said. 'Pack your stuff. The place is crawling with Krauts.'

Sonny had to rush upstairs for his manuscripts and his canteen. He met Frau Schmit again.

'I'll be back for you. I promise.'

And he ran into the woods with the corporal and Major Oliver, who had to keep adjusting the straps of the fire tank on his back.

2

IT NEVER SHOULD HAVE HAPPENED. The Allies were nearly a stone's throw from the Rhine. But the high command must have been half-asleep. With its regiments roughed up in the Hürtgen, the Fourth had to patrol thirty-five miles of hard terrain along the Luxembourg-German border, a section of the Ardennes Forest. The Allies were dancing along a depleted string. And rather than crawl deep into Germany and create a defensive line, the Krauts had their own breakthrough in the Ardennes – it was the Führer's last deadly serenade to GI Joe.

For two weeks in December, there was utter chaos. So much of it was caused by one man, Otto Skorzeny, a lieutenant colonel in the SS, a six-foot-five giant with curly black hair who had a wicked scar along his left cheek and mythical status among the Krauts. A whoremonger, barroom brawler, and bon vivant, Skorzeny would have been tossed out of the SS, delivered to an internment camp, and beaten half to death if he hadn't been Hitler's favorite *Kommando*.

'My mischievous Otto,' the Führer supposedly said, 'my beloved Scarface.' He seemed to like the idea of this giant who wrecked one

SS canteen after the other and always had some madcap scheme in his skull.

It was Skorzeny who rescued Mussolini from La Maddalena, an obscure island in the Tyrrhenian Sea, with his own company of gliders and SS paratroopers. The gliders swooped down on La Maddalena. Skorzeny's commandos marched into Mussolini's hotel and brought him to Berlin without having to fire a shot. Skorzeny himself had planned every detail of the rescue mission.

Now Hitler relied on Scarface to infiltrate the Allies in the Ardennes. He gave the giant his own castle in Oranienburg, Schloss Friedenthal, outside Berlin, where Otto could train his volunteers and recruits in *Kommando* tactics. They all had some basic skill in English, and a few of them were actual linguists. Schloss Friedenthal seemed like the Kraut equivalent of Fort Holabird, where Sonny himself had trained after joining the CIC. But these commandos had much of Scarface's own mischief in their blood. They were murderers as much as counter-intelligence agents and spies. They would become the heart and soul of Operation Greif – or Grab – an attempt to destabilize the Americans in the Ardennes. As such, they were given captured American uniforms and jeeps. They spent hours watching Hollywood films, such as *My Friend Flicka* and *Sergeant York*, to learn the American idiom and use of slang. And they were smuggled across the border, four commandos to a jeep, as the Kraut panzer divisions advanced into a salient of the Ardennes, creating an ominous wrinkle in the American lines.

The havoc was immediate. These commandos cut telephone wires, slaughtered MPs, led Allied convoys astray, and stalled military traffic, until Lieutenant Colonel Blunt himself made the connection between such mishaps and Otto Skorzeny.

'It's the giant. I'm convinced of it. It's a Skorzeny trick. It has all his fingerprints.'

Forty jeeps had slipped through, at least forty. They seemed to know the current passwords. But none of these commandos had mastered the idiom of baseball. And that's how Sonny and his mates at the CIC tripped them up, though it took persistent cunning. The CIC established checkpoints, manned them day and night. But Sonny couldn't stop every damn bird colonel and his retinue in a jeep. He would have caused havoc of his own. And some of these colonels didn't know their baseball any better than the Krauts. So he had to look for a suspicious flick of an eye, or a mismatched uniform on the driver. And then he would pull the jeep over to the side of the road, with Corporal Benson and some other CIC man clutching a submachine gun.

His first catch is what stuck in his mind – four overconfident Krauts.

'The Brownies of St. Louis, yes,' said the trick lieutenant who sat next to the driver. This one, it seems, had memorized whatever baseball he could at Schloss Friedenthal. 'Georgie McQuinn at first base.'

'And who's on second?'

The trick lieutenant pawed his chin. 'On the second base sits someone I can't recall, Sergeant. But I am not such an addict.'

'Get out of the jeep,' Sonny said, with his .45 in the trick lieutenant's face. 'And no fancy moves.'

Of course, they were a little foolish, Skorzeny's commandos. The lieutenant wore an armband with a swastika beneath his field jacket. Perhaps it was to convince his brothers that he was a genuine commando once he crossed the German lines again – after all, the CIC could have played the same trick. They knew their *Deutsch*. They could have pretended to be Skorzeny's fellow commandos, members of Operation Greif. And so the *Greifers* needed some sign of certainty. And that's what betrayed them.

Even while the Krauts advanced deeper into the Ardennes, and the Allies were in disarray, Major Oliver mocked Skorzeny. He had to give up his flamethrower. He couldn't command a company in the middle of a retreat while he had a hose in his hands and that metal hump on his back.

'The giant's a joke. Do ya know how many of his missions misfired? That *Greifer* didn't really grab Mussolini. The Guineas gave him away. The soldiers guarding Mussolini were on Hitler's payroll – pure fascists. We'll catch every Kraut jeep that got through the lines. And we'll also catch the giant. I hear he's in the Ardennes.'

And while Sonny stumbled in the snow, during the worst December in recorded history, as the temperature dropped to ten below, he was on the lookout for the big prize – Otto Skorzeny, who might have obscured his scar with a muffler, but not his gargantuan height. The CIC had the best spotters on the western front, hawkeyes, every one, yet Skorzeny couldn't be found – not in a jeep, not on the battlefield, with all its violent tugs and pulls.

The *Greifers* had had their little victory. You couldn't always trust a GI guarding some gate. He could have been one of Skorzeny's men planted there. If he stuttered over the current password – *Quicksilver* or *Big Blue* – Sonny had to arrest the poor guy and take him behind the lines to an interrogation center. It took valuable time when they had none to give. And so this battle in the Ardennes had become Skorzeny's war, no matter what the major said.

'We have to catch the fat fuck,' Sonny muttered, but he couldn't. Skorzeny had become more than a myth. He was as relentless and mysterious as a snowdrift in the Ardennes.

And then a huge lump of a man with a scar on his left cheek wandered out of the snow.

'I'm lost, son,' he said as he tottered about. *Schnapps*, Sonny told himself. Scarface was a notorious tippler. He didn't have the slightest German accent, but he must have been schooled by half a dozen linguists.

'What's the password for this sector, sir?'

'How the fuck would I know?' the giant grumbled. 'I'm Colonel Darl from Division.'

'And I'm Minnie Mouse. You'll have to come with me.'

They were challenged half a dozen times as they marched into a blizzard. But Sonny had the password for each sector. The big guy cursed and complained.

'Can't help you, buddy,' said one of the military policemen. 'This boy is with counterintel.'

But it was quite different when they arrived at CIC. Major Oliver happened to be inside the center, and he saluted the big guy. 'Sorry, sir, the sergeant is overzealous at times.' And he whispered in Sonny's ear. 'That's Darl of Division, you idiot.' And then he went back to Darl.

'Would you care for a snifter, sir? It's cold as a witch's tit in this damn sector.'

He handed Colonel Darl a bit of brandy in a paper cup. Darl tossed back the brandy, shook his head, cried 'Hiyaaaah!' and stared at Sonny.

'Our lines are crumbling everywhere,' he said, 'and I have to deal with shit like this.'

Then he wandered out of the center and into the blizzard, as lost as he'd ever been.

'Salinger,' the major said, 'you don't arrest a guy like that. He could wreck our entire company with one command.'

'But isn't he Skorzeny's double… with that scar?'

'No,' the major said. 'He doesn't look like Skorzeny at all.'

3

THEY WERE STRANDED, ISOLATED IN THE SNOW, company separated from company; the Twelfth could not hold its ragged, invisible line. E Company was all alone. The Krauts advanced into the woods in their snow-white battle suits like a band of sleepwalking ghosts. Some of them were children. Sonny was amazed. There were boys of fourteen and fifteen, and they looked like pitted old men. They were marching to Antwerp, an Antwerp of the mind. Hitler threw his last resource at the Allies – his Children's Brigade. He'd nurtured them for this battle, fed them, outfitted them in wool and white fur. Children and old men, with two divisions of seasoned warriors and seven rocket brigades, had created a wedge in the Allies' imaginary wall on either side of Echternach. The so-called battle lines were 'fluid.'

You couldn't afford to fall asleep in your foxhole. Without some movement, some scrambling about, you'd freeze to death in this subzero weather. The wounded didn't survive. Sonny had gone from interrogator to rifleman in a wisp. He knew that some of his buddies were trapped inside the walls of Echternach. It had become a German stronghold, or 'iron fist,' as they liked to call it. But the Allies bombarded Echternach until the ramparts no longer stood – there were great wounds in the outer wall. The watchtower was gone. The house on the rue des Ramparts where Sonny and the corporal had stayed was now a tiny hill of rubble. Sonny hoped that Frau Schmit and her husband had survived. He'd promised the couple that he'd come back for them...

It had become a battleground of hallucinations – soldiers sighted who were never there. Entire columns seemed to drift out of the snowfall and then vanish in a blink. The boys of E Company, whatever was left of them, those who hadn't succumbed to trench foot and frostbite, celebrated Christmas in their foxholes – with K rations they were lucky to have. Sonny thought of the Christmases he'd had at Schrafft's with Miriam, Sol, and his big sister, Doris, who hadn't been married at the time. Doris despaired of ever finding a husband.

'I'm twenty-one,' she said, 'and have a look. Not even an engagement ring.'

'You're a child,' Miriam muttered. 'Eat your turkey leg.'

It was their annual feast – almost a ritual. Sonny was wearing his bar mitzvah suit on this occasion – slate gray. Yes, he'd been bar mitzvahed in this half-Jewish world of the Salingers. His father, the seller of pork and ham, had read bits and pieces of the Torah with him.

Doris had dark eyes and looked a lot like Sonny's older twin. She was morose as she watched Miriam devour her lobster Newburg and creamed cauliflower.

'But that isn't kosher, Mother dear. And you're at the same table with the bar mitzvah boy.'

'Doris,' Sol said, gritting his teeth, 'stop making a nuisance of yourself.' He wore a Swank tiepin and cufflinks made of solid silver. He had a silver mustache, and his hair was silver, too. That's how Sonny recalled him – Sol, the silvery man.

'Then tell Sonny to strip and take off that morbid undertaker's suit. We are a wonderful family of Gentile Jews.'

Sonny adored his sister, but Doris' dark eyes had all the menace of harpoons. No one was safe around Doris Salinger, not even Sonny, and she adored him, too.

'Jesus, Sonny, don't just sit there. Take off that damn gray rag.'

'Rag?' Sol repeated. 'Rag? That suit didn't come off any rack. It was handmade. Cost me a fortune. Goldfine's a genius.'

'Who's Goldfine?' Doris asked.

'My tailor,' Sol said. And he appealed to the bar mitzvah boy. 'Get up, son, and slap your sister in the face.'

Sonny didn't move. He'd finished his main course – chicken à la king – and was digging into his butterscotch sundae with a very long spoon. He stopped eating and stared at the enormous spiraling *S* stitched onto his napkin, which was the hallmark of Schrafft's. The immaculate marble floor had a black-and-white-checkerboard pattern. The lamp on the table had a blue shade.

'Papa dear,' Doris said, 'why didn't you invite the rabbi to join us? He can recite the Torah while we devour the family Christmas feast.'

'Sonny,' Sol said, 'slap your sister in the face.'

Sonny stood up and slapped Doris with his partially cupped

hand to soften the blow. Then he returned to the table and finished his butterscotch sundae, while Doris sat there like a mute. But all the relish was gone. His hand was shaking. He couldn't spoon the butterscotch properly. The sundae was sickeningly sweet.

He still had the taste in his mouth, inside a foxhole in the Ardennes. He'd always remember the defeated look on his sister's face, that sense of eternal doom.

A man with a blanket over his head moved all along the crooked line of foxholes. It was Oliver himself, with snowflakes on his lip. 'Saddle up, you guys.'

'Where are we going, Fireboy?' asked one of the newbies.

Oliver grimaced at him from under the blanket. 'Shut your mouth and saddle up, soldier.'

'Yes, sir, Mr Oliver, sir.'

But Sonny knew where they were going – back to Echternach to flush out whatever Krauts were left. The Wehrmacht lacked a *Schwerpunkt* in their own military parlance – an attainable goal, as Sonny had been taught by his CIC instructors. The Krauts couldn't get to Antwerp with their rockets, their bicycle boys, and their baby shock troops; they couldn't cut off Ike's main source of supply. No longer the invincibles of 1940, they didn't have a real destination in 1944. By Christmas, they were floundering in the forest they had owned these past four years.

'And don't forget to piss on your rifles, or they'll never thaw,' the major growled, an icicle forming on his chin.

And so Sonny stood there with the rest of his buddies, unbuttoned his fly in the numbing cold, and peed on his M1. Not even the stoutest of them could form a steady stream in this bewildering weather.

They packed their gear and climbed out of the foxholes, one by one, following the major, who led the attack. They discovered a few shadows in the thick strings of fog.

'Don't shoot, don't shoot,' the major shouted. They'd stumbled upon several scouts who'd lost touch with their own company.

And these scouts attached themselves to the major and his men. Like the rest of them, they'd ripped off the inner lining of their helmets and used it as a mask with eyeholes. But Sonny had ice on his eyebrows, and his cheeks burned from the blasts of cold.

Still, they marched through the white pines. Some of them disappeared into a snowdrift and had to be carried out feetfirst. They couldn't afford to stop and stand in place. The terrain was much too treacherous. They found frozen dogfaces sitting in a disabled jeep; the dogfaces had all turned blue, with blue beards and blue mustaches. One of the major's men wanted to take a mitten off a frozen GI.

'Soldier,' the major said, 'that's sacrilege. Leave the dead in peace.'

'But he won't miss that mitten, sir, and I will.'

'We're not grave robbers,' the major said.

'But it ain't a grave, sir. It's a jeep. And Graves Registration hasn't gotten to 'em yet.'

'Leave that mitten, soldier,' the major said, 'or I'll have you guard the jeep until Graves Registration comes.'

The wind whipped them along. The major had his compass, but the needle froze.

'First damn time that's ever happened.'

'It's the Ardennes, sir,' said another newbie.

Then they saw Echternach. It could have been a miniature Pompeii, a city in ruin, buried in dust, bits of mortar, and black snow rather than volcanic ash. The ramparts looked like rows of rotten teeth. Sonny wondered how many aerial raids Echternach had endured, how many bombardments, how many tons of TNT. All within a swirl of snow and soot.

They could have been wandering into a pillaged graveyard. The ground itself seemed molten. They marched across a great gap in the outer wall, as if they were jumping off into another world. Whatever buildings still stood were wrapped in the charred remains of Nazi banners. This little town had been the

Wehrmacht's nerve center until a few days ago, where the Nazi warlords had assembled to plot out the details of Hitler's grand disillusion, that the Allies could be kept forever on the far side of German soil.

But Sonny did not feel like a conqueror; more like a living shadow – dangerous as ever – that had intruded upon a tiny town and a country caught between bigger, fatter nations with a host of killers and killing machines. Sonny was a killer, too, a reluctant one perhaps, but a killer nonetheless. He did not have Major Oliver's sense of being on a religious crusade. He hated the Krauts as much as the Krauts hated him. But he mourned the dead fifteen-year-old boys who lay all curled up in mounds of rubble along the rue de la Montagne in their soiled snow-white battle suits, though they had once been as fierce as any soldier and would have ripped out Sonny's guts if they'd ever had half a chance.

Their bodies were strewn everywhere, mittenless hands outstretched like broken claws, with filthy fingernails. There was no longer a hospital on the rue de l'Hôpital, nothing but snowdrifts and rubble. The inner walls of the old Echternach abbey had been bombed and fire-burnt to the ground. The basilica had been dynamited by the Krauts themselves while they withdrew, yet parts of it remained untouched – it had two arched steeples rather than four. Half the basilica stood. Sonny did not believe in miracles. P-47s flew right past the basilica and didn't strafe a single window, though Reich commandants and their aides had probably been hiding under the pews before they ran from Echternach.

The Allies had bombed the old Echternach bridge; it sat half-sunk in the water, like some gnarled monument that reminded Sonny of a monstrous lion's paw. Where were the inhabitants? They couldn't be hiding in the rubble. The major and his men had come to a flattened town. Yet Sonny could have sworn that he heard the faint thread of a chant coming from inside this basilica with pieces bitten off.

He didn't believe in ghost choirs.

He stepped across the charred lintel. All the pews had vanished and had been replaced by an entire country of desks and chairs, with wrecked typewriters and Teletype machines with humped backs that reminded Sonny of the fuel tank that Fireboy carried with his flamethrower. This ancient abbey had been the command post of Hitler's generals until a few days ago. It was overrun with rats. They squealed and ran under the desks with their whiskers and long tails. And still Sonny heard the sound of that choir. It bewildered him. E Company had run out of morphine and he'd taken none for his little wounds and cuts. He'd seen hallucinations in the forest, had conjured up children in their snow-white battle suits, had shot at them a couple of times. But there were no monks or priests in this broken basilica, nothing but gutted Teletype machines and an invasion of rats.

Yet the chant continued, faint as it was, like a prolonged musical whisper. And it startled him when he said to himself, *I'm in Jehovah's house.*

He walked out onto the grim gray streets of Echternach, with bits of slate on the ground. He could hear the calm wake of the water. It couldn't reassure him, bring him back to his own destiny as Sargeant Salinger of CIC. The chant was still there.

PART SEVEN

Kaufering Lager IV

April 1945

1

THERE WAS THAT STING IN THEIR NOSTRILS, and the sting wouldn't go away. Sonny and the corporal would ride into some quiet little town in Bavaria that hadn't been strafed by Allied fighter-bombers and had its roofs ripped off, and after the Twelfth had cleared it of die-hard, suicidal Krauts, with all the debris of abandoned artillery held by horse-drawn carts – the horses often limped and had bloodshot eyes. Sonny's nostrils burned all the time, and he couldn't quite identify that lingering acrid odor. He took over the *Rathaus* in the tiny village square, its picturesque cobblestones smeared with horse dung and its half-burnt Nazi banners still dangling from the dormer windows, and began to interrogate suspected war criminals and saboteurs. The local population wouldn't help him at all. Sonny was rather suspicious of the town jeweler and his hairy hands. This jeweler had all the bearings of an SS torturer, with his Olympian shoulders, bullish neck, and leering smile. His papers were in perfect order, perhaps a little too perfect. Sonny knew they were forged. They'd been worked on by a wizard, a member of the SS elite.

Sonny sat him down in an uncomfortable chair, with a naked light bulb in his eyes. The athletic jeweler never blinked.

'Herr Linder, isn't it strange, that awful smell? Does your nose ever sting?'

'Never, Herr Kapitän.'

'*Mensch*,' Sonny growled, 'you see the stripes on my shoulder. Call me Sergeant Salinger.'

'*Gut*,' the jeweler said, with that same smirk, 'yet you, a simple sergeant, have the authority to question me. That is what is strange, not the metallic aroma of war. I use carbolic acid all the time. And I assure you, the smell is much worse.'

The jeweler had a logbook that offered every little detail of his whereabouts; he hadn't left the village in two years. But Sonny could tell that this 'jeweler's' logbook had been inked less than a month ago, as the Twelfth had punched its way into Bavaria. None of the entries had faded, or turned brown. But Sonny still had to play the fox.

'Herr Linder, why aren't you with the Wehrmacht? You're no invalid.'

'Ah, but I am. I have a terrible hernia. And it cannot be corrected.'

The doctor's elaborate notations were right in the jeweler's logbook, with the same forged hyperbole, the same crafty design.

Sonny motioned to the MP beside him. 'Take the jeweler back to Division and put him in a cage. Let him sit. I'll deal with him another time.'

'This is preposterous,' the jeweler said. 'I will complain to your superiors.'

Sonny smiled. 'They will send you back to me. And you won't have a *Rathaus* to protect you, with witnesses. You might not survive our next little chat.'

Sonny closed the interrogation room and walked out onto the steps of the *Rathaus*, where he met Lieutenant Colonel Blunt. He watched the mayor of the quiet little town climb on a ladder and remove the Nazi banners. The mayor had tiny feet.

'Sir,' Sonny said to Blunt, 'I'd like to arrest the entire village. I think they're all in cahoots with the Gestapo and the SS. They're hiding officers, helping them to forge their logbooks.'

Blunt winced at him. 'That'll look terrific on our dossier. "CIC arrests a Kraut village, claims they're all complicit with the SS." Division will break my bones. Salinger, do your job.'

But Sonny was persistent. 'Sir, isn't there some kind of terrible tickle in your nose? It feels like it's burning my nostrils right off.

Blunt growled, as if he were talking to a rebellious child rather than an agent of the CIC. 'Salinger, we're investigating that smell. Meanwhile, get back to work.'

But it happened again and again. Local printers and proprietors with impeccable credentials and the build of Olympians, and he couldn't break them under the lights no matter how hard he tried. He had a premonition about their tricks. He was interrogating fellow interrogators. They were prepared for Sonny, every single one of them, with their smoothness and martial manner. And he sent them all back to Division. He would break them there, disrobe them of their cover stories. He went on to another Bavarian village seized by the Twelfth.

And then the stink grew unbearable. Sonny and the corporal followed behind the invaders, rode across the city of Landsberg, with its medieval inner walls and houses with orange roofs that seemed to exist at a slight tilt, so that Sonny had the illusion they were about to fall and he would be buried in all the rubble. He had been ordered to keep clear of Landsberg, and he didn't know why. But all he had to do was follow his nose – and the path of E Company.

And nine miles or so from Landsberg, Sonny and the corporal happened upon a *Krankenlager* – a camp for sick slave laborers who worked at some munitions factory. But it made little sense to Sonny, this *Krankenlager* in the middle of nowhere, surrounded by barbed wire. They met several of their buddies at the front gate. These boys marched about in delirious circles. A few of them were crying. Others muttered to themselves. And then Sonny saw Major Oliver, who no longer had the luminous eyes of a zealot.

'Salinger, don't go in there – don't go through the gates. We've been abandoned. The Lord has left the lights out in Bavaria.'

'I can't believe it,' Sonny said. 'Fireboy has lost his faith.'

But he shouldn't have mocked the major. A chill went through his bones. He could identify that atrocious smell – a mingling of excrement, stale urine, charred and rotting flesh. This was no

Krankenlager – that was just a prettified name. It was a charnel house. Sonny had heard reports about them back at CIC – 'concentration camps,' they were called. But no dogface had ever seen one. The SS had always kept them hidden, it seems, except for the acrid smell that pervaded the countryside. What a dope Sonny had been not to have guessed the source of that stink. He'd fooled himself, as if he were back in the time of Charlemagne, with warrior fighting warrior, like in *The Song of Roland*, not SS gangsters attacking the sick and the lame. He shouldn't have pitied those child warriors in the snow. They must have known about this camp, Kaufering Lager IV, and others just like them.

'Open the gate,' he barked at the MP on patrol.

'Sarge,' the corporal whispered, 'are you sure you wanna see it? Fireboy said it was an abomination. And I believe him.'

'Drive,' Sonny said, 'and that's an order.'

All the SS guards and officers had abandoned Kaufering IV, had melted into the atmosphere, or had found a new identity, like Herr Linder, the muscular jeweler, who would be sitting inside that cage at Division, sitting for Sonny. Skeletons in black-and-white pajamas approached the jeep. They wore some kind of philosopher's cap inside the Lager. Their skin was translucent, with cheekbones that stuck out like horns. They wanted to clap for Sonny and the corporal. But they did not have enough skin on their hands. So their clapping was so faint that it was like the muffled caw of a forlorn bird. But these were the lucky ones. They could still stand and run after two GIs in a jeep.

The corporal wanted to toss K rations at them, like some grand seigneur.

'Don't,' Sonny said. 'They'll choke on our chocolate. They have to be spoon-fed.'

'Like babies?' the corporal asked.

'Yes, like babies,' Sonny said. 'That's how much their stomachs must have shrunk. Their masters have been starving them to death.'

Look for the narrative. That's what his instructors always told him. And it didn't take him very long to find it, despite the horrors that tore through his system and drained him of his strength. Their guardians had run away once they realized the Twelfth was rolling in. And they hid whatever evidence they could. There was a railroad siding that ran along the length of the Lager, with several boxcars on the single track. The ground was strewn with naked bodies that looked like dolls, with their arms and legs stretched out, as if they'd been caught in the middle of some strange and abrupt ecstasy. For one tingling moment, they reminded Sonny of the mannequins in Bloomingdale's window. Doris had been a window dresser for a while, and Sonny had once watched her handle Bloomingdale's dolls. They had the same macabre, distant eyeless gaze...

Sonny climbed down from the jeep. He saw several axes near the siding, axes covered with blood. The guards must have been in a great hurry. They'd slaughtered prisoners of the camp even while they were herding them into the cars. Sonny found several bodies without heads, hands, or feet. He could follow the path of their butchery, footprints etched in blood. Next to the railroad siding was the stationmaster's shack, covered in ornate shellac, like a gigantic cuckoo clock. And Sonny was startled when he found the stationmaster still inside the shack. He hadn't left with the guards, officers, and doctors on the last death train from Lager IV.

The man had whimsical eyebrows. He was wearing some kind of uniform, but without the SS shoulder patch of double lightning bolts. He had ragged cuffs. His hands were trembling. And Sonny couldn't find any compassion or comprehension in his pale, lusterless blue eyes.

He isn't compos mentis, Sonny muttered to himself, *a dispatcher who's lost his mind and can't leave his itinerary of toys.*

'We'll have to arrest you, *Mein Herr.*'

'That is nothing,' the man said. 'You must do much worse – come, come, I will give you a tour of our wonderful camp.'

And he motioned to Sonny with his clean, elegant hands, while

Corporal Benson wanted to remain there in the jeep, hiding from all the deviltry surrounding him, in this village of corpses without a *Rathaus*. Sonny couldn't make sense of Kaufering. Lager IV went beyond his ability to imagine, or to think.

'Follow us, will ya?' he growled. And the corporal crept behind them in his jeep, over the charred earth, with its trails of excrement and blood, and bits of SS paraphernalia – unpolished belt buckles and boots with missing toes. The officers and guards must have been shedding their uniforms and identities while they ran, recasting themselves as ordinary citizens of the Reich.

'Stationmaster,' Sonny asked, 'did you help those bastards escape?'

'Of course I did,' this train dispatcher said, caressing the buttons on his uniform. 'That was my job. I would have been remiss had I not done so. And I am very good at my job. But come, let me give you a guided tour of our Lager. It was my home. I slept here every night. I had my lunch and dinner right in the shack. The trains never stopped running. Kaufering would have been a pathetic shell without me.'

'And the screams never bothered you, the butcherings right in front of your face?'

'Of course it bothered me, Herr Unteroffizier. I fed these poor fellows as much as I could, from my own lunch pail. But I couldn't interfere. I would have been executed on the spot. But you are distracting me – come, or you will remain a tourist and never see the camp.'

The stationmaster led Sonny to three barracks that were partially underground, like wooden bunkers, but these bunkers had been nailed shut and set on fire while still packed with 'citizens' of Kaufering, the camp's slave laborers. Sonny had to wear a handkerchief over his mouth and nose, or he would have fainted right in the Lager. He couldn't fathom how the stationmaster had survived the stench, the crippling acid of rotten flesh.

'Open the barracks,' Sonny said, 'every one.'

'But that is impossible,' the stationmaster said. 'It is not my job. I am responsible for the trains.'

'Open,' Sonny said, handing him a bloody ax. 'Or I'll execute you – on the spot.'

The stationmaster saluted Sonny with a sudden respect. 'Yes, Herr Unteroffizier.'

He chopped away at the wood, pried out the nails, and opened the barracks, one by one. Some of the charred bodies were still smoldering. They were packed so tight, skull-to-skull, covered in shreds of their own burnt hair, that they had a perverse, horrifying beauty, as if they'd been sculpted out of fire.

'Come,' the stationmaster said.

'But we can't leave them there – like that.'

'And what do you propose?'

That's when Sonny recited Major Oliver's blessing from the burial service in the Green Hell.

Naked came I out of my mother's womb...

Sonny was shivering. He couldn't abandon this assembly of forgotten souls – Gypsies, Serbs, Jews, and half-Jews, like himself – in their three Kraut coffins.

'Come,' the stationmaster said. 'You must see for yourself.'

And Sonny followed the stationmaster along an earthen path until they arrived at a flower garden. None of the flowers had wilted among all that carnage and blood. They entered a barrack that had been converted into some kind of Swiss chalet with its own carpentered porch and shellacked window shutters.

'Herr Salinger,' the stationmaster said, still clutching the ax. '*I* refurbished this – with my own hands.'

'When did you have the time?' Sonny said as his cheeks began to twitch. He wanted to split the stationmaster in two with the ax, cleave him with a single blow, and watch the blood pour out.

'I made the time,' the stationmaster said. 'I turned this pigsty into an officers' club.'

They strode onto the porch and went into the chalet. All the files had been removed, all the records of Lager IV. The chairs had missing legs. The SS had left their own office in a shambles, as a parting gift to the Allies. But Sonny wandered into another room, with red wallpaper and fanciful couches and a vanity table that must have come from Berlin. It was the camp bordello. And his rage deepened, nearly blinded him. He found yet another victim, hiding under the vanity table. A girl of twelve, perhaps, with enormous eyes. He realized in a second that her tongue had been torn out, as she delivered a muted shriek.

'Herr Stationmaster, who is that?'

'*Ach*,' said the dispatcher, with a flutter of his free hand. 'She's nobody, a *Polska*, Little Alicja. We picked her up in a garbage pail, from another camp. She's our mascot, Herr Salinger, our pet.'

Sonny pulled the girl out from under the vanity table. She was wearing an SS officer's tunic with nothing underneath. He gave her his own field jacket to wear and fed her tiny gulps of water from his canteen. He patted her head, and the shrieking stopped.

'Don't be afraid, *Liebchen*,' he said. 'We will not harm you. We are your liberators.'

He realized how foolish he must have seemed to the girl. *Liberators*. No one could liberate her. Alicja's tongue had been torn out. She was covered in filth. The SS officers must have pissed on her as part of their play. He undressed Alicja, as if he had become her servant. The stark terror in her eyes had receded. He stood her over the sink and scrubbed her with an SS officer's towel.

'Herr Salinger,' the dispatcher said, 'why are you bothering with such a person? She's nobody – a toy.'

'Shut up,' Sonny said.

It soothed him to scrub her narrow shoulder blades. He did not even blink at her nakedness, the patch between her legs, like a silken beard. He bundled her up in his field jacket; then he seized the ax from the stationmaster and chopped at all the family photographs that the SS had displayed on the walls of their wives and children – this strange quest for normalcy they must have had, the remembrance of another life, before they were butchers and firebugs. Then he carried Alicja on his shoulders, as if he had become a hobbyhorse at Lager IV, and marched out of the officers' playland.

'Corporal,' he said to Benson, who stood outside, smoking a Camel from his K pack, 'I'm done.'

'What about me?' the stationmaster whined.

'You can stay here – and guard your little kingdom.'

'But I will be *kaput* when the other soldiers come.'

'Not at all. You're invaluable. You have all the secrets of this camp. You can give another guided tour.'

And Sonny climbed into the jeep with Alicja on his shoulders.

'Who's the *Mädel*, Sarge?'

'A friend of mine,' Sonny said, and he knocked on the windshield with one musical rap of his knuckles – that sound ricocheted right through him, as if he were a tin man. He felt like tin.

PART EIGHT

Krankenhaus 31

June–July 1945

1

HE'D GONE ROGUE FOR A WEEK and didn't report to his desk at Division; neither did he rejoice on V-E Day, drink piss-water champagne with the dogfaces of E Company, nor with his fellow CIC agents at the Villa Oberwegner, in the Bavarian village of Weißenberg, where he was stationed, near a sea of rubble. He could barely get out of bed. Yet he did deliver that tongue-torn *Polska* to a Catholic orphanage outside Nuremberg before the MPs could grab her. She had no papers, no identity cards. She'd been a plaything at an SS brothel in a Bavarian death camp. But Sonny was CIC, and he used the force of his credentials with the Mother Superior at the Catholic orphanage.

'She's vital to our cause,' he told her. 'She has seen certain atrocities. And I have marked them down. We will need her as a witness.'

'But she cannot speak,' said the Mother Superior, who wasn't unkind. She had a tiny stain on her sleeve, a smear of blood.

'I've taught her sign language,' Sonny said.

The Mother Superior smiled under all that white armor. 'I cannot flout the Allied authorities, Sergeant Salinger. They will come here and put her in a camp for displaced persons.'

'Then hide her,' Sonny said. 'I'll pay for her upkeep.'

The Mother Superior covered the stain with an ink blotter. 'That will not be necessary. We will find a way... But why does your cheek twitch, Sergeant?'

Sonny recalled the chiseled cheekbones of those men in the camp, sticking out like horns, and that's all it took to dismember him.

'Habit,' he said. 'My own wartime souvenir… I don't want her behind barbed wire ever again.'

But the girl wouldn't let him go. She clung to Sonny, like some wild creature that had mated with him. And all the terror of Lager IV returned to her eyes. He stroked her face with his rough soldier's hand.

'Alicja, I cannot keep you with me. Wish I could.'

Fear became frenzy, and she tore at him with her fingernails. He had a gash under one eye – another wartime souvenir at the very end of war. The *Polska* went limp, and Sonny sat her down in a chair while the Mother Superior removed her first-aid kit from a drawer.

'That's a nasty cut, Herr Salinger. You will have a scar, I'm afraid.'

She swabbed his wound with a dark solution and dressed it with a bandage while Alicja rocked on her feet and shrieked a tongueless song to soothe all the savagery locked inside her thin, pathetic frame.

Sonny remained gallant. He kissed Alicja's unwashed hand, gave the Mother Superior all the occupation currency he could collect from his pockets, and strolled out of the orphanage with his torn, twitching cheek.

2

HE WAS LYING IN BED in the room he shared with Corporal Benson at the Villa Oberwegner, but the corporal was out playing poker at the divisional canteen. From his balcony window on Nürnberger Straße, Sonny could look out upon the ruins of the last B-17 bombing raid of the war. The villa had been spared. It was a beige-and-brown stucco 'mansion' with a tiny bull's-eye window under a slanted slate roof. The villa also served as CIC headquarters in Bavaria for the American Army of Occupation. Suspected spies, saboteurs, SS officers, and Nazi Party officials were questioned in an interrogation room on the ground floor, and some were later shackled and sent to the Army of Occupation's prisoner of war cage at the northern edge of Nuremberg. But Sonny had unmasked very few spies or Nazi officials, high and low, in the past few weeks.

There was a knock on his door. He ignored it until Lieutenant Colonel Blunt marched into the room and growled, 'Sergeant, may I come in?'

Sonny nodded. He was clutching his Colt .45.

'Jesus Christ,' Blunt asked, 'do I look like an enemy agent?'

'Yes,' Sonny answered with a trenchant smile. 'You could be a Kraut in disguise.'

The lieutenant colonel was silent for a moment and then his mouth puckered like a fish searching for oxygen on dry land.

'Sergeant, holster that firearm, or I'll have you put away.'

Sonny thrust the Colt .45 under his bed. 'Is this a social call, sir?'

Blunt began to pace the narrow room. It had two beds, two night tables, two lamps, two chairs, a closet with a moth-infested curtain, and a chipped mahogany bureau.

'I was chatting with the mayor – *that* was a social call. He mentioned the bombardment. The entire city was covered in a shower of dust. The dust didn't clear for days. Fifteen buildings were either damaged or destroyed, he said – no, sixteen, counting the Wehrmacht barracks. And Weißenberg had never even been targeted. That's a fact, son. It was a logistical error.'

Sonny stared at him with the same trenchant smile. 'What does that have to do with me?'

'Very little – and quite a lot. We're guests in this town.'

'I thought we were conquerors – or occupiers at least,' Sonny said.

'Don't get smart,' Blunt said. 'We have to show these Krauts the American way of life, or we'll go from a shooting war to a fickle mind game... Sergeant, it's impossible to read your reports.'

'Something wrong with my English, sir?'

'No,' Blunt shouted, with a rawness in his eyes. 'It's your handwriting. I can't decipher a word. No one can.'

'Ah,' Sonny said, covering the twitch in his cheek with one hand, 'I always had a problem with penmanship. It drove my teachers crazy.'

'But *we* didn't have this problem – until now. Why are you wearing a bandage?'

'A little girl scratched me,' Sonny said. 'I rescued her from Kaufering Four.'

Blunt stared at him. 'Sergeant, we're not in the business of rescuing little girls.'

'I know,' Sonny said. 'But I couldn't leave her there, in that hell house. I took her to a Catholic orphanage, and made a bargain with the Mother Superior.'

'That's illegal,' Blunt said.

Sonny had captured the lieutenant colonel now in his own little bag of tricks. 'Everything we do is illegal – we're CIC.'

'Not quite,' Blunt said, pleased with himself and his 'band of angels,' as he called the CIC agents under him. 'I'll grant you that little girl. It's the kind of initiative I like. But don't take advantage of me, Salinger. I want those reports. And don't give me any more crap about penmanship.' He paused to scratch his chin, and his entire manner shifted. 'I'm grateful to you, kid. You took care of me on Utah Beach. I had a mental lapse. Corporal Benson would have left me there to rot. You didn't. Why did you save my ass?'

'We're CIC,' Sonny said. But that wasn't the reason. Blunt seemed vulnerable, lost, alone, right after the landing. His eyes were static, dull. He would never have made it off the beach alive. Sonny couldn't abandon him – just like that.

'No more mistakes,' Blunt said. 'It's harvest time. We're grabbing Nazis by the bushel.'

'Yes, sir,' Sonny said, saluting Blunt. 'By the bushel.'

Sonny didn't believe in the CIC's *denazification* program. Some local schoolteacher was put in a cage, while rocket scientists and aeronautical engineers were treated like little kings and chauffeured to America on heavy bombers converted into transport planes. Sonny despised the unfairness of it all, the brutal unfairness of the peace that arrived right after war.

Blunt returned his salute. 'Salinger, behave!' And he sauntered out of the room.

He's nuts, Sonny said to himself, *nuttier than I am*. And suddenly he recollected his trip to Poland when he was eighteen. His father has sent him to discover the pork business after he flunked out of NYU. And Sonny went off to the town of Bydgoszcz, where he had to learn to slaughter pigs from the king of the slaughterers, a huge man with a broken face who called himself Roman. For two months Sonny had to walk around with butcher knives and bathe in pig blood. The stench wasn't nearly as awful as Kaufering, but it was awful enough. He would go on excursions with Roman the hog butcher, at three in the morning, in a wagon full of slaughtered animals. Roman carried a shotgun to protect him and Sonny from rival hog butchers. Sonny felt like he was living inside a tale by Gogol or some other surreal master. But not even Gogol could have invented Roman, who hitched himself to his own horses and plowed through the snow and sleet, shooting whatever target met his eye – winter crows, fellow wagoners, bear traps, the roofs of barns, all with a merriment and meanness that were unfathomable...

3

H E HAD FOUR COMMENDATIONS, FOUR bronze battle stars and was due a fifth, but his cheek continued to twitch and his hand couldn't stop shaking. He could have gone to a military facility – U.S. 15 Evac. Hospital – but that would have meant a Section Eight discharge for being mentally unfit for service. So he checked himself into Nuremberg's General Hospital, which had its own psychiatric clinic – Krankenhaus 31 – an ornate stone building on a quiet street, with civilian psychiatrists and not one link to the U.S. Army of Occupation.

A nervous disorder, Sonny said. He did not mention battle fatigue, nor did he wear his uniform and his CIC armband to the clinic. He'd requested a two-week furlough from Blunt to wander around in the Bavarian Alps, and Blunt had granted his request.

He didn't lie to the inquisitors at the front desk of Krankenhaus 31. He revealed who he was, a secret soldier with the Counter Intelligence Corps. He wasn't put in with the other patients in the psychiatric ward. He had a room of his own on the second floor; it faced a garden surrounded by a wooden fence that looked like the loops of a gigantic leather belt. There were bars on Sonny's window, but his room wasn't somber or bleak. He had a sleigh bed with a bright coverlet that could have been knit by a child, with a child's sense of spectacular colors. He had a simple desk and a handyman's bench, where he could have worked on his Holden Caulfield novel. He hadn't written a word since he fell upon Kaufering IV with his driver. His typewriter collected dust on a shelf at the Villa Oberwegner. He no longer had the knack of placing word after word, like musical footsteps. The footsteps were gone. His CIC commander had been wrong. Sonny's handwriting wasn't indecipherable – it had vanished, along with his psyche. Sergeant Salinger wasn't here, there, or anywhere.

An intern entered. She was tall and had dark hair, with bloodred fingernails and lipstick. She introduced herself as Frau Doktor Sylvia Welter, an ophthalmologist who was in training at Krankenhaus 31 under the guidance of Herr Doktor Ulrich Fleck, director of the psychiatric clinic. This tall ophthalmologist was wearing silk stockings and high heels, both a luxury in a defeated land that lived on coupons and ration books, and had no coffee, chocolate, tea, or milk.

It was like an opening gambit. Sonny could have come to the clinic wearing his CIC armband and arrested Herr Doktor Fleck, who had been with the stormtroopers and the SS, but he didn't want to create havoc at the one hospital in Nuremberg that could care for him. So he left the Herr Direktor in place – for the moment. And here was his disciple, a volupt-u-u-u-ous ophthalmologist with bloodred nails. She was Sonny's age, it seems, and he was drawn to her – no, driven – like a melancholic under a witch's spell.

'I am told you are a reader – and a *Schreiber* of short novels, Herr Sergeant Jerome Salinger. And you have inscribed yourself at the clinic for a rest. This is not the first time our paths have crossed. I live in Weißenberg and work at the little hospital there… when I am not at the clinic. And I have seen you many times in the street, outside your headquarters.'

Sonny stared at her. She touched his cheek, and it stopped twitching.

'Frau Doktor, why didn't you say hello?'

She laughed, and her voice had such a musical lilt that the enchantment grew.

'I didn't dare,' she said. 'You had a brooding look on your face, like Ishmael in Herr Melville's novel. But you must call me Sylvia. And I will call you –'

'Sonny. But what is an ophthalmologist doing at a mental clinic?'

'Ah,' she said, with a sudden, almost savage movement of her wrists. 'You can tell many things from a patient's eyes. The blood vessels are like a soothsayer's map.'

Sylvia was wearing a light blue smock that revealed the sweep of her hips. She plucked a tiny flashlight from her pocket and looked into Sonny's left eye.

'Oh, I am not a magician, Herr Sonny. But the sadness is there in your blood vessels... a kind of morbidity.'

Morbidity. Yes, he had a kind of morbidity. 'Fräulein Sylvia, I am already bedazzled. The director sent you here from your little hospital as his little spy, didn't he?'

'Yes,' she said, with all the music gone from her voice. 'He is frightened of your American Gestapo.'

'But why did he accept me as a patient?'

'He is a doctor,' Sylvia said. 'He must accept you.'

'Hide me, you mean, from my own Army of Occupation.'

'Call it what you like,' she said.

He was cracked, wasn't he? Inside a loony bin with bars on the window. And so he seized Fräulein Sylvia, like some resurrected Rhett Butler right off the screen at the RKO 86th Street in Manhattan, and kissed her on the mouth. It was ludicrous, but she didn't resist: a movie romance inside Krankenhaus 31, with Sonny as his own projectionist. And then a kind of miasma gripped him, a melancholy he had never felt with such force, like an iron crown screwed to his skull.

'Please,' he said. 'You can tell Herr Fleck. I won't arrest him – not while I'm in his care. But I've seen his file. The CIC will come to collect him very soon.'

Sylvia preened at Sonny with defiance, like an exotic bird of prey. 'And will they collect me?'

'I'm not so sure,' he said. 'I'm not so sure.'

4

S HE APPEARED IN HIS DREAMS, utterly undressed, her hips as sharp
as razor blades. He hadn't been with a woman during his entire
European junket. He'd dreamt of Oona recently, but it wasn't at
a Nazi cellar on the Avenue Foch, and it wasn't at the Stork – it
was at Schrafft's, on Madison and Seventy-seventh, with cupcakes
in the window, and Doris in residence with their mother and
father. He was no longer the bar mitzvah boy. He was wearing his
military tunic with his CIC armband and bronze battle stars. Oona
Chaplin O'Neill. He couldn't dance the rhumba with her on the
checkerboard floor. Schrafft's had a soda fountain and waitresses
in smart black uniforms, but not even one solitary musician. And
now he had this Fräulein. And their lovemaking – in his dreams –
was akin to madness. He tore at pieces of her flesh. She straddled
him, and his orgasm was like a bitter, suffering song…

She didn't appear again at the clinic. He had nurses who
bathed him, sat with him in the garden, read to him from *Moby-
Dick*. Residents asked him ridiculous questions about his sexual
fantasies. But Herr Doktor Fleck seemed to avoid him. And then
he had a visitor – Hemmy.

The commandant of the Ritz wasn't carrying a Colt or a
submachine gun. And he didn't have his band of Irregulars. He'd
come alone to Krankenhaus 31. He'd been attached to the Fourth
Division as a correspondent for *Collier's*. He'd gone through the
Hürtgen campaign and the Ardennes, though Sonny had never
seen him once at Division. The Fourth had been shipped home
in June, and Hem was currently unattached, an abandoned war

bride. His cockiness was gone, the bravado of a civilian marauder with his own little mob of soldiers and Resistance fighters. Sonny could see the panic and pain of Hürtgen in his eyes, the despair of a haunted wood.

'Hem, how did you find me?'

'Easy, kid. I got it right from the horse's mouth.'

'Was that a military horse?' Sonny asked.

'Righto. Lieutenant Colonel Blunt.'

He'd been the fool of fools. Blunt had outwitted him all along. He must have known that Sonny's Bavarian Alps was a stone building with a garden – Krankenhaus 31. That's why the inquisitors at the front desk had awarded him a private room. It all came with the compliments of CIC. Sergeant Salinger was a Nazi hunter who hadn't really left the hunt.

'It must hurt like a bitch.'

Sonny could tell that Hem wasn't talking about the bandage on his cheek; he was almost prescient as Papa pursed his lips.

'*Oona.*'

A ripple went right up to Sonny's throat. He was back at the Stork with Winchell and Hem and the playwright's daughter with her dark lashes and dark hair, her bosoms floating above her strapless gown, her bare arms like fucking musical flesh – it was worse than any nightmare, because it was tinged with both acid and delight.

'I'll survive,' Sonny said. 'We survived the Hürtgen.'

'Did we?' Papa asked. 'I haven't sent a dispatch in for months. *Collier's* calls me their celebrated ghostwriter. And I was rear echelon, not like you. I dined with the generals at Division, and it was still that bad. The artillery never stopped. There wasn't a damn inch of stable ground.'

Sonny was also *rear echelon*, some of the time. His desk was at Division, where CIC was headquartered. Sonny had several tunics in his sack. A CIC man wasn't supposed to reveal his sergeant's stripes, and he never did at Division. It was the rule of law, since a CIC agent often had to bark at men who outranked him; he had to boss those men around, and they might not have listened to a staff sergeant. But he always wore his stripes at the front. He was Sergeant Salinger, dammit, Salinger of E Company, and it was his chevrons that gave him whatever identity he had, and a bit of peace… until Lager IV, when *all* his identity fled into some forest that could have been another Hürtgen.

'Salinger, you weren't there when we said good-bye to the bravos of the Fourth. They were shipped back home last month. Major Oliver asked about you. "Where's my CIC man?" he said. He missed you. A lot of the guys did. They admired their rifleman who came over from Division.'

Sonny couldn't bring himself to attend that reunion, that last hurrah. He was as skittish as a cat locked in a closet. He kept to his quarters at the Villa Oberwegner, right across from the Kraut barracks that had been firebombed as the Allies whooped into Bavaria with their war cries. He couldn't seem to face these men, as if he'd been at fault, a spy among them, put there by the CIC. But he'd never spied, not once.

'Can you sleep, kid?'

'Not much.'

'I'm a casualty,' Hem said. 'I keep losing wives – with every war… Bad dreams, bad dreams.'

'It feels like we're still in that damn forest,' Sonny said. 'The wind keeps howling, even in my deaf ear.'

This Falstaff with his own arsenal must have shed fifty pounds since Sonny had last seen him at the Ritz. Hem had been chastened, spanked, not by General Patton or the provost marshal, but by the unfortunate and chaotic melodies of battle, the continual, relentless barrage in a dark wood. He'd lost his enthusiasm, his appetite. He had a chicken neck; his shirt and trousers didn't fit. He was all skin and bones, with a scraggly beard. He could have been a hobo who'd come in off the street to visit a staff sergeant who was largely invisible at Krankenhaus 31. He was the most recognizable and revered writer in the world, and Sonny pitied him.

'Hem, forget the fucking dispatches. Have you gone back to writing fiction?'

One side of Hemmy's mouth curled, and he had a satanic smile. 'I don't have all my marbles, kid. Nothing is left in the barrel.'

5

IT WAS HEM WHO MUST HAVE HEALED HIM a little with his own sense of grief and despair. Sonny opened his sack, put on his tunic with the chevrons, wore his armband, and paraded around the clinic as a CIC man. Nurses ran from him. 'Ach, the American Gestapo is here.' He went into the psychiatric ward, and was startled by what he saw. It was filled with German soldiers who lay abed in their uniforms, some with their boots still on. They must have endured the Hürtgen and the Ardennes. The Krauts had lost the privilege of their own military hospitals, and the casualties had come here, to this ward. The soldiers kept kneading their hands in some kind of gesture that Sonny couldn't fathom. They had an aura of dullness about them, a sense of absolute oblivion. Sonny wasn't even sure they had noticed him. He could have been a cosmic Santa Claus delivering K rations, but he had no rations to give. He wiped the spittle from one soldier's mouth with his handkerchief.

'Danke,' the soldier said in a mechanical voice. 'Dankeschön, Liebling.'

Sonny found Herr Doktor Fleck waiting for him when he returned to his room. Fleck was a tall man with perfect posture and a monocle in one of his oceanic blue eyes. There was a slight tremor in the cheek that held the monocle. That was the only sign of his rage.

'This will not do, Herr Sergeant Salinger. You have been frightening my other patients. You must not wear such a uniform at the clinic. You are my personal guest.'

'And yet you never visited me once – until now. I had to rattle you like a toy.'

'I am not your toy, Herr Salinger. I assure you. And why did you come here?'

Could he talk to this Nazi about his own collapse? For a moment he felt like Raskolnikov, an ax murderer.

'I came here,' he said, 'to rest.'

'But we are not the *Queen Mary*. We are a *Krankenhaus*. I deal with mental traumas, wounds of the mind. And you mock us when you wear that uniform.'

Sonny was wild, wild. He couldn't say what had gotten into him, like the demons in one of Dostoyevsky's novels. He wanted to harm this healer who had served with the Nazis, was a Nazi himself.

'Herr Direktor, you cannot heal *and* walk among the murderers who built Kaufering Four.'

Fleck removed the monocle. 'Then you have come here to arrest me. And that is why you wear your uniform. It is an *Amerikanische* game of cat and mouse. But I will not play. Come, arrest me in front of my staff. Did your forget your handcuffs, Herr Salinger?'

He had no handcuffs, and wouldn't have used them even if he did. And then, without a bit of warning, he floundered in front of the director, lost his train of thought, as if he'd endured an eclipse and had been diminished somehow. Sonny started to speak. The words wouldn't come. He was as forlorn as Alicja, without her tongue. He fainted, it seems, fell into Fleck's arms. That's the last he could recall.

He woke up in his bed at the clinic, wearing government-issue pajamas rather than his military tunic, and someone attended to him, a creature with bloodred nails. He wasn't sure whether it was Fräulein Sylvia or not. He didn't have all his marbles, as Papa had said. But she was tender with him, this nurse… or Nazi from another clinic.

Suddenly, Herr Fleck appeared with a flock of residents in white gowns. The doctor scribbled in a pad with blue lines.

'How long have you been considering suicide, Herr Salinger?'

'Since the war ended,' Sonny said. 'I never felt like a real soldier, and I wouldn't know how to be a civilian again.'

'And I suppose you meant to use a firearm,' the doctor said.

'My Colt.'

'*Richtig*. Your Colt – like a cowboy from the Colorado. But you're not a cowboy, Herr Salinger.'

'I used to be.' He'd had a fight with Doris when he was four and decided to run away from home, to be free of all the Salingers forever. He put on the cowboy suit that Sol and Miriam had bought him for his birthday, with a child's Stetson, boots, and a pair of cap pistols, and waited with the doorman until his mother came home from shopping at Saks. They were living on West End Avenue at the time in a seven-room apartment with so many winding hallways that Sonny often got lost.

He was crying in his Stetson and blue bandanna when his mother arrived.

'Mama,' he said, 'I'm running away, but I wanted to give you plenty of clues, so you wouldn't have to call a fire truck to look for me.'

Miriam observed him from her Olympian height, replete with wondrous bags from Saks Fifth Avenue. She didn't seem startled at all.

'What happened, Sonny?'

'Doris bit my ear, and she said she would drown me in the toilet bowl… if I went into her closet again and put on her clothes.'

Miriam was perfectly reasonable, like Herr Doktor Fleck. 'But why would you touch what belongs to her?'

'To be nasty. And now I'm running away. But I had to tell you, Mama, or it wouldn't be fair.'

And they went into an elevator that rocked like a stagecoach...

The doctor scribbled voraciously as Sonny recapitulated his encounter with Miriam on West End Avenue when he was four and had so little fright. 'That is a miracle, such a tale. And I beg your pardon, Herr Salinger. You were once the perfect little cowboy... But you did not bring your Colt to the *Krankenhaus*.'

'I left it in Weißenberg.'

'And you do not have such a desire to shoot yourself – at the moment.' The doctor smiled after Sonny nodded. 'Then that is progress.' And he left the room with all his disciples in their white gowns.

Sonny could hear a faint, prolonged murmur from the psychiatric ward below throughout the night.

His driver came to fetch him the very next day. He walked downstairs in his civvies and checked himself out of the clinic. Herr Fleck stood in the garden, smoking an American cigarette.

'You are my talisman, Herr Salinger. No one would dare arrest me while you were in residence. How much time do I have?'

'Very little,' Sonny said. 'But tell me, Herr Direktor, why do the patients on the ward wear their uniforms in bed?'

'It comforts them. They still feel like soldiers, even as their minds wander. That is the *last* stability they have left – soldiers without a war... And will you come back to arrest me yourself?'

'No, Herr Doktor,' Sonny said. 'I doubt that I will have that privilege. The CIC won't give me a second chance. My commandant is afraid you might capture me again.'

Herr Fleck's eyebrows rose halfway up the garden wall. 'But we did not capture you, *Mein Herr*. You came of your own volition.'

'Indeed I did.' And Sonny left Krankenhaus 31 with his driver.

PART NINE

The Grand Inquisitor

July–August 1945

1

H<small>E RETURNED TO THE INTERROGATION ROOM</small> at the Villa Oberwegner and was the grand inquisitor again. One of his first 'customers' was Frau Doktor Sylvia Welter, the ophthalmologist who had watched over him while he was delirious. She was suspected of having been a Gestapo informant while she studied medicine. It seems Sylvia had wandered from university to university – Erlangen, Munich, Prague, Königsberg, Freiburg, and Innsbruck. It was considered a typical Gestapo trick – gather information from fellow students and move on to yet another school.

'Why did you move around so much, Frau Doktor?'

She smiled at him, wasn't frightened of the naked bulb and the arid emptiness of the interrogation room – not a window or a picture on the wall. 'You must call me Sylvia, Herr Interrogator. We have been intimate, I think. Do I have amnesia, or didn't you kiss me at the clinic?'

'I did,' Sonny said. 'And I believe you came back and nursed me while I was ill.'

'More than nursed you,' she said with the same wicked smile. 'I bathed your little balls.'

'But I was delirious, Fräulein.'

'No,' she said. 'Not all the time.'

Ah, he told himself, *she's much wilier than I am*. But he wouldn't permit Sylvia to turn the interrogation around.

'That was in a different place,' he said, 'a hospital in Nuremberg.'

'And isn't this a hospital?' she asked with a defiant air.

'How is it a hospital, how? You have a blinding light in your eyes. You cannot see my face, Fräulein.'

'But you deal with the same damaged souls,' she said. 'And your voice can tell me what I cannot see.'

He wondered who was the real interrogator now. Had she been trained by her Gestapo masters to resist a naked bulb and a hard-backed chair? He would not win this contest with her – perhaps he didn't want to win.

'You worked at a clinic run by a doctor who had once been with the SS.'

'*Mensch*, I didn't have much of a choice,' she said with a sigh. 'How many hospitals are there in Nuremberg that have a psychiatric clinic?'

'But you are an ophthalmologist, a doctor of the eyes,' Sonny said.

'And where else could I deal with trauma cases?' she asked. 'It was a golden chance, and Herr Doktor Fleck gave it to me.'

Sonny tossed her file onto the table. 'We're finished here,' he said.

'And will I be escorted to the cage by your military police?'

'You're free to go, Fräulein,' he said, snapping off the light. 'But I would advise you not to consider a sudden change of address.'

He couldn't deal with her dark eyes and that regal beauty of hers – a princess among the ruins.

'We cannot kiss,' she said, 'but may I clap my hands, Herr Interrogator?'

'Clap all you like,' he said.

But she didn't clap her hands at all. She reached for her purse and left the interrogation room while his own corporal crept up behind him like a ghoul.

'Sarge, she's a Fritzie. I can tell. She was trained...'

Sonny stared at the stark wall. 'Maybe, maybe not.'

And he called in his next customer, Colonel Blunt, looking as skeletal as ever. Blunt wasn't even in uniform at the Villa

Oberwegner. Blunt was wearing a Hawaiian shirt in Weißenberg this afternoon. 'Salinger, come with me.'

They went into the canteen, which was cluttered with CIC agents, with their armbands and bayonets. They were guarding a lone giant who sat in his SS colonel's uniform, drinking schnapps from a paper cup. Sonny recognized the scar that rifled down his left cheek and the side of his mouth. Somehow, the CIC had captured Hitler's favorite commando, Otto Skorzeny, the mastermind of Operation Greif in the Ardennes, which had utterly bamboozled the Allies and helped slaughter hundreds and hundreds of men. Otto the Terrible was an outlaw and shouldn't have reigned at a CIC canteen with schnapps in a paper cup. His knuckles were as big as doorknobs.

'It's a wonder,' Blunt said. 'Nobody recognized him, and Otto landed in our lap. They haven't much of an intelligence team at Division. Otto's our gift.'

Sonny's cheek began to twitch. He shouldn't have been pulled out of the interrogation room so that Blunt could parade his elegant crocodile.

'Sir, do you know how many boys we lost on account of Skorzeny and his little battalion of jeeps?'

'You exaggerate,' Skorzeny said. 'Only ten jeeps got through the lines.'

'Shut up, Otto,' Blunt said, clutching his own paper cup of schnapps. 'We don't need any more of your lies.' Then he turned on Sonny. 'Sergeant, does this look like an interrogation room?'

'No, sir.'

'We've already interrogated the big fat fuck. That's not why I brought you here. When Otto was training his saboteurs at Schloss Friedenthal, all he did was show American flicks. And I can't answer a single one of his questions.'

Sonny couldn't hide his twitch. 'I don't understand, sir. I have to give this butcher a lesson on Louis B. Mayer and MGM? What about his plan to kill Ike and bomb the Allied high command?'

'Pure fable,' Blunt said. 'Half of Otto Skorzeny is our own invention.'

Sonny wanted to trace Otto's scar with a finger, nick it if he could. Yet he barely contained himself, he was trembling so. 'What about the other half? I witnessed the massacre, Colonel. Soldiers shot in the head because of Krauts in American uniforms, riding in one of our jeeps. I dug their graves.'

'Don't be impolite,' Blunt said. 'The fucker has confessed.'

Skorzeny appealed to Sonny as some strange comrade in arms. 'Please. Plenty of Yanks crossed the lines in German trucks. We didn't invent that trick. The Ardennes was our last push. It was really a suicide mission. And if I hadn't been wounded, Sergeant, I would have died with my boys. But the war is over. And I have many questions.'

'I'm not in the mood, Herr Otto,' Sonny said. The Villa Weißenberg had become a madhouse, a haven for captured Kraut colonels who were treated like movie stars. But if Sonny was with lunatics, he'd have to talk the language of lunatics. 'What would you like to know?'

Skorzeny grew pensive, suddenly absorbed. 'Please. We watched movie after movie, and it was so fickle, a sea of faces, each face talking so fast. We could only catch every other word, and we had to mimic all the facial twists. Confusion upon confusion. We had little time to accomplish so much. Who is your favorite movie star, *Mein Herr?*'

'Groucho Marx,' Sonny said.

This butcher with a butcher's hands started to giggle. 'Groucho Marx? But he is not beautiful. He is a clown… Ah, I love Deanna Durbin. And Gary Cooper, of course, as Marco Polo and Wild Bill Hickok. And don't forget Tyrone Power as Zorro and the Black Swan… or Errol Flynn as Robin Hood and General Custer.'

Sonny heard a rumbling sound from deep within the giant's chest – it was his show of laughter. 'This Yankee general with the yellow gloves was a much bigger butcher than Otto Skorzeny.

How many Red Indians did he slaughter, eh? But you cannot deny Hollywood's interest in male beauty. That was the first thing we noticed at Schloss Friedenthal. Errol Flynn had much more charm than Olivia de Havilland. She could have been his nanny.'

The giant turned to Sonny with the cup of schnapps half-squeezed in his huge fist. 'Be honest with a poor captured colonel. Were you not struck by this male beauty within the Hollywood calendar?'

'My favorite,' Sonny said, 'was Darcy Doyle.'

The giant muttered to himself. '*Was ist das?* I do not know from this Darcy Doyle.'

'He was the star of a silent serial, *The Royal Whisperer.*'

The giant seemed agitated now, as if Sonny had swindled him. 'But this is foolish. How could my commandos at the *Schloss* learn American English from a *silent* serial? Colonel Blunt, why did you bring this man? Was it to mock me?'

'Salinger,' Blunt said, 'I told you. This is not an interrogation.'

'Well,' Sonny said. 'Herr Otto, I would like to know one thing. When your birdmen, your glider patrol, swiped Mussolini from La Maddalena, what did they see in his eyes?'

The giant ruminated for a moment. 'There was nothing in the official report. But my boys said that Benito was scared to death – he wanted to remain on his island retreat. And now he would have to face the Führer. He was a pompous, lazy man.'

Blunt was waspish now. 'Enough intrigue. Sergeant, you can return to your interrogations. I don't like the sound of this Welter woman. I've seen her dossier. She could have been a Gestapo courier. I'm sure of it. Will you detain her?'

'We'll see,' Sonny said. He didn't like Colonel Blunt's display of Skorzeny in the canteen, the commando prince with his tell-tale scar. He didn't return to interrogation. He went outside the villa and smoked a Camel from an old, abandoned K pack. He wouldn't arrest Fräulein Welter. She was a tiny flower compared to the Führer's Errol Flynn – a tiny flower indeed.

2

ONE AFTERNOON, WHILE FLOATING ALONG, he met Sylvia outside the Villa Oberwegner, almost by accident. Weeks after he'd interrogated her. And they went to her flat on the Kehler Weg, amid mounds of rubble and stalactites of exposed brick that looked more like a macabre stage set than the blurred design of a broken city.

Sylvia had several antiques, including a carved oak bed with a canopy, and a boarded-up window – there were no more glaziers in Weißenberg, no more glass. He was alarmingly passive. Sylvia undressed him, as if she were still his doctor-nurse at Krankenhaus 31. She stroked him, played with his balls. And yet she aroused a passion in him that was also alarming. He pinned Sylvia to her carved oak bed, like a brunette butterfly with gorgeous wings, while swirls of dust came through the boarded-up window.

He stayed with Sylvia in that tiny flat on the Kehler Weg, though he held on to his room in the Villa Oberwegner, as a kind of camouflage. And he continued to interview *collabos* under the inquisitive gaze of Lieutenant Colonel Blunt. He didn't hang out at local beer halls, or spend much time at the CIC canteen and commissary. He was *always* with Sylvia when she wasn't at the little hospital in Weißenberg, or at Krankenhaus 31 with that Nazi, Fleck. On weekends they rarely left the flat. She had some perverse hypnotic power over Sonny. He told her about Oona, detail upon detail, each nuanced moment of his desire, and he watched her strange metamorphosis, as she began to mimic Oona's catlike walk, even the purr of her voice.

Soon Sonny was besotted, under Sylvia's spell. Part of him had melted into her in some bizarre way. She was the interrogator now, and Sonny, the CIC man in tatters, was the *collabo* and courier of what had become their own private love and hate fest.

'And what are your plans, Herr Sonny?'

'I have none,' he said, 'none at all.'

Sylvia smiled. 'Won't you marry Chaplin's widow when you return to America?'

Sonny was shaking. 'Never said Oona was a widow.'

She'd sat him down in a wicker chair and dug her knee into his chest. 'But you Americans are wonderful widow makers – that is your most conspicuous talent. You could get rid of Herr Charlie.'

She was trying to goad him into warfare, a fistfight on the Kehler Weg. And Sylvia succeeded. Each gave the other a bloody nose. And then she would hurl Sonny onto her antique bed, undress him with a fierce deliberation. 'Close your Gypsy eyes and pretend I'm your high school princess in her gym clothes. Call out to her.'

'*Oona*,' he whispered in spite of himself. And then he'd cast off Sylvia's spell, just in time.

'What about your own suitors, Sylvia? I see them on the stairwell, like starved animals, waiting for a lick.'

There was a businessman from Berne who wanted to marry her and whisk her family out of Nuremberg.

'Oh, him – Karl,' she muttered. 'Poor Karl doesn't bring out my dread. He's not an enchanter – a Yankee devil. Karl cannot greet me with a love potion, not like my Sonny.'

There were no boundaries between peace and war. They'd pummel each other, and he'd promise never to see her again. He lay in exile at the Villa Oberwegner for a week and then returned to the Kehler Weg, dispatching all her suitors with a display of his badge.

'I'm CIC.'

They all fled Nuremberg in a nonce.

Thus it went on and on like some bitter Bavarian fairy tale of the

American occupation, with Sylvia threatening to move to Berne, and Sonny wearing his holster while he made love.

It was dizzying, disastrous.

'Whore, I'll leave you here.'

Sylvia laughed and laughed. 'You can't. What American Fräulein would caress your balls? I dare you. Name me one.'

They'd battle until he was all black-and-blue. And then Sylvia kneaded his forehead and taught him how to levitate. They rose above the rooftops of Weißenberg, crossed Bavaria in some endless wanderlust, while she whistled an old tune, and arrived irrevocably at Hürtgen Forest.

'I can't go back, I can't,' Sonny shouted into the vast summer foliage of white pines, his voice a feeble echo in the forest.

'But you are back, darling.'

And he had no answer as he clung to Sylvia and could conjure up the unregistered graves, the hellfire of each Kraut attack, the blistering cold, newbies going mad in the vanishing light, and the relentless whimper of the pines that was like his own private call of doom.

PART TEN

Dracula's Daughter

May–June 1946

1

MIRIAM WAS INCONSOLABLE.

She couldn't understand why Sonny had stayed a whole year among Hitler's tribe of people after the war had ended. Why didn't he come home like other GIs? He'd been discharged last October, and still he stayed. Now he had a civilian contract with the CIC, hunting black marketeers and war criminals around Nuremberg, which even Miriam knew had once been the Nazi heartland, where Hitler had held his biggest rallies.

'Give him time, give him time,' Sol said, ticking away like a broken clock. 'The boy's confused.'

And Doris, the divorcée, chimed in: 'He's like a PI, Mama. Sonny's our Sam Spade.'

It didn't make sense. Miriam had knit him woolen socks all through the war, but she stopped knitting right after V-E Day. Why would Sam Spade need woolen socks? And then, like a punch in the solar plexus, this war bride appears right out of the blue – no announcements, no invitations, nothing. A French girl, Sonny said, Sylvie something. It sounded suspicious. What was a French girl doing in Nuremberg? Sonny called her a 'letter carrier.' Miriam's storytelling son was a teller of tall tales. But she hadn't seen a published story by him in months. She perused the pages of *The Saturday Evening Post* and couldn't find one mention of J. D. Salinger. He'd given up writing, God forbid. He sent a photo of the war bride. She was a brunette with pale skin and dark eyes, and Sonny asked her and Sol if they could see the hump she had on her shoulders – a letter carrier's sack. It was another one of his mystifications.

'Mama,' Doris said after parsing the letter, 'he's ribbing you.'

'It's torture,' Miriam said.

She couldn't seem to get Sonny on the line. She had a working phone number, more than one, but the overseas operator could never connect her to Sonny himself. Sometimes she got a captain who had no idea where Sergeant Salinger was, or if he existed at all. But he did exist. Once he even called, pretending to be a general, and said that Sergeant Salinger was on secret maneuvers and would get in touch the moment he could.

'Sonny,' Miriam screamed into the phone, 'you're killing me. Can't you admit who you are?'

He parroted the voice of the overseas operator. 'Sorry, Mrs Salinger, but your party has disappeared.' And the line went dead.

Several letters did come in a row, like a fleet of fighter-bombers. Sonny chatted with her as if he lived right next door, in Nuremberg. 'Mom, we're swell, we really are. Sylvie sends her love and a deep *bonjour*.' And then there was a long silence that pinched her vitals, until she couldn't eat for days. And after another month of silence, a tiny scribble on a piece of GI tissue paper: Her boy was coming home with his war bride on a Liberty ship, the freighter *Ethan Allen*. They even had the landing schedule. They picked up Doris at Bloomingdale's and rode down to the piers along the West Side Highway in Sol's company car, a 1946 Cadillac Fleetwood sedan, borrowed for weddings and funerals and other important engagements, like Sonny's return from Hitler Land. The highway had an eerie look. The Hudson was packed with Liberty ships that lay at anchor, like rusting carcasses with a vast scatter of smokestacks. Sol was moody, but Miriam was much too excited to remain silent.

'Doris, I haven't seen my son the secret agent in so long, how will I recognize him?'

'Mother, he's not a secret agent,' Doris insisted. She had Sonny's cheekbones and great dark eyes.

'But that's what I told Ralph.'

Ralph was the doorman at 1133, and a vast conduit of misinformation.

'And Ralph has told half the world,' Doris said, rolling her dark eyes like Eddie Cantor or Fanny Brice. 'He's not a secret agent; he hunted Nazis for a whole year and visited orphans at DP camps.'

They parked on West Street, in front of the piers, and waited while the *Ethan Allen* nestled into its berth like some night rider with darkened windows. It was puny, and Miriam couldn't imagine it as a Liberty ship that had carried her son across the ocean with his war bride.

'I'm so excited,' Miriam said. She sat in the back of the sedan, on her own private cushions, like a reigning queen. While the passengers disembarked, a sudden anger seized her, a sense of betrayal, as if she'd never had a son. And then, there he was, her Sonny, coming down the gangplank with his bride and a big black mutt – a schnauzer, a Nazi dog. Miriam climbed out of the car, with Sol and Doris behind her, barely keeping up with her pace. Her arms flew like an engine out of control. But Miriam never lost sight of her target. She stared at this brunette creature with the pale skin and bloodred lips, at her hauteur, her swagger, and knew right away that this Sylvie wasn't French. It was all a ruse. Sonny *was* a secret agent. He'd come out of Germany with a German war bride.

2

SHE'D BEEN SEASICK FOR THE ENTIRE TWELVE DAYS of the crossing. He brought her cups of soup and strong black tea from the captain's own cook. She never left the cabin, except at night, when he'd wrap her in a shawl, and they'd stand on the main deck as Sylvia breathed in the salty air, with the wind in her face and Benny at her side, on his leash. The schnauzer had his own passport, with a litany of shots from the veterinarian in Nuremberg and different stamps from government officials. The provost marshal had to agree and some guy from Special Services. Benny was like a liberated prisoner of war. If Sonny hadn't been with counterintel, he could never have taken the dog.

The schnauzer had kept the marriage from unraveling. They loved the dog, doted on him. How the hell did it happen? That black dog appeared one day on the Kehler Weg, and wouldn't leave Sonny's side – it was utter, desperate devotion at first sight. Sonny didn't have to think or brood. 'Benny,' he barked at the dog, and Benny it was. The mutt belonged to both of them, and would growl at any of Sylvia's other suitors. She had to send them away.

And so, in the midst of his Bavarian enterprise, Sonny had become the papa of a black dog with whiskers and a beard. Now he had to take care of Benny and Sylvia. Sonny wasn't supposed to fraternize with German nationals. He could have been fined a hefty sum and sentenced to six months in the stockade. But he was much too clever for the Army of Occupation. He had Corporal Benson prepare a forged passport, and Sylvia became a French national overnight – *Sylvie Louise Welter.*

The corporal was going back to the States. He wouldn't consider another six months in Nuremberg with counterintel. 'Sarge, I hate to leave you here alone. You're like a baby.'

'But I'm not alone,' he insisted. 'I have Sylvia.'

'That's what I mean. *You have Sylvia.* She'll tear your heart out. It's an old Kraut trick. You should have put her in the cages when you had the chance.'

'Well,' Sonny said with a slight stutter, 'we're in lo-o-o-v-e. We levitate.'

'Levitate all you want, but love's nothing in Nuremberg,' the corporal mused. 'One more commodity. Everything's for sale – everything.' He started to sniffle. Sonny had never seen him cry before, not in the Hürtgen, not at Kaufering IV, with all those corpses and skeletons on fire. But the corporal knew that he wouldn't have survived without Sonny, wouldn't have survived at all.

'Jesus, Sarge, 'member the time our own planes were shooting at us and we had to jump from our jeep right into a ditch? You broke your damn nose and it never healed right.'

Sonny laughed. 'Ah, it's only bent a little. I can still breathe through both nostrils... and become a movie idol.'

'But you have a sixth sense in battle, like the king of all the alley cats. You're a spotter, Sarge. You know how to spot trouble. 'Member the time we were interrogating that Kraut with the eye patch and he whipped out a knife and went straight for my gullet? You were faster than Billy the Kid – whacked him right on the schnozzola.'

'It was pure chance.'

'No, no. It's your sixth sense. But it sure ain't there when it comes to the Fräuleins.'

The corporal ran off with his duffel bag to catch a bus to Zeppelin Field, the old Nazi rallying ground, which had been converted into an airstrip. Sonny watched and watched until the duffel bag disappeared, and then he realized how much he would miss this corporal from rural Pennsylvania who had never heard of Friedrich Nietzsche or Franz Kafka, and wasn't even curious about Sonny's stories in the *Post*.

He married Sylvia a month later. And now he was back in the land of Fleetwoods and Frigidaires, coming down a wooden plank with a seasick wife and their schnauzer, who had acted like a referee, holding the marriage partners together with a dog's miraculous mirth. It was Benny who had the sixth sense, not ex-Sergeant Salinger, Benny who could paw at his mistress and master, bring them out of their gloom with some silly trick, like hiding Sonny's hat, or stealing Sylvia's sock. And at least Sonny could laugh, while Sylvia was terrified of this new country of conquerors and Sonny's own conquering tribe, the Salingers.

But it was Sonny who seemed a bit shell-shocked, even with

a big black dog who was half a clown. He was like poor Alicja, without a tongue. Sol stood in the background with his spectacles and trimmed mustache, as if he were staring at a stranger, or worse, a war criminal, and his illegitimate bride. It was Miriam and Doris who danced around Sonny and Sylvia at the bottom of the plank.

Sylvia had her usual pale skin and bloodred lips, and the dog had a long black beard and eyebrows that looked like chicken feathers. But Miriam was transfixed by Sonny.

'Sol,' she said, 'they hurt my boy – look at his nose. Not even Joe Palooka ever had a nose like that. We'll have to take him to Mount Sinai, right from the docks.'

Sonny would have to get used to her hyperbole again.

'Mother, it's nothing,' he said.

She mimicked him. '*Nothing*, he says. Doris, you're my witness. He comes back from Hitler's hometown with a bride and a broken nose, and calls it nothing. Please, Sonny, introduce us to your wife – and your big black dog with the beard.'

He had his regrets, right on the pier, among the warehouses of West Street, but he couldn't have signed up with CIC for another six months. He'd spent most of his time with young orphans in a DP camp outside Nuremberg, steering them through a bureaucratic maze, but these children were already marked no matter what Sonny did for them, no matter how hard he fought; they wore a numbered tag rather than a name. He organized volleyball matches for the boys, put on playlets for the little girls from a sister camp near Munich, helping them sew the costumes, providing whatever material he could, but orders came down from the provost that Sonny should stop interfering with 'the internal business' of the DPs. He couldn't stray from the master plan invented by the Army of Occupation and its diabolic clerks. This camp outside Nuremberg was a former SS barracks, with barbed wire and the odor of unwashed flesh. He fed these children contraband candy, allowed the more daring ones to smoke a Camel with him, his fingers stained with nicotine. He'd been smoking since he was seventeen.

'How are you today, Five two one B?'

'I was lucky, Herr Salinger,' said a Talmudic-looking boy who'd risen from the dead at Dachau. 'I did not have to wait so long outside the latrines. I could move my bowels. It is a wonder. But I wish we had some toilet paper.'

'There's a short supply this week,' Sonny said, despairing that he was part of this regime. He could not create a family for 521B, who would go from a reconditioned SS barracks to some orphanage in Upper or Lower Silesia, where he would walk around in ill-fitting clogs and drink soup from a tin cup. And so Sonny quit and returned to America. And now he had to face what he didn't want to face, the sovereignty of the Salingers.

'Mom, Dad, Doris, meet my Sylvie… and our Benny.'

He could feel that tinge of iciness, though Doris hid it better than Miriam and Sol. Doris was the worldly one. She'd made regular trips to Europe on the *Queen Mary* before the war, as empress of fashion at Bloomingdale's, a fashion buyer at a very unfashionable store, which sat in exile, far removed from the emporiums of Fifth Avenue, such as Bergdorf Goodman and Saks, and catered to the riffraff of Third Avenue and a maelstrom of Park Avenue maids.

She'd once been friendly with Coco Chanel, had visited all the fashion houses near the place Vendôme. She wore a summer cape that Coco's couturières had designed. She'd been Sonny's ally all through childhood, though they fought a lot. She married Billy Samuels in 1935, a wholesale grocer who chased after every skirt in town until the Salingers got rid of him less than two years later. Billy was a blue-eyed Adonis, a ne'er-do-well who played Russian roulette with Doris' life. Sonny admired him in some dark way – his zest, his willingness to destroy and create anew, his manicured mustache and fingernails like a mask of confidence. Sonny had none of this as he climbed down from the *Ethan Allen*. His hands still shook and his cheek still twitched.

It was Doris who sensed the root of his pain. He was rudderless, without his craft. And he had all the trappings of someone who had settled in. But he'd settled nowhere, and he had nowhere to settle – not Nuremberg, and not 1133 Park Avenue. And yet he was returning to his childhood nest, with a wife and a dog. Sonny's homecoming, Doris sensed, was a subtle form of suicide.

3

HE WAS SILENT ON THE RIDE UPTOWN, into the sinews of Manhattan. Yet it was almost surreal. Trained in reconnaissance at Fort Holabird, he couldn't get rid of that hawkeye of his so easily as he calibrated each shift in the landscape – a hardware store on Columbus and Sixty-ninth where a hardware store had never been; a dinette that had once been a hole-in-the-wall; a candy shop on Madison that was reincarnated as a dry cleaner's…

He had to bear the unbearable weight of the Salingers, with the schnauzer at his heels and Miriam planted between him and his wife. She clutched Sonny's hand and gripped Sylvia's, too, and wouldn't let go. He would have had to strangle his own mother and still might not get free.

'Lovebirds,' she crooned. 'Where did you lovebirds meet?'

'At the clinic,' Sylvia said.

'Clinic? What clinic?' Miriam asked.

Sonny broke his silence. 'Mother, I had a breakdown. I wrote Doris – remember?'

Miriam was bewildered. 'She said it was a rest cure… at a health spa for GIs.'

Doris had a subversive smile. 'A health spa, Mama, in Nuremberg?'

'Solly,' Miriam said, 'stop the car. I will not be jostled in so rude a fashion by my own son and daughter. There has to be a reckoning – right now.'

'Miriam,' Sol said, 'we're on Madison, in the middle of traffic.'

'That's not my problem,' Miriam shouted, her coiffure ablaze, a nest of burning red snakes.

I will have to strangle her one day, Sonny muttered to himself. But it was Doris who was the real captain of the ship. 'Mother,' she said, with the same subversive smile, 'calm yourself, please. You'll have your reckoning. We'll settle this upstairs.'

And it was Doris who steered them home. They got out of the Fleetwood in front of 1133, and the doorman, Ralph, pranced out from under the green awning to welcome the half-forgotten war hero.

'Sergeant Salinger,' he said with a crisp salute, the blade of his hand striking the bill of his cap. 'And your lovely bride. What an honor, sir.'

'Ralphie,' Miriam said, 'pipe down. We're not in the mood.'

And for a moment, with all that rattling, Sonny thought he was back in the Green Hell, where the bombardments never ceased. And it wasn't Doris, his older 'twin,' who rescued Sonny. While Sol went to park the company car, Sylvia seized Sonny's arm and led him into this brick and limestone palace, taller than the Nuremberg Castle and the *Frauenkirche* – the Church of Our Lady – much, much taller. She was surrounded by men in uniforms, who looked like overdressed beetles. One of the beetles ran the elevator and drove them up to the Salingers' palace apartment, with the help of a metal stick. Frau Salinger thanked this beetle, who stopped on the sixth floor, and they marched Sonny into the apartment, which wasn't even locked. *Scheiße*, she muttered to herself, *they don't have locks and keys in America*.

4

THEY DIDN'T LIKE HER, THAT'S ALL. And it wouldn't have mattered what she did or said. She got rid of that French veneer. And Sylvie was suddenly Sylvia again. But it wasn't *gemütlich* to be a German war bride in America, not during the Nuremberg tribunals, when images of Dachau haunted every newsreel. The Salingers had a Hungarian live-in maid, Maja, and Sylvia recruited her as an ally. She had to use her own counterintel against the Salingers. Maja must have been forty-five or fifty. She had a narrow, pinched face, with swollen eyes. And she was a reservoir of information about the Salingers and the building, and America. They would meet in the maid's room, while Maja did the ironing, and devour half a box of white Belgian chocolates that Doris had brought from Bloomingdale's, and smoke Pall Malls from Sylvia's pack, kept in a lizard skin pouch.

'Maja, is it true that Sonny and Doris were child prodigies… that they were on the radio as little wizards – quiz kids?'

Maja giggled with white chocolate in her mouth. 'It's an invention, *Liebchen*. He is always lying, that Sonny, making fibs. He was never on the radio. He was a normal child.'

'And Doris?' Sylvia asked. '*Gott*, they look like twins… doubles with the same dark eyes.'

Maja smoked and ironed and gobbled chocolate, all with the same intensity and concentration. 'Ah, she is the clever one, that Doris. But she can get you any blouse or skirt, take it right off the racks at Bloomingdale's. I have an entire wardrobe, thanks to Doris Salinger. But she was not so lucky in love. Her *Mann* was a gigolo... I'll tell you a secret, Sylvia. He couldn't keep his hands off me. He came into my room at night.'

Sylvia was befuddled. 'You live here – in this room – with the Salingers?'

'*Dummkopf*, of course,' Maja said, teasing Sylvia with her swollen eyes. 'I am a live-in maid. I would not accept such a position otherwise. I have been with the Salingers for sixteen years, before they moved to Park Avenue. I have always had the finest employers. Herr Salinger is a gentleman. I call him "*Vati*".'

Sylvia was still perplexed. 'But they do not seem so fond of the German language.'

'I don't care. He is *Vati*. But Doris' *Mann*, he sent me love notes. He was without shame. He was also a crook. He stole from Doris and Herr Salinger. He wanted to steal from me. All of us, we had to push him out the door. It was a terrible scandal. And now that you and Sonny are here, Doris has come back to live with us, in her old room.'

'The two quiz kids reunited,' Sylvia said. 'And Madame Salinger, what about her and her red hair?'

Maja pounded the ironing board with a steam iron that looked like an enormous clubfoot. She was removing a crease in a pillowcase. 'We fight like cats and dogs. She threw an ashtray at my head once. We had to call an ambulance.'

'Then why do you stay?' Sylvia asked.

'Because,' Maja said, 'I *crave* the excitement. It's in my blood. Being around the Salingers is like living in a cabaret. Frau Miriam loves Sonny, but she is not always so kind. She has found a name for you.'

'Well?'

Maja pounded the board again. 'But you must guard it as a secret – *swear*. I could lose my job, and I've grown lazy and fat, on white chocolate.'

Dark pellets appeared in Sylvia's eyes. 'What does that *Rotkopf* call me behind my back?'

'"Dracula's Daughter",' Maja said.

Sylvia inherited her husband's habit – her cheek started to twitch.
Dracula's Daughter.

'Is that what they think of me?'

'What do you expect?' Maja asked. 'A *Mädel* from Nuremberg.
But you must not give me away.'

'Maja,' Sylvia said, 'I will guard your little secret – with my life.'

But she stopped eating Doris' white chocolate. She shouldn't have
come to America with a husband who had lost the art of making love
to her. Yet she wanted to heal him somehow. She'd spent much of
her childhood in Switzerland, in Luzerne. She could have joined the
Bund Deutscher Mädel – the Nazi Girl Scouts – at her gymnasium in
Nuremberg, but she did not. Yes, she was loyal to Herr Doktor Ulrich
Fleck, the director of Krankenhaus 31, but not because he had been
with the stormtroopers and the SS. He was devoted to his patients,
whoever they were. He understood *das Trauma*, the annihilation
of the spirit and the psyche under mental and physical duress. He
would not permit the German generals or the Gestapo access to his
clinic. He guarded his patients, mostly uneducated farm boys who
were just as afraid of killing as of being killed, guarded them with
his own stubborn stamina, until the Army of Occupation arrested
him and removed his picture from the wall of Krankenhaus 31. The
new director did not have Herr Fleck's gifts. He could not deal with
a farm boy's calvary, could not wander through the psychiatric ward
for hours, seeing patient after patient, singing to them, holding their
hands while they wept. The new director rarely visited the wards.
And she was not welcome there, under his pale stewardship.

5

SHE WORE WHITE PAINT TO DINNER, like a mime or a master clown. Sonny didn't interfere. And not a word was said, though Doris had that familiar subversive smile. Sylvia didn't understand the strange habits of the Salingers. Maja, the maid, sat at the table and dined with the family, like a minor relative, or a jester right out of *King Lear*. It was Miriam who cooked and Miriam who served – the *Rotkopf* herself. The dining table had four leaves and could have sat ten or twelve, if there had been more Salingers.

They had roast beef and cauliflower and yams, and Jarlsberg from Herr Salinger's own company stock, and a bottle of Bordeaux that he'd saved from his minuscule wine cellar in the basement of 1133. As the *Vati* of the clan, he opened the bottle, savored the cork, let the bottle sit, then hopped around the table as he poured, and proposed a toast to the bride and groom.

'To our Sonny,' he said, 'and to Sylvie, his ravishing French bride.'

Now it was Sylvia who had the subversive smile. She stood up and said, 'We must put an end to this little farce, please. I am not French and I never was. Your son had my papers forged. I am a German citizen, Mrs Sylvia Salinger. And I am not a letter carrier. I was an intern at the psychiatric ward in Nuremberg.'

'You're still welcome,' Miriam said without standing up. 'But why the white paint?'

Sylvia knew she was betraying Maja, and that they could never be allies again. But she had to risk that rupture.

'Frau Salinger, I couldn't be Dracula's Daughter without some white paint on my face.'

Miriam sat where she was and stared at Maja as if she meant to stick Sol's corkscrew between her eyes. 'Someone at this table has a big mouth.'

Maja's face reddened, but it was almost like a rash. She wasn't frightened of Miriam, wasn't alarmed in the least.

'Madame, did you want me to lie to the war bride?'

'Ingrate,' Miriam said. 'It was a private matter, between family members.'

But Maja wouldn't be swayed. 'Isn't Sylvia a member of the family now?'

'That's not the issue,' Miriam said. 'Don't play semantics with me. You sit with us at *my* table. You eat our food.'

'And wash your underwear – wash, wash, wash.'

Sonny's hands were trembling. He couldn't even cover the twitch in his cheek. Doris had to intervene.

'Mother, you will apologize to Sylvia, and you will not call her Dracula's Daughter ever again.'

But Miriam was on a tear, and she wouldn't be tangled with. 'Look who's taken the high road, the princess of Bloomingdale's, the buyer of buyers.'

The house telephone rang. It was Maja who picked up the phone. 'Yes… yes.' She cupped her hand over the mouthpiece. 'He's here,' she said.

'Don't be so damn mysterious,' Miriam said. 'Who's here?'

'Billy Samuels.'

'That's impossible,' Sol said. 'We haven't seen that *gonef* in years. What's he doing here – at dinnertime?'

Maja kept her hand over the mouthpiece. 'He wants to congratulate Sonny and his bride.'

'Send him away,' Miriam said.

Sonny stood up. His cheek was no longer twitching. 'I like Billy – I always did.'

'He stole from us,' Sol said. 'But Sonny's the war hero… whatever he says.'

Doris was bristling. 'He was *my* husband, for God's sake. Shouldn't I be consulted?'

'Certainly,' Sol said. 'You're the boss in this matter.'

'Ah, the hell with it,' Doris said with a wave of her hand. 'Show him up.'

And they all waited while Sol muttered, 'That *gonef*.' A prince among Park Avenue Gentiles and vice president at a pork and ham company, yet he never forgot the Yiddish of his childhood.

The doorbell rang. A kind of panic arose around the table; even Benny, who sat between his master's legs, began to growl. It was Miriam who was the first to collect her wits. 'Maja, be a darling and let the *gonef* in.'

Maja curtsied like an eloquent rag doll and opened the unlocked door. Billy Samuels wandered in wearing sharkskin shoes. He had a blond handsomeness, with sideburns and a blond mustache. And Sonny realized why he had once worn a mustache in occupied France. He was cultivating Billy's debonair look as a kind of talisman, but he shaved off the mustache once they got to the Hürtgen and had to live for a month among all the devils in a darkened wood.

Billy hadn't prospered without the Salingers. His cuffs were ragged and his necktie was unclean. He was carrying a bouquet of wilted roses for the bride. Sol had helped Billy build his career in the wholesale grocery business, then abandoned Billy to his own fate. Billy seemed to twist about in some invisible wind. He nearly tottered, but he still managed to wink at Sylvia and give her the wilted flowers.

'Sonny, I couldn't resist. Home from Germany, and here I am. I had to introduce myself to the lucky girl.'

'Billy,' Sol said, 'we've hardly seen or heard from you in seven years.'

'A mere detail,' Billy said. 'My heart has always been with the Salingers. May I sit?'

'Maja,' Miriam said with a gruffness in her voice, 'set the table for our Billy. Give him some silver. He can't eat with his fingers.'

It was Sonny who got up, went into the sunken living room, swiped an armchair, and put it at the far edge of the table, near one of the unfolded leaves. He listened to the clatter of silverware as Maja set a place for Billy. Sol poured him some wine with a half-turn of the wrist, like the most experienced sommelier.

'*Mazel*,' Billy said, 'to Sonny Salinger and...'

Sylvia sensed a new ally in this raggedy blond man. They were both outcasts at 1133. 'Sylvia,' she said. 'My name is Sylvia.' She put the stem of a wilted rose, with its prickles, between her breasts, while Billy began to gobble up all the roast beef that was on his plate.

'Stop,' Sol said. 'We haven't said grace.'

Sonny's hand was trembling again. 'Dad, what's this? We never said grace, not once.'

'It was your mother's idea,' Sol said. 'We started to recite a benediction while you were fighting in France.'

'Was it a wager with God?' Sonny asked. 'Dad, were you playing the odds, like a bookmaker? I was in a death camp, and there were no damn angels on my shoulder.'

'Darling, you shouldn't blaspheme,' Miriam said. 'We recited a prayer for your safe return.'

Sol clasped his hands together, shut his eyes, and chanted, 'Oh Lord, bless this meal. We are humbled in Your presence and grateful that You have given Sonny back to us.' Sol opened his eyes. 'Now, Billy, you can dig in.'

'No, Dad,' Sonny insisted. 'You have to bless the living *and* the dead, and those who lost their limbs.'

'Darling,' Miriam chirped, 'it's a benediction, not a battlefield.'

'Then I can't accept your blessing,' Sonny said, 'and I can't eat this meal.'

He got up from the table, thrust his napkin down, and went into his old room, with the schnauzer trailing behind.

Sol was bewildered, forlorn. 'I don't understand. Miriam, did I do something wrong?'

It was Doris who went after Sonny, galloped across the living room and the foyer in three great strides and entered her brother's room, which he now shared with Sylvia. Their trunk had yet to arrive from the piers, and Sonny had gone shopping with Sylvia at Saks and Bloomingdale's, with Doris as a kind of commandant. Sonny still had his clothes in the closet from the time before he was drafted. He preferred his old suits, and wouldn't even buy a new fedora. He had a signed picture of Pete Reiser, Brooklyn's batting, running, and fielding wizard, on his nightstand. Sonny had always been a Dodger fan. But he had a particular affection for Pistol Pete, who kept crashing into the far wall at Ebbets Field and fracturing his skull as he reached for impossible fly balls. Both Sonny and Pistol Pete were born in the same year – 1919. And Sonny loved to compare Pete Reiser's acrobatics in the outfield to a writer's quest to discover his own style.

'Doris,' he would say, 'Pete has his music and I have mine. But it's all about the reach, the desire to do what can't be done.'

'And his reward,' Doris would say, 'was a broken head.'

'Same as mine,' Sonny would answer like an acolyte, 'same as mine.'

Sonny was lying on the same narrow hardwood bed he'd slept in as a child – Miriam and Sol had made scant accommodations for Sylvia. She had to share whatever Sonny had. Doris fondled the covers of the worn Dostoyevsky classics in Sonny's bookcase. Her brother read rapaciously, like a hawk, outlining sentences, savoring words. He had the same desk he'd had as a child, an old shoemaker's table. He'd brought his army-issue Corona back from the war. There was a manuscript on the desk, a scatter of pages with scribbles all over them; Doris couldn't decipher a single word.

'Sonny, is that your Holden Caulfield? When was the last time you worked on it?'

He was lying facedown, like a floating corpse. 'I can't remember, sis. It's been so long ... Even before we drove into that death camp.'

'Then why did you stay in Nuremberg a whole other year? You could have come back with the Fourth Division.'

'Yeah,' Sonny said, 'the hero with the nervous tic. Nuremberg made more sense. I could structure my days as a counterintelligence agent. But I was worthless as a Nazi-hunter. I couldn't break the bastards down, catch them at their tricks. So they sent me to deal with the orphans in the DP camp, like some exalted playground director. But they didn't like my deals. I was too emotional, they said, too involved with the DPs. I wouldn't treat them like numbers in their own trick deck – kids, for God's sake. I wasn't going to help them stack the deck. So I came home to 1133 with Sylvia. It's not her fault that she married a guy who's made of glass. I shatter every now and then, and she glues the pieces together as best she can.'

'With white paint?'

'Ah,' Sonny said, 'that's her way of dealing with Mom and Dad.'

'Don't hit them so hard on the benediction,' Doris said. 'They were worried… and that's how they coped.'

She lured Sonny back into the dining room, with the schnauzer at his heels. He took his seat at the table, Benny between his legs.

'Dad, I'll make the benediction. I'll bless our bread. Will you all bow your heads, please… Oh, Lord, we all deserve to die.'

'Sonny,' Sol said, 'that's enough.'

Doris stared her father down. 'Dad, let him finish.'

'But if live we must,' Sonny chanted, with his head bowed, 'then let us not live in vain. Let us give our possessions away, and devote ourselves to utter stillness. It's in silence that we will thrive… Now we can all eat. As Dad said, dig in.'

There was a great clatter around the table. Sol hummed to himself. Miriam smiled at her brood. 'We've had our benediction. And God returned Sonny to us – in one piece.' But Billy wasn't listening. He wolfed down whatever he could. It was Sylvia who picked up the great sadness in his face. She'd seen the same sadness on the ward at Krankenhaus 31, of a psyche spinning out of control in front of her eyes. He hadn't come to bring her flowers and welcome Sonny home. He had a darker motive.

'Herr Billy,' she asked, 'what is wrong?'

Billy didn't answer at first. He devoured every bit of roast beef that was left on the table, wiping his mouth with one of the monogrammed napkins that Maja had ironed that morning. Miriam had borrowed the enormous rounded *S* from Schrafft's and had the Salinger crest – *Miriam & Sol Salinger, 1133* – sewn on every napkin, every pillowcase.

Billy belched once, wiped his mouth, and muttered, 'I'm dead.'

'*Gonef,*' Sol shouted across the table. 'We can't hear you.'

'Dead is dead.'

Miriam grew surly. 'Must you come here and speak in riddles? Dead men don't swallow enough roast beef to choke a horse.'

'I got involved with a bad crowd,' Billy said. 'I owe them a lot of gelt.'

'You swindled,' Sol said.

Billy wiped his mouth again with the Salingers' monogrammed napkin. 'You're the swindler, Solly, not me. Didn't the government fine you for making phony Swiss cheese?'

'We settled,' Sol said in a rage, 'settled out of court. But I'm not the one who's on trial – you are, Billy. Was it the Scheherazade crowd?'

His ex-son-in-law had gotten involved with a notorious café on the Upper West Side, ripe with gamblers, extortionists, and guns for hire who shrouded themselves in a Roumanian poets' society. These were poets who had a gift for scribbling letters that threatened to break your fingers and your head. Billy must have performed cartwheels for the Roumanian poets, been their bagman, and borrowed from the poets, heavily.

'Yes,' Billy said, 'those bandits, with their passion for poetry.'

'And you want us to bail you out?' Sol asked, his eyes hidden under the wire frames of his spectacles.

'Not at all. But I would like to give them a dose of Sergeant

Salinger. They're all draft dodgers. Anything to do with the military would scare them out of their pants. If Sonny himself could go to the Scheherazade in his uniform and *play* Sergeant Salinger, the Nazi-hunter and intelligence whiz, like Don Winslow of the Navy, well, that would do wonders for me.'

Sol removed his spectacles. His jaws were trembling. 'Billy Samuels, you're insane. Get the hell out of here.'

'Dad, wait,' Sonny said, with the blank, wild-eyed stare that Sylvia recalled from Krankenhaus 31. 'I don't have my uniform, Billy. I had to surrender my badge and my armband to the CIC. All I have is an Eisenhower jacket with bloodstains on the collar.'

'Beautiful,' Billy said. 'That would add a little menace.'

Sonny remembered wearing that Eisenhower as a windbreaker on the *Ethan Allen*. It was his last memento of the war.

'I could pay a thousand dollars – cash,' Billy said, winking at Sylvia. 'Don't I get to kiss the bride?'

'No,' Sylvia said. 'We will have to kiss another time, Herr Billy.'

'There is no other time,' Sol said. 'Billy, my boy was in a clinic. He can't come with you to the Scheherazade. It's madness.'

Billy banged his elbows on the table. The silverware shook. 'Let's negotiate.'

Sol pointed to the front door. 'Out, I said.'

'Not a chance. I haven't had my dessert.'

Billy turned and appealed to Doris. 'Help me. You were my wife. We shared certain vows… We made love right under this table.'

'I'll return some of your love,' Doris said, and poked him in the ribs. He fell back, and Sol shoved him out the door, with the help of Maja and Miriam. It was like the last time, six or seven years ago, when he owed a bundle to some other poets' society of swindlers, and went into the master bedroom, ransacked all the drawers, and nearly walked out with a fistful of cash and securities. Maja caught him in the act and screamed. The Salingers swooped down upon Billy and had him banished from the building for three whole years.

6

SONNY SLIPPED OUT THE BACK DOOR in his Eisenhower and sat in the service car. Corporal Benson was waiting outside in his jeep. He'd come all the way from Pennsylvania.

'Corporal, how's civilian life?'

'Aw, it ain't so terrific. I run a hardware store, with my battle stars in the window. No one's really heard of the CIC – not one article in the news. We were a couple of ghosts, and that's how we went right through the war. Where are we goin', Sarge?'

'To the Scheherazade,' Sonny said.

They drove down Park Avenue in their jeep, the corporal marveling at the floral gardens in the little island that went along the entire length of the boulevard, with row after row of tall buildings on either side with the same majestic look that grew monotonous after a while.

He turned right and rode onto the ramp at Eighty-fifth Street that delivered them into Central Park. They had the only jeep in town, as far as the corporal could tell. Drivers saluted them and whistled at Sonny in his sergeant's stripes. 'Hurray, soljer boy!'

Benson asked about the clot of barn-like buildings and stables on the left side of the Eighty-sixth Street Transverse Road, with its gathering of horses. 'Sarge, is that some fucking lost platoon?'

'No,' Sonny said. 'It's the Central Park Precinct – with its horse patrol.'

It had once been his favorite spot in the park, even more crucial than the old carousel of gallant hand-carved horses that went up and down a series of greased poles.

He'd go on field trips with Doris into the park and visit this quaint precinct that most New Yorkers had never heard about. Sonny was eight at the time and Doris fifteen, a flapper with dark eyes, like a long and lean Clara Bow. Doris had become the household pet of this hidden precinct, with Sonny as her tag-along partner. She would dance the Charleston or the Black Bottom or do the Shimmy Shake for the detective squad and members of the horse patrol in the muster room. They couldn't take their eyes off Doris and her frenzied moves, the way she would kick out a leg and flap her arms while she stood with her chin near her knees. Sometimes Sonny would dance along with her. But he couldn't do the Shimmy Shake, not like sis. Afterward, the stable hands, who were also cops, would let Sonny climb onto a horse and ride along the narrow lanes, like a lone jockey.

Doris had a crush on a young detective with a drooping mustache who called himself Vic. Years later, Sonny would say that Vic reminded him of Billy Budd, the foretopman in Melville's sea tale. This young detective had Billy Budd's innocent, almost angelic smile, though he carried a blackjack, and must have cracked many a skull. He also stuttered, like Melville's sailor. But he wouldn't allow any of the other detectives to fondle Doris or whisper in her ear. He protected her at the precinct.

Still, his wife arrived one afternoon while Doris was doing the Black Bottom, and she put an end to the performance. 'Vic,' she said in a savage but modulated voice, 'get this baby bitch outa here.'

The Billy Budd of Central Park shrugged his shoulders.

'Sweetheart, it was only f-f-f-f-un.'

'I'll show you fun,' she said, and whacked him with her pocketbook. He didn't flinch once. He escorted Doris and Sonny out of this precinct of refurbished stables with little windows for the horses' heads. Doris sulked, and Sonny had to steer her away from the traffic on the transverse and lead her along to the West Eighties, where they lived at the time.

'I'm so ashamed,' she blubbered, and never went back to the Central Park Precinct...

Sonny remembered the look of desolation on Doris when she no longer had her young detective and free rein of the horse patrol. Billy Samuels became her suitor several years after that, Billy with his bouquets and his cockeyed schemes to make a buck in some fanciful market. He was always scheming, always alert about hard cash. He would gamble and lose a tiny fortune, and Doris would have to bail him out. But Billy had a kind of zest that the Salingers never had...

The two ex-soldiers left the park a few blocks north of the old redbrick Museum of Natural History, and found the Scheherazade on Amsterdam, near a nursing home and a string of ramshackle hotels. It wasn't the kind of cafeteria with the aplomb of Schrafft's. Sonny could never have ordered a butterscotch sundae at the Scheherazade. It was quite dark inside. He and Benson had to find the poets' corner. And there they were, in their suspenders; curiously enough, this poets' lair reminded Sonny of Table 50 at the Stork. But Winchell didn't preside here, not among these gangster-poets. He recognized another man in the shadows, the baron de Boeldieu, that *caïd* from Le Sphinx, on the boulevard Edgar-Quinet.

'Boldy, what the hell are you doing in Manhattan?'

But it wasn't Boeldieu, just someone in velvet who happened to look like him. His name was Andrei. There was also a poetess who wore white paint, like Sonny's own German wife. She was called Michaela. The other poets sat in the semidarkness and never uttered a sound. They all seemed to know who he was.

It was Sonny who had to speak. 'I'm here to settle Billy Samuels' account.'

The poets cackled at *their* Table 50. 'That's inconsequential,' said Andrei, who seemed to be the president of this little society. 'It was only a lure, Sergeant, to bring you here. Billy was our bait. Tell us your secrets.'

Sonny was baffled. He had imagined these Scheherazadians discussing the fire that a poet had to collect between every word – ex-Sergeant Salinger had lost whatever he had. Language lived in that fire and that fire alone. It didn't matter that the Roumanians were thieves and draft dodgers, as long as they were guardians of that feathery flame. He wanted to commune with them in his Eisenhower jacket, bang his way back into the drumbeat of words.

'I have no secrets,' Sonny said, 'none.'

'Then what use are you to us?' asked Michaela with the white face.

'We've been sitting here for months,' said Andrei in his velvet jacket. 'Yes, we've cut an occasional throat. It serves as inspiration. It was wonderful during the war. We operated in the middle of a blackout. We were all air-raid wardens, registered and certified. It was *beautiful* during the blackouts.'

'A heavenly nest,' whispered Michaela with her eyes shut. 'We wrote all the time.'

'We didn't have one dry spell,' said Andrei, 'not one.'

'And what happened?' the corporal asked. There weren't any poets' societies in Pennsylvania.

'Peace,' Andrei said. 'That's what happened. No more ration stamps. We had to return our wardens' helmets. We couldn't forage in the dark. We all went cold – and completely flat.'

And Sonny had to plead with this fraudulent society of poets. 'What secrets could I possibly have? I'm absent without leave as a writer, AWOL.'

'But you must have a secret,' Andrei insisted, 'you must.'

Perhaps, Sonny thought, dancing on his feet, as if he were back at the station house with Doris, doing the Black Bottom, perhaps it was that imperceivable lick of fire caught in a sudden freeze. That was it. Sonny wanted to write sentences that would scorch the reader's soul like shards of burning ice. But he was impotent, even in his Eisenhower.

The Roumanian poets weren't shielded at the Scheherazade.

There was a police raid, detectives and patrolmen from the Central Park precinct, who charged into this cafeteria with shotguns and billy clubs, and a couple of crowbars. They were looking for illegal merchandise, and they found a storeroom full of stuff. Sonny recognized Doris' old flame, that young detective, Vic, who had a paunch now and dull, watery eyes.

'Sergeant, what are you doing here with this g-g-g-gang?'

'Reminiscing,' he said.

'Well, you ought to reminisce somewhere else. This is a mean bunch.'

'But they're poets,' Sonny said.

'When they aren't burglars and g-g-guns for hire.'

Sonny couldn't resist. 'Don't you remember me? I was the squirt who played with your handcuffs a long time ago. My sister, Doris, danced for you in the muster room… until your wife broke up her act.'

The dull, watery eyes didn't blink once. 'I don't remember any D-d-d-doris.'

It pained Sonny. The gift of remembrance was all he ever had. But nothing he said could bring Billy Budd back to that moment in the muster room almost twenty years earlier, when Sonny was a pisser in short pants.

The poets were led out of the Scheherazade in handcuffs. Language depended on their largesse. These poets couldn't produce without their plunder. They were as impotent as Sonny in peacetime, adrift without their wardens' helmets.

He marched out of the cave-like cafeteria with Corporal Benson. They got back into the jeep, but Sonny couldn't seem to sit still. He ballooned upward, was swept right out of his seat. He couldn't even say good-bye to the soldier who'd escorted him back from Krankenhaus 31, when he still had the shakes.

Buffeted by the wind, he lost sight of the corporal, and flew among the water tanks above the palatial apartment houses of Central Park West, where many of the silent-movie stars still lived, forgotten in their fifteen-room flats. He crossed over the Central Park Reservoir, which looked like a bright green layer of faultless glass from his altitude, and arrived at the castle on Ninety-fifth and Park, with its crenellated towers and turrets, like some trick façade from the Middle Ages, an abandoned movie set. The Squadron A Armory, as it was called, had been designed and built to mimic a thirteenth-century French fortress, Sonny was once told by the castle's night watchman. Gentlemen soldiers from the armory, most of whom had lived on Park Avenue and were polo players, had fought in the First World War. The armory fell into disuse after that, and served as an occasional indoor polo grounds. But its drill hall and dressage field had become Sonny's private playground, *after* he had moved to 1133, a secret home he shared with his sister once or twice, before she was engaged to that wastrel with the mustache, Billy Samuels, the wholesale grocer who retailed whatever he stole from his most current employer.

Sonny touched ground in the ruins of the castle. But he wasn't wearing his sergeant's olive drab. He was a boy again with a fifteen-year-old sister, with whom he shared a bathroom, a sister with reddish brown hair and his own sad eyes. It was the Salinger look, which might have gone back for centuries in some Eastern European settlement, at least on his father's side. And there was another person in this revamped polo grounds for Park Avenue players – a witch with a painted face who looked more and more like Sylvia. The witch had appealed to the child in Sonny, appealed to him now. She could feel the turbulence in his mind with her fingertips.

'*Kinder*,' she said, 'you must come with me.'

'But where are we going, Auntie?' Doris asked, wiser than Sonny.

She smiled under that white mask. 'Does it really matter?'

'I have school, Auntie Sylvia,' Doris said.

'*Ach*,' the witch said, 'I will teach you what no school can teach.'

'And what is that?' asked Sonny Salinger, gullible as ever.

'How not to exist.'

Sonny screamed. He hadn't left his chair at the dining room table.

'What's wrong?' Miriam asked. 'Sol, he's ashen. Go to the medicine chest. Get him a bicarb.'

'I'm fine,' Sonny said. 'I was dreaming. Happens all the time. Your soul decides to travel. It has no anchor. It always comes back.'

'Bicarb,' Sol said, bemused by his son's *mishegas*. 'It's the best remedy for runaway souls.'

'Dad,' he said, staring at his wife's painted face. 'I'll bet it is.'

PART ELEVEN

Doris

July 1946

PART ELEVEN

1

THEY GOT SYLVIA A BERTH on the *Queen Mary*, second class. She didn't want to stay another week with the Salingers, so Miriam decided to use her own ingenuity and some of her son's counterintelligence craft. She avoided the travel agency on Madison, since the clerks there were very inquisitive and might discover Sylvia's ultimate fate, and reveal it to *everybody*. Therefore, Miriam went down to the Cunard Line on lower Broadway to book a cabin on the *Queen*, paid in hundred-dollar bills, and left the ticket for Sylvia in an envelope on the breakfast table. Sonny seemed in a daze, but the Salingers worked around him. He wouldn't permit them to call her a Nazi.

'But you interrogated her,' Miriam said, 'you caught her in a dragnet and let her go free. And you falsified her papers. Isn't that right, Solly?'

Sol remained neutral. He would have liked Sylvia a little better if she hadn't worn that white paint.

'I'm telling you,' Miriam muttered, 'Dracula's Daughter.'

'Mom,' Sonny said, 'you promised not to say that ever again.'

He was guilty as hell. He hadn't touched Sylvia in months – desire had run to the wolves somewhere in a forest way beyond Sonny's comprehension. He was trapped, bewildered, too. Perhaps he was still Sergeant Salinger of the CIC, in civilian garb, and she was the Fräulein he had once interrogated, now crystallized in his mind. He heard the wolves of desire howl from afar in his dead ear.

It was her idea to return to Europe, and the Salingers supplied the fare. Sonny slept on the living room couch, and Sylvia occupied his old room. She paced most of the night, like a trapped panther. A deep anger began to build. She would appear at two in the morning, sit beside Sonny in her white paint. He would rouse himself and see the narrow slits of her amber eyes.

'Did you ever love me, Sergeant Salinger?'

He wasn't even sure. Was he still mourning Oona and her abrupt departure from his life? But the image of her, that dark voluptuousness, grew fainter and fainter after his pilgrimage in Hürtgen Forest. He could no longer draw her outline on a windowpane at 1133. The *art* of Oona was gone.

'I seduced you,' Sylvia said. 'I did. I waited for you outside your headquarters. I saw how helpless you were. My tall, handsome American Gestapo agent. You did not have the will to arrest me. And I wanted French papers, forged or not forged. We arrived at an impasse, my poor darling. You could not stay in Germany, and I cannot remain in this Park Avenue prison. You have stopped writing, Sergeant Salinger. Is it really on account of me?'

'No,' he said, still half-asleep.

'And yet my very existence seems to make you suffer. You fondle Benny all the time, like a lover… and have so little gentleness left for me.'

Sonny couldn't even say why. She'd been his German wife. They dashed about in a fire engine red Škoda, lived in an apartment at CIC headquarters with their schnauzer, and the sadness accumulated on his shoulders like a letter carrier's sack. He attributed the sack to Sylvia, but it was really his. She stopped working at the clinic, or perhaps the clinic was frightened of her past association with Herr Doktor Fleck and had fired her. It made little difference. Caring for Sonny had become a full-time job.

He'd gone with her and Benny on long walks in Central Park, and rarely said a word. She could see the strange fissure in his face, like a crack somewhere in his mental clock. He belonged on the ward with the German soldiers in Krankenhaus 31. He'd never healed, and perhaps he never would around her.

'You will not write me, I'm sure, after a month. I already feel invisible.'

He'd burrowed inward, into some armored but invalided core. She did not want him to accompany her to the piers. She'd miss Benny, not the Salingers, and might have insisted on taking the dog. Benny could have been a bargaining chip. But the dog would have complicated her departure, and she had her papers to worry about. And so she left Park Avenue early one morning, nuzzling Benny; she'd cried during half her stay in Manhattan. She did not kiss her CIC man good-bye. She never believed in sentimental departures. It was Doris who went downtown in a hired limousine with Sylvia and her steamer trunk. Doris was the strong one, made of Salinger steel. She'd watched Doris maneuver between her bosses and her underlings at Bloomingdale's, like a lady matador. Doris knew when to linger and when to go for the kill. She flung aside her assistants as expendable items she could file away somewhere. Her underlings would follow her from floor to floor while Doris inspected every counter, and went to the display windows, shoving aside the window dressers and dressing the mannequins herself, a general amid her entourage. Sylvia could have dealt with Miriam and Sol, but Doris was a formidable foe.

Gott, *I should have taken lessons from this girl.*

She did not talk about her time with Sonny. That was spent material.

'Doris, will he ever write again? You are my sister-in-law at the moment, so I have that privilege to ask.'

Doris was very slow to answer. 'He'll write again, but meanwhile he has the willies.'

Sylvia's brows knit with consternation. She could not grasp this American slang. 'Willies?'

'Spooked,' Doris said. 'My baby brother has been spooked by the war. Don't worry. We'll ride the Silver Meteor to Florida. He'll bake in the sun, and the words will come back. Sonny fell, and you've become the victim of that fall.'

'A victim with a wedding ring,' Sylvia said. 'It was Sonny who picked the band. He was excited about the wedding – and our dog. My *Vati* was against marriage. He said you Americans are a barbaric tribe. But perhaps that is the fate of all conquerors.'

Barbaric, Doris thought to herself. *This bitch calls us barbaric.*

'Sonny isn't much of a conqueror,' Doris said, with the same flicker of contempt she had bestowed upon the window dressers at Bloomingdale's. But it only lasted for a moment. Sonny had always been a handful, even as a child. He had no business getting married to a Fräulein in a foreign town, no business getting married at all. He should have come back with Benny, and Benny alone. His letters had become chaotic and unreadable; lines disappeared on the page, as if he were writing in invisible ink. Doris had to puzzle out every word. Her brother was a hospital case with a bride.

'I'm grateful,' Doris said.

Sylvia laughed with a bitter ball of phlegm deep inside her throat. 'Grateful for what, my soon-to-be-forgotten sister?'

'That you brought him back to us in one piece.'

'I was not his *handler*, Doris. I was his wife. I could have made a child with Sonny. That might have saved the marriage,' Sylvia said with a certain bravura.

Doris' dark eyes went even darker, with a hint of hate. 'I doubt it, Sylvia. It would have been a disaster. He barely has the stamina to brush his teeth. How could he have raised a child?'

Doris got out of the limo at Rector Street and paid the driver. 'If Sonny doesn't answer your letters, Sylvia, you can always count on me.' She stuffed an envelope with cash into Sylvia's pocket and darted into the traffic without a proper kiss goodbye. Her sister-in-law was an entanglement that had to be torn apart from Sonny at whatever cost.

Sylvia saluted Doris like a CIC agent from her half-open rear door and shouted, 'Auf Wiedersehen.'

Glad as she was to get rid of the last family member, she couldn't stop crying. She had a false passport in her pocketbook, and a settlement from the Salingers, a bride's purse of cold cash. *A barbaric tribe*, she told herself, and it seemed to soothe her. She should never have looked into his dark eyes at Krankenhaus 31. But Herr Doktor Fleck had begged her to watch over this young American who had committed himself to the clinic's care.

'*Ein Spion*,' the doctor said. And she had been foolish enough to volunteer, when she should have run from the *Krankenhaus* and this devil with the dark eyes.

2

THEY RODE THE SILVER METEOR from Grand Central. The imprint of silver wings on both sides of the coaches and sleeping cars reminded Sonny of Buck Rogers. Doris insisted that Sol and Miriam not come along. She didn't want all the complications of the Salinger clan, all the fuss. Miriam would have pestered him, asked about his chronic constipation, and supplied him with a bounty of Ex-Lax. And Sol would have wondered aloud if he was ready to work as an adman at Hoffman & Co. They wouldn't have to mingle with other passengers. Doris had booked a private berth, a roomette, where Sonny could doze and she could sit beside him. But Sonny began to twitch after a while and wanted to go for a breather in the dining car.

She worried that he might misbehave, not out of malice, but his own curious whim, and most travelers weren't used to his arsenal of word tricks and weird observations. It was off-season, and the prices at the Sheraton Plaza in Daytona Beach were a steal. The lush hotel with its terraces and canopies – the Salingers' favorite resort – had shut down during the war and been turned into a barracks for the Women's Army Corps; it reopened, again as the

Sheraton, with central air-conditioning and a refurbished lobby, but without its old allure. Doris wasn't worried about the hotel and its private beach; it was the dining car on the Silver Meteor, with all its little snares, that she had to deal with. They were crossing the Appalachian foothills, and Sonny could see the wealth of forest from his spacious window in the dining car; he expected the Fourth Division to rise out of the crags and follow the path of the Silver Meteor in its rush toward Florida. Doris was a bit perturbed.

Sonny kept staring at a man in uniform eating across the aisle.

'Were you sent overseas?' Sonny asked.

'I was stateside,' the man said, coming out of his own reverie, 'instructing air cadets. I didn't see much of the war. And you?'

Sonny seemed frozen. 'I missed all the action. I have an undescended testicle, and it decided to descend. Caused a big stink.'

Doris managed to maneuver him from the table and steer him back to their berth without much of a fuss. She ordered breakfast and lunch in their little sleeper after that and they arrived in Orlando the next afternoon. A bus from the hotel was waiting for them across from the railroad tracks. They were the only passengers on the fifty-mile ride.

3

IT WAS THE PRELUDE TO THE FALL SEASON, and Doris had to convince her boss that she could skip a week amid all the fury around Seventh Avenue, and its top designers, who still had to be courted, and the window dressers, who were a wayward band of children without her.

'Doris, we'll lose a beat. It's a crippler, this change of season.

The stylists are lost without you. We'll have naked mannequins, for Chrissake.'

'Charlie,' she said, 'Mr Dellavedova. I've collected all the paper, every trace – it's like a coloring book, one-two-three. My brother's a war hero. I can't just abandon him.'

'Was he at the Battle of the Bulge?' asked Mr Dellavedova, a senior vice president at Bloomingdale's.

'Yes. He liberated Germany – in a jeep.'

The displays would be in shambles if she was gone more than a week. But she had to take the chance, risk her own career. Sonny loved the beach and that burning sand. He never wore a bathrobe, just a towel across his shoulders. He sat right on the sand in his bathing trunks, but Doris had a beach chair. They did look like twins, but his skin was pale white, as if he'd gone through the war in an overcoat. His hair was browner than hers. She'd inherited a bit of red from Miriam. But they had the same dark eyes in deep sockets.

The manager at the Sheraton Plaza was rather smug, and offered them a suite that looked out upon the parking lot, and the bellboys she knew by name were gone. But they hadn't bulldozed the beach. The break of the water had always soothed Sonny. He sat there, relaxing, one wrinkle at a time. For a moment, he thought a silver string would rise right out of his navel and return him to Normandy, but nothing happened. No amphibious tanks appeared on the beach, no armless or legless boys, no barrage in his dead ear. But Doris was staring at him. He could feel the rivet of her brown eyes.

'Sonny, that letter carrier's sack you said was Sylvia's. It's where you carried your novel all through the war – about Holden Caulfield.'

'He died,' Sonny said, 'in the Pacific.'

'I know, silly. It's the adventures of a dead boy – before he died. You were always fond of ghosts.'

'I'll get back to it… Sis, do you remember that detective from the Central Park Precinct?'

Doris was suddenly uncomfortable on her beach chair. 'What detective?'

'Vic, Vic. You did the Black Bottom for him, and his wife came into the muster room, and...'

'Oh, that Vic,' she said. 'I forgot about him in five minutes.'

His blondness was still like a stab. They'd never kissed, though he'd held her face in his hands once, and she could feel the shiver in his blue eyes. What was Billy Samuels to her, that *pisher* who came into her life and stole everything but her bloomers? And she had once danced for a blond detective, like the Salome of Central Park West, and never even knew his last name. How many buyers had she met at Bloomingdale's, with their proposals, and invitations for this and that? But nothing struck her like the moment when she crossed that transverse in the park and entered a precinct that stank of horse manure and captured the first glance of her blond detective, who swiveled his shoulders and smiled like some tall cherub with stubble on his chin.

'Sonny,' she asked, 'what about you?'

The beach was deserted, except for a few children sculpting a sand castle; there were four of them, a tiny tribe.

'Vic reminded me of Billy Budd.'

Doris laughed. 'What does a detective with a wife who went bonkers have to do with Billy Budd?'

'He had such gentle eyes, not like those other detectives. He was different.'

She felt that stab again, and it bothered Doris, pissed her off, that whatever little romance she'd had in her life, whatever real hunger she'd had for a boy, should have happened in a goddamn converted stable in Central Park during her freshman year at high school. Doris was in her thirties now, midway on a rocket ride to some sanitarium for the enfeebled. And all she had in her treasure chest were Vic's blue eyes.

'Sonny...'

But Sonny was gone.

He went off to play with those four brats and their sand castle. Sonny felt like he was with a bunch of Seabees, or army engineers. These kids hadn't built one castle but an entire city, a fortress town from some mythical future they had invented on their own. It had moats and rocket launchers and rivulets in the sand that must have served as this town's convoluted water supply. It had endless winding streets that made Sonny think of Nuremberg. And then he realized that it wasn't a town they had built but a cosmos that had flowered in their minds. The streets could have been stars, and the rivulets celestial gas. These builders couldn't have been older than eight or nine – three boys and a girl. It was the girl who was the genius of this lot. She must have been bent a little by the war.

He decided to interrogate her with all the hidden talent of a CIC man.

'Miss,' he asked, 'what are you and your builders building?'

She squinted at him. 'Don't you dare patronize us,' she said. 'What's your name?'

'Sonny Salinger.'

She peered at him now through her thick lenses. She must have been very nearsighted. 'Did you serve?'

'Yes,' he said.

'What rank did you hold?'

'Staff sergeant,' he said.

'Well,' she answered, 'my dad saw action. He landed three months after D-Day… What about you?'

'I was with the second wave,' Sonny said.

The four builders tried as best they could to mask their curiosity. 'What second wave?'

'On Utah Beach.'

They marched around Sonny in the sand. 'Can't you tell, Sergeant Salinger? We're rebuilding the continent – from scratch.'

'I see,' Sonny said. 'With rocket launchers and moats – to keep out the panzer divisions… What's *your* name?'

'Dot,' she said. 'That's short for Dotty.' And she introduced her three other playmates and master builders. 'That's Robert and Matthew and Maxwell. Max is a refugee from the British Isles. My family is keeping him until he can relocate.'

'Relocate?' Sonny asked.

'His mother and father lost their lives in the London blitz. And we cannot locate his next of kin. And so we've been given custody of poor Max in the relocation program.'

Sonny had never heard of such a program and he'd been dealing with war refugees.

'Oh, it's temporary, mind you,' Dot said. 'His kin will be found. Mama is certain of that. But it was Max's idea to rebuild the continent – to our liking and specifications.'

'May I help?' Sonny asked.

Dot took off her thick lenses and sized up Sonny. 'You are awful tall, Sergeant Salinger, and tall people, in my limited experience, are rather clumsy. You might sabotage the project. Stumble all over Italy or Transylvania.'

'I'll try not to stumble,' Sonny said, though he couldn't see the markings of Italy or Transylvania. All he could discern was a web of streets and houses and rivulets that widened in the sand into the cosmos of a continent. And so he stooped beside these four master builders, packing the wet sand until it turned into clay, and with his palm as a kind of trowel, he sculpted a tiny version of the Villa Oberwegner in Weißenberg.

A woman with cream on her nose arrived. She had very broad shoulders and was wearing sandals and a white robe from the Sheraton Plaza.

'Dorothy,' she shouted to the nearsighted girl, 'why are you bothering this young gentleman?'

'Oh, Mother,' Dot said, 'he's not a gentleman. He's just one of our volunteers.'

And Sonny had a sudden lightning bolt in his dead ear. '*Hurricane*,' he said.

The woman seemed very suspicious. 'I don't...'

'You saw Dorothy Lamour in *Hurricane* and that's how you named your daughter.'

'My God, are you a charlatan of some sort?' the woman asked. 'How did you ever know?'

'It's simple,' Sonny said. '*Hurricane* was a big hit. And Dorothy was one of the most popular names of 1937.'

'I'm enchanted,' the woman said. 'But Dotty dear, you must come right now. And don't forget Max.'

'Oh, Mother,' the girl said, and she signaled to her companions, who proceeded to stomp on all the sand castles and demolish the continent they had built. And Sonny, who had been shaping with both hands for the past fifteen minutes, began to shiver.

'You're builders. Couldn't you set aside one piece of your brand-new continent?'

'Oh, Sergeant,' Dot said. 'You are not a sand person. I can see that. The breakers will destroy it all. We'll be back tomorrow and rebuild.'

And she ran off with her mother and her three companions, while Sonny stood among the ruins and runnels in the sand as a kind of syncopation entered his skull. Not words, not lines of music, exactly, but musical beats, as if he were doing the Black Bottom right in the runnels.

Dammit, here he was with a melody in the scoop of his hands.

> *Slap your knees and dance a little,*
> *Slap your knees and dance a little,*
> *And d-o-o-o the Black Bottom…*

And he started to dance, like the Crazy Man of Daytona. There wasn't one beach umbrella, one beach boy around. It was late in the afternoon, near dinnertime at the Sheraton Plaza. And then he heard the clap of other knees than his. Doris had joined him in the ruins of that vanished continent. She was singing and laughing and crying.

'Oh, Sonny, we did have fun, didn't we?'

And he wished he knew how to answer Doris. He'd been through some insane baptism that he could never share with any other serviceman – or civilian. The sergeant with stripes he wasn't supposed to display, the secret soldier. He'd seen the senseless killing at Slapton Sands and on the Far Shore. He'd survived Hürtgen and the *Krankenhaus*, mingled with a battalion of dead souls. Perhaps the soldier in him hadn't survived, and that's why he stayed so long in Nuremberg, a Nazi town – to linger with the dead. But he was with Doris now, in the middle of a dance.

CODA

Bloomingdale's on Sleepy Hollow Lane

February 1947

1

DORIS, YOU'LL REDECORATE,' MR DELLAVEDOVA said, 'and that's that.'

The bastards wanted her to redo all three tiers of Bloomingdale's bargain basement, the 'Downstairs Store,' as they had dubbed it, and took away most of her other privileges. That's how they saw their fashion queen, who'd been to Paris, had a *café crème* with the finest couturières, even stayed at the Ritz with Coco Chanel, before Coco was denounced as a collaborator.

And now Doris was in a kind of temporary exile, underground at Bloomingdale's. She couldn't pick her own architect, but had to work with whoever was on hand. And still, she gave the Downstairs Store what was soon known as 'the Doris punch, the Doris flair.' It didn't matter that the entire edifice shook every seven or eight minutes, whenever an elevated train roared on the Third Avenue tracks; Bloomingdale's was composed of several buildings that were cobbled together, so that above ground the floors buckled and didn't match, but Doris could end that warp in her basement paradise with a pair of carpenters, and she did.

No one ever suffered from vertigo in the Downstairs Store. She got rid of all the ugly bins that were crammed with mountains of merchandise. And she had a series of fashion islands installed at each level. She collaborated with Seventh Avenue, and had her own fashion shows in the basement, with models she borrowed from designers who were in her debt from some past favor bestowed.

'Doris, it's a miracle,' said Mr Dellavedova. 'There's no difference between downstairs and upstairs – it's just as classy.'

They wanted to pluck her out of the basement and give her 'an island' or two on an upstairs floor, where she could present her fashions shows, but Doris preferred to rule Downstairs. And she invited Sonny to her subterranean kingdom. She also helped him move out of 1133, right after his twenty-eighth birthday, and together they were able to find him new quarters in Tarrytown, twenty-five miles north of Manhattan, despite Miriam's protests and Sol's prediction that the boy with five battle stars would end up a bum in a garret. He did live in a loft, actually the rebuilt upper half of a garage near Central Avenue and Storm Street that supplied a curious comfort to Sonny, since it reminded him of the cages in Weißenberg, where the CIC kept its prisoners. Sonny's loft had one tiny window, and he relished its single shaft of light – his morning moonbeam.

It was Doris who chipped in half the rent, as her own idea of a 'housewarming,' and took him by the hand to the Downstairs Store. But he wouldn't shop at one of her fashion islands underground. He bought shirts, sweaters, jackets, ties, and suits – all of them in charcoal or the blackest black – from the bargain tables. And that's how he dressed for his butterscotch sundae at Schrafft's.

But Doris didn't scold or discourage her baby brother. He ranted about Western elitism, epitomized by Bloomingdale's. 'Doris, it's a store that caters to the rich.'

'The rich,' she said, trilling those words on her tongue. 'Like all the debonair damsels who come off the El, and illustrious writers who live above a garage.'

'Well,' Sonny said, relishing his sundae with one of Schrafft's famously long spoons. 'I'm not going to write for the slicks anymore. I've had it. They change my titles, and run amuck with my prose. I'm a piece of merchandise. Like one of your bargain bins.'

Doris was furious. 'Don't knock the basement, darling. You could be a mannequin who marched right out of the Downstairs Store.'

But she softened to Sonny after a few seconds, since she realized that writing had become his sole religion, his sacred quest. He'd returned from the war with a sadness that chiseled his features, until half his face was in shadow, except for his big ears. She would often find him meditating in his loft when she visited Tarrytown with bags of groceries. He'd first started to meditate in the Green Hell of the Hürtgen Forest, he said. But that's not when the sadness – and the rage in him – began. It was long before Hürtgen and the war. Doris remembered that rage from the time of Sonny's bar mitzvah, in 1932. They were living on West Eighty-second Street, in luxurious quarters, with Maja, their aristocrat of a maid, who was always a blabbermouth. Doris couldn't abide Maja's haughtiness, her Hungarian airs. But she was loyal and kept close to Miriam, who often brought her along to Schrafft's as a sidekick. And it was Maja who prepared the menu for Sonny's bar mitzvah, which wasn't at the local synagogue, but in Sol Salinger's enormous living room on West Eighty-second. It was Sol who had given Sonny Hebrew lessons, or so it seemed.

The bar mitzvah was a kind of showpiece, staged for Sol's parents, Simon and Fannie Salinger, who had come all the way from Chicago, where Simon was a medical doctor with his own private practice in a neighborhood of the poorest Jews in the world on Chicago's South Side – Simon had financed his medical studies by serving as a rabbi in Louisville, a town of goyim with its tiny ghetto. He was a hard man not to notice. His left eye had been torn out of its socket in a pogrom. It happened in 1880, while Simon was a member of the volunteer Jewish police in the Lithuanian town of Taurage; scuffling with the czar's drunken soldiers outside the central synagogue, he was gouged with a bayonet. No one had to pity him. Simon gave much more than he got. He left two of the czar's louts lying with smashed skulls on the clay road. A renegade now, on the czar's death list, he had to run to America. But that gouged eye intrigued Sonny. Simon didn't cover it with a velveteen patch. His empty socket looked like a sinister tunnel with a flap of skin…

Sol had hired an itinerant rabbi with a Torah in a silver case to please his father and mother, but Simon disapproved of this charlatan, and he knew that Sonny recited from the Torah without understanding a single line. Yet he loved the boy, felt a kinship with him. He could sense that zeal in Sonny's dark eyes, the boy's search for God. Grandpa Simon hadn't lost his predilection for mayhem. He took the itinerant rabbi with his Torah and tossed him out of the apartment, and then he had a shouting war with Sol in one of the back bedrooms, while Sonny spied on them, like a secret agent wrapped in a prayer shawl.

'You had no right, Pa.'

'Faker,' Simon cackled, 'I had every right in the world. I would break your bones if it weren't for the boy. You never taught him the Haftarah. He doesn't even know about the Prophets.'

'I did teach him – I tried. And I found the best rebbe I could.'

And that's when Grandpa Simon discovered Sonny in the crack of the door. He had tears of anger and frustration in his eyes. He'd been a battler all his life. But he couldn't slap Sol's big ears back in front of Sonny. He welcomed the bar mitzvah boy into the room.

'It's nothing,' he said. 'Pay no attention. I never got along with your father. He loved to swindle, and I never could.'

He wiped his eyes with a handkerchief that was as long as a dish towel and walked Sonny out of the room…

They rode the Fifth Avenue bus together, sat on the upper deck, where Simon took delight in the different streets and covered his empty eye socket with the flat of his hand in order not to embarrass the bar mitzvah boy in front of the other riders. While Sonny watched families parade in their finest winter hats and coats, Simon pointed to a fashionable department store, made of solid stone.

'Altman B., isn't that where your sister works?'

'Grandpa, Doris works off Fifth Avenue, way uptown.'

'Too bad,' Simon said, brushing his lip with a gnarled finger. 'Sonny, you can't read Torah, can you?'

'No, Grandpa.'

'Then why didn't your father have a ceremony of ham and cheese? I might have enjoyed that, rather than a rebbe who was no rebbe at all.'

'Grandpa, I disagree.'

The ceremony had excited him – it was, after all, a kind of bloodletting. On that afternoon in January, he was *another* King David, a molder of words, a warrior, and a master of art and song. He was surrounded by friends from summer camp and school, and some of Sol's neighbors in the building, in this enclave of Upper West Side Jews. Sonny and his male companions were wearing skullcaps and prayer shawls made of pure silk. They drank cups of kosher wine and gobbled hunks of honey cake with almonds, then sat down to a walloping meal, while Simon frowned and argued at the table with his son.

'You could have invited us without this fake bar mitzvah.'

'Papa, what are you saying?' Sol cried out in despair. 'A Jewish boy should have a Jewish service.' 'Our little king,' Sonny's friends yelled, their mouths sweetened with wine. And Sonny delivered a speech in his prayer shawl.

'We are the purveyors of justice, the conquerors of Goliath. I need little more than my lyre and my slingshot. We seek honor over wealth. We cherish the holiness of songs. We will sway the Lord with our own sweet wine.'

Even Grandpa Simon was touched, but the boy's glory as little King David didn't last.

A few months after Sonny's bar mitzvah, the Salingers abandoned the Upper West Side and moved to 1133. They were now the Salingers of Park Avenue, and Sonny was ripped right out of public school and enrolled at McBurney, a private school affiliated with the local YMCA. But the sadness didn't really start with that. One Saturday afternoon, during lunch at Schrafft's, Sol announced that Miriam wasn't Jewish.

'She's Catholic,' Sol said. 'Her name was Marie, and she called herself Miriam to please my parents. But she never converted.'

And the young King David peered at his father with a whole arsenal of slingshots. 'Dad, what does that mean?'

'We're not really a Jewish tribe. We never were. I import ham, for God's sake.'

'But I sang from the Torah,' Sonny said. 'I recited the Lord's prayers.'

'To please my papa, who worked like a dog to put bread on the table,' Sol said with a cherubic smile.

Sonny clapped his hands over his ears. 'I'm going mad. I studied for months – months. You yourself called me your "little Jewish king".'

'You are, darling,' Miriam said.

'At McBurney, with a chapel for Christian prayers.'

'It's a private school,' Sol insisted, 'one of the best. You don't have to attend chapel. That's in my contract.'

It was Doris who intervened, Doris who shared a toothbrush and a bathroom with her brother. 'But you didn't have to trick us, Dad.'

'Doris Salinger,' Sol said, without that cherubic look, 'leave the restaurant. We don't have to dine with traitors.'

'No,' Sonny said. 'I'll leave. It's not Doris' fault.'

And school became a deepening quagmire. He had to drop out of McBurney after a year – he just didn't have the grades. He was an ordinary boy with an ordinary IQ – 111, according to McBurney's measurements. Sol decided that Sonny needed the discipline of a military boarding school, a kind of junior West Point. The Salingers selected the Valley Forge Military Academy, in Pennsylvania. Sol didn't attend the interview – he looked too Jewish, despite his Park Avenue credentials, and Valley Forge had its quota of Jews, like most other academies.

It was Miriam who arrived at Valley Forge with her red hair, and Sonny was enrolled. Corporal Salinger seemed to thrive under the military rigor at Valley Forge, and would graduate as a sergeant major, Doris recalled. Valley Forge was the only school that would ever grant him a diploma. But he returned to Manhattan with the very same sadness etched deep into his eyes. And that was the sadness Doris saw at Sleepy Hollow Lane, as Sonny had decided upon his address in Tarrytown, since his loft had a separate little road, and Washington Irving, who had written 'The Legend of Sleepy Hollow,' had lived in Tarrytown. Sonny adored Ichabod Crane, the acrimonious schoolteacher in that acrimonious tale. He called anyone he admired Ichabod or Ishmael, no matter what their names were – or Bartleby and Billy Budd. Often these names were transferable from one to another, and Doris could barely tell the person apart.

'How's Bartleby?' he asked as she entered with her groceries. He had a tiny fridge and one gas burner. He lived like a monk in that loft with a low ceiling, a shower curtain that couldn't even cover the shower stall, and one sink that delivered only hot water. The toilet seat sat in the open. Sonny called it 'King David's can.' She had to ask him to step outside onto the tiny porch whenever she wanted to pee, for God's sake.

'Which Bartleby is that?'

'Ya know, the new doorman at Eleven thirty-three.'

She was living on Lexington now, a block from Bloomingdale's, but Sonny kept his old address. It was Doris who had become his letter carrier, Doris who delivered his mail. If he had used Sleepy Hollow Lane, nothing at all would have ever arrived. Sleepy Hollow Lane didn't exist in Tarrytown, except in her brother's fancy, and perhaps it was there that he dwelled, a disused soldier who found little nourishment in civilian life.

'Oh, Frank. He's fine. He guards your mail like an ogre. He's your biggest fan, tells one and all that the eminent writer and war hero, Sergeant Jerry Salinger, once resided in the building, and that Frank himself has become your custodian. I hope he doesn't get fired for blabbing so much. You know how prissy the management is.'

'What about Ishmael?' Sonny asked.

Doris had to reflect for a moment. And then she recalled that Ishmael had become Sonny's name for Sol.

'Oh,' she said, 'he still thinks you'll return to the primeval roost. He's betting that you'll fail in your own craft and that you'll be the next little King David of Hoffman ham and cheese... You're coming, aren't you?'

Sonny seemed a bit muddled. 'Coming where?'

'To our Bargain Basement Bazaar. You promised. It's the grand opening.'

'Doris, the Downstairs Store reopened months ago. Didn't we grab every bargain we could find? I have a brand-new designer wardrobe.'

'I know,' Doris said, as if he was still the booming bar mitzvah boy, 'but it's in my honor.'

'Will Ichabod be there?'

Doris didn't have any doubt this time about the shifting personalities. Sonny meant her boss, Mr Dellavedova.

'Of course,' she said with a blink. 'Now step onto the verandah. I have to pee.'

2

HE TOOK THE HUDSON LINE TO GRAND CENTRAL, wearing his charcoal gray topcoat and black argyle socks. He always loved to follow the slow roil of the river, the way it would sink out of sight and suddenly reappear again through a crush of trees or some builder's dream of a cluster of cottages near the south shore. He stopped at the Automat, where he marveled at the cashier, who could deliver a fistful of nickels with a numbing, blind accuracy that didn't allow for errors. He had coffee and a slice of apple pie, fresh out of the little window. The pie here, in this enormous womb of a cafeteria, was better than Miriam's and Maja's, or the pie maker's delight at Schrafft's. Its crust was crisp and flaky, and wouldn't disappear inside a customer's fork, and the warm chunks of apple were never overcooked…

Ichabod was waiting with other executives, buyers, and designers at the escalator that led to the bargain basement's top tier. Doris was among them, wearing the latest fashions from Seventh Avenue – a mini cape, a flared blouse and skirt, and red leather pumps, while Sonny looked like a cadaver with big ears.

'Ah, Mr Dellavedova,' she said, 'you've met my brother, J. D., he's moved to Tarrytown. He lives in a loft on Sleepy Hollow Lane – writing stories and a novel. He carried that novel right through Normandy, in a sack.'

'Ah, Sergeant Salinger, the war hero,' said Ichabod, alias Mr Dellavedova. 'You were with the OSS, like Cagney in *13 Rue Madeleine* – all that cloak-and-dagger stuff. How many Krauts did you kill with your bare hands?'

'Very few,' Sonny said. 'I was with the CIC.'

'Never heard of that outfit.' He prodded another exec. 'Walt, did you ever hear of the CIC? They were also in the commando business, it seems.'

But none of the execs had the faintest notion of the CIC.

'We worked in the shadows,' Sonny said. 'We didn't have James Cagney on our side.'

'Well, Doris swears by you,' said Mr Dellavedova. 'You don't have to hide in Tarrytown, son. You can work for us at Bloomingdale's.'

Sonny had an ache in his gut, a rawness he couldn't get rid of, as he imagined writing copy about the latest sales at Dellavedova's department store. He joined the others as they ambled down the escalator to the first tier. It had tidbits from Bloomingdale's shelves and its soda shop near the Third Avenue exit. It had floor-walkers who carried around slivers of food on a silver tray. It had live mannequins who mingled with customers, and the Seventh

Avenue stars who had designed their outfits and fretted over every inch of crêpe. It was bedlam to Sonny, a madhouse of merchandise and well-wishers, including his mom and dad, and Maja, the queen maid with her own quarry of other live-ins. Doris didn't seem to have any friends, only accomplices and other buyers, who congratulated her. She'd devoted herself to one particular craft – Bloomingdale's. Perhaps next year she would board the *Queen Mary* again and visit the place Vendôme, bring the *parfum* of Paris to Lexington Avenue. But this year she was in her own palace...

Sol was impressed, and told that to Mr Dellavedova. 'What traffic, what volume. The crowds never stop. There's no lunch break at the Downstairs Store.'

'That's right, Mr Salinger,' said Ichabod. 'Your daughter's a classic. No salary in the world can tempt her to move back upstairs.'

'She's stubborn,' Miriam said, 'like our Sonny, in his garage on Sleepy Hollow Lane.'

'Mrs S,' Ichabod whispered, 'he shouldn't wear black on black. It gives the wrong impression. He's a war hero, a rival to the OSS.'

'He stayed too long – in Nuremberg,' Sol said. 'He brought back a German girl with a shady past.'

'Sol,' Miriam said, 'you shouldn't give out Sonny's secrets, not to a stranger.'

'Mr Dellavedova is Doris' boss, for God's sake. And didn't we help Sonny get rid of Dracula's Daughter?'

Doris stepped in and elbowed her mother and father away from Mr Dellavedova.

'Shush, Papa, or I'll strap you to the escalator.'

'Doris Salinger,' Miriam said, 'you can't talk to your father in that tone of voice.'

'Yes, I can,' Doris said. 'This is *my* Monopoly board – all of it.'

'Then we're leaving,' Miriam said. 'Maja, come – I won't tolerate such rudeness from my own daughter.'

'But there are bargains – everywhere,' Maja said.

Miriam pierced Maja with a maddening gaze. 'Come.'

Then she turned to Sonny. 'You never call, you never write, Mr Sleepy Hollow. You have your dog, and a sister who's as good as a grocery clerk. Why would you need a mother?'

Sonny was the same bar mitzvah boy, with a black turtleneck instead of a silk prayer shawl. 'Stay, Mama.' Miriam had nourished him through the war with her bundles of woolen socks, her letters, her clippings about the latest Hollywood gossip – the love tiffs between Bogart and Betty Bacall, Carole Lombard's death in a plane crash while selling war bonds, and Gable's grief over the crash...

'I'll do it,' Miriam said, 'for your father's sake. But Doris must apologize. She's grown wild in this basement, wild.'

Sonny signaled to his sister with a telltale wink, honed at the movies, during the silent era, when actors had no melodies to aggrandize themselves with and had to act with their eyes.

'Oh, Dad,' Doris said, 'oh, Dad,' and went back to her minions, who stood in the middle of each fashion island, giving out free bars of soap and offering silk scarves at a ridiculous price. It troubled Sonny, this whole idea of a basement bazaar and its wonderland of goods, while all he could remember was desolation, from Normandy to Nuremberg.

He took walks with his schnauzer in the little park near Sleepy Hollow Lane. That was as much companionship as he could bear, except for Doris, his postmistress, and an occasional chat with his landlady. He was growing mute in America. He'd always be that bar mitzvah boy who fell from grace, the cadet from Valley Forge who began writing stories in the middle of the night with a flashlight under his blanket, an errant sergeant major with his lone degree. He was trained as an interrogator, the mysterious noncom who could chastise generals and had to hide his stripes, but the Nazis he'd unmasked were as broken as he was, men with frozen faces. The war itself was one great marshaling yard. In the end, the Allies were better marshalers than the Krauts. He'd gone to Paris, which had been the cultural capital of the Third

Reich – Hermann Göring had ruled from the Ritz, with his morphine and his slippers studded with diamonds, and the German high command preferred the amenities of Le Sphinx to the battlefields of Normandy. And now Sonny had Manhattan with the rocking noises of the El. The basement bazaar was a little boomtown. He saw his own somber reflection in the mirror, black on black. And Doris watched him break into a cold sweat.

'Sonny, I can have Mr Dellavedova's driver escort you back to Sleepy Hollow Lane.'

'Sis, I'll be fine,' Sonny said. He was beginning to shake.

'Sergeant Salinger,' she said, like a drillmaster, and had one of her minions find him an empty chair, while Sonny continued to shake.

'Doris, do you remember the bananafish?'

'What bananafish?' she asked, growing concerned about her brother's sanity.

'It was one of the rare times, ya know, when Dad was nice – at Daytona Beach. He told us that story when we were wading in the water.'

'Jesus,' Doris said, 'you must have been two.'

'I was older that that,' Sonny said. 'Dad was the real daredevil. He'd plunge us into the water, like some crazy baptism, and tell us about the bananafish when we came up to breathe.'

Doris was still skeptical. 'What the hell are bananafish, anyway?'

'I'm not sure, sis. They swim into holes, looking for bananas.'

'That's silly,' Doris said. 'Bananas can't grow in the sea.'

'But Dad's bananafish did – only the bananafish never survive the hunt. They grow so fat they drop dead. That's what I remember of Dad and Daytona Beach.'

And Sonny sat right in the middle of Doris' basement bazaar as men and women maneuvered around him, searching for bargains and free gifts, nearly knocking him over, until he was caught in the crush and the crowd carried him along with his chair. Sonny was in a kind of free fall, with hats and coats fluttering around him like headless horsemen on Sleepy Hollow Lane. He had no idea where he would alight, and with whom.

He must have been near the escalator, because he tumbled onto that movable track. Somehow he'd lost his chair. And he seemed like the lone passenger on this descent – it was a curious ride. Whole landscapes passed in front of him. But nothing made sense, really. He was in the canteen at the Villa Oberwegner one moment and in a forest of white pines the next. Then he was at Slapton Sands, digging graves for the unburied dead caught in that miscue, where GIs landing on the beach were fired upon by Allied warships and massacred in their footsteps. And it was Sonny's task to collect the dog tags and hide every trace of their existence. He watched himself sobbing. Sonny had his own arc of time on the escalator, could wheel in and out of his past as passenger and participant. He was Sonny Salinger, not little Alice in her subterranean wonderland, but he still had to endure some kind of plunge into a metal rabbit hole at Bloomingdale's bazaar.

He was back at Tiverton Castle again, prince of his lordly room in the tower. No one could contradict him, not the generals or the ambulance drivers. He went about in his jeep, visiting those refugees who had been plucked from their homes because of the training exercise and put into a relocation camp near the castle; these were the ones who had no relatives to take them in – the lonely and the lost. The one solace he had was a small treasure of Hershey bars. He was like some pirate from the Fourth Division, distributing whatever bounty was on hand. The widows and orphans grabbed at him with a wistful smile. 'Father Christmas in May, dearie. A bit late in the season, aren't ye?'

And he watched his own wistfulness in the reflection off the escalator rails. And then the landscape vanished in a wisp.

He could feel the silk of his prayer shawl and also see himself wearing it. He'd sniffed human flesh on fire, and it clung to his nostrils on this ride. And then time slowed to a crawl on the escalator, and he was with Hitler's giant, Otto Skorzeny, at the CIC canteen in Weissenberg. But the location and the subjects were all scrambled. Otto was his rebbe in an SS uniform, and Sonny was a bar mitzvah boy with chevrons and a prayer shawl.

'Scarface, you have nothing, nothing to teach.'

'And you, I suppose,' said this chimera of Otto the Terrible, 'have nothing to learn.'

'I'd like to learn about bananafish.'

'There's no such creature,' the chimera cackled in Sonny's face. 'It's all vanity – and madness of the mind.'

It's not madness, Sonny thought, *and even if it is, the copyright is mine.*

As he bumped along on the escalator, Sonny realized that he wasn't at the canteen in Weißenberg, but inside the muster room of the Central Park Precinct, with its panoply of stables. And the muster room wasn't filled with detectives and members of the horse patrol, but with Sonny's fellow Jewish *Injuns* from summer camp in Maine, lads he hadn't seen in years. The SS giant had insinuated himself into this group as counselor in chief of Camp Wigwam, with his scars and bloodred Nazi armband. He was a fiendish sultan and grand rabbi of his own congregation of camper commandos.

Crazy as it sounded, Otto must have taught him another kind of Torah, because Sonny's songs had come back with each bump of the metal stairs. He could recite, and sing, and bless every camper in his own ride toward manhood. Whatever music he had lost in the carnage at Slapton Sands, at Hürtgen, and among the smoldering corpses at Kaufering IV had come back. He could hear it on the movable stairs, like dancing metal bones in his dead ear.

'I am Sonny Salinger,' he shouted, 'and I sing to my heart's content.'

And then fat Otto disappeared, as if time could cannibalize and devour the living and the dead, and Sonny was back inside the ruined basilica at Echternach; despite all the babel of the Downstairs Store, that agony of constant shoving in the desperate search for goods, Sonny could still hear the songs and prayers of the vanished monks and priests, a chorus that went fainter and fainter, until it was an almost imperceptible chant that flew right out of the fashion islands themselves, as if the bargain basement had become a basilica and somehow Sonny had stumbled into God's own department store.

Doris found him on the bottom stair of the escalator.

'Sonny, what happened? Jesus, you disappeared.'

She grabbed at him, and they both landed on the floor of the basement's second tier, with Doris a prisoner in her own palace. A pile of corsets covered her legs, as if girdles and scarves had become runaway items in all the human wind of a basement sale.

'I miss Grandpa,' Doris said, laughing and crying. 'I wish he could have come from Chicago with his missing eye.'

'Doris,' Sonny said, 'he's eighty-six.'

His sister wasn't impressed. 'He came to your bar mitzvah, didn't he?'

'That was fifteen years ago.'

'So what?' she said, with someone's shoe in her face. They crawled into a neutral corner and sat there like a pair of penitents beside the escalator that was crammed with people, half-mad in their search for the biggest bargain.

Grandpa Simon had recognized Sonny's talent, that desperate need for silent songs – that was his real Torah. Sonny didn't have much of a choice. He had nowhere else to go but Sleepy Hollow Lane. He had his dog, his army-issue typewriter, his toilet seat, Sol's bananafish, and that single shaft of light. Even as he rose out of that corner with Doris and battled his way back into the crowd of shoppers, he knew he'd have to descend into a long, long winter of words.

'Sonny, where are you?' Doris asked in a sudden panic.

'Sis, I'm right here.'